TAKEN

Out of the fog leapt a burly humanoid, painted green like a toad. It slammed into Fargo, almost knocking him off the Ovaro. Quickly, he grabbed the saddle horn, and had nearly straightened up when another dark shape hurled itself from on high.

They're jumping out of the trees! Fargo ducked, but not low enough, and the creature crashed into him full force and they fell, locked in combat. The warrior shrieked a ghastly cry just like those Fargo had heard during the night, and within seconds the fog disgorged more green-skinned, brutish forms. Five, six, seven of them flung themselves on top of him, struggling to pin his arms and legs.

Fargo resisted. He punched one, kneed another, slugged a third with his Colt. He almost broke loose but there were too many. As he surged upright, an iron hand clamped onto his ankle, and he toppled. His legs and arms were seized. The Colt was ripped from his grasp. The unthinkable had happened.

He was a captive of the Shadow People. . . .

D1040869

A GIANT TRAILSMAN ADVENTURE

WOODLAND WARRIORS

by

Jon Sharpe

A SIGNET BOOK

SIGNET
Published by New American Library, a division of
Penguin Putnam Inc., 375 Hudson Street,
New York, New York 10014, U.S.A.
Penguin Books Ltd, 80 Strand,
London WC2R ORL, England
Penguin Books Australia Ltd, Ringwood,
Victoria, Australia
Penguin Books Canada Ltd, 10 Alcorn Avenue,
Toronto, Ontario, Canada M4V 3B2
Penguin Books (N.Z.) Ltd, 182–190 Wairau Road,
Auckland 10, New Zealand

Penguin Books Ltd, Registered Offices:
Harmondsworth, Middlesex, England

First published by Signet, an imprint of New American Library,
a division of Penguin Putnam Inc.

First Printing, December 2001
10 9 8 7 6 5 4 3 2 1

The Trailsman

Beginnings . . . they bend the tree and they mark the man. Skye Fargo was born when he was eighteen. Terror was his midwife, vengeance his first cry. Killing spawned Skye Fargo, ruthless, cold-blooded murder. Out of the acrid smoke of gunpowder still hanging in the air, he rose, cried out a promise never forgotten.

The Trailsman they began to call him all across the West: searcher, scout, hunter, the man who could see where others only looked, his skills for hire but not his soul, the man who lived each day to the fullest, yet trailed each tomorrow. Skye Fargo, the Trailsman, and the seeker who could take the wildness of a land and the wanting of a woman and make them his own.

The Candian border, 1861—
Where legends come to life
and fear runs rampant.

Prologue

One moment the deep woods were alive with the warbling of songbirds and the chattering of a red squirrel high in a towering spruce. The next instant an unnatural silence descended. A silence so complete Camilla Kemp stopped searching through the high weeds that overran a clearing beside a gurgling stream, and straightened in alarm. "There it is again," she said. "This makes the third time today."

Her assistant, Harry Baxter, absently grunted. A Bostonian in his early twenties, Harry adjusted the spectacles on the end of his thin nose while poking about with a stick. As a concession to the uncommonly warm autumn weather he had removed his coat. A baggy woolen shirt and beige pants clung in loose folds to his skinny frame.

"Tonekotay says it is a bad sign," Camilla mentioned, smoothing her plain work dress, a garment that did little to conceal the shapely contours of her full figure. Her lovely oval features mirrored concern as she gazed deep into the shadowy depths of the dense forest. Swiping at a blonde bang that hung over her green eyes, she sought the reason for the sudden quiet.

Harry snorted in ill-concealed scorn. "He's a Delaware, for crying out loud, as superstitious as the year is long. He's always looking for omens and portents in the most trivial of things."

"He's a Lenape, actually," Camilla corrected him. "It means the 'original people', or words to that effect."

Harry snorted again. "Original as opposed to whom? Are they claiming they were the first Indians on the continent? I daresay there are fifty other tribes who would dispute the fact." He bent lower. "Whites have been calling his people Delawares since before our country was founded. That's good enough for me."

Camilla sighed in mild exasperation. "You puzzle me sometimes, Harry. For the life of me I can't understand why you've chosen our line of work. Your attitude toward Indians leaves a lot to be desired."

Now it was Harry who unfurled and regarded her closely. The thick lenses of his eyeglasses made his eyes seem three times as big as they really were, lending him the aspect of a gangly owl. His Adam's apple bobbed slightly as he looked her up and down. "Do you remember when we met?"

"What does that have to do with anything?" Camilla asked. "It was seven years ago, on the first day of college. You were behind me in line at the Registrar's Office."

"We talked some, remember?"

Camilla reflected a few seconds. "You were acting shy, so I introduced myself. We discussed which courses we planned to take."

Harry nodded. "It always amazed me how friendly you were. Girls never liked me much when I was younger. They shunned me as if I were covered in poison ivy. The boys, too, pretty much left me alone because I didn't care for the same activities they did. Most were only interested in wrestling and hunting and the like. I liked books. I liked to study. In the lower grades I was virtually an outcast."

"I don't see your point."

"I really didn't know what I was going to do with my life. I thought about teaching history, perhaps. Or geology. Then I met you, Cammy." Harry coughed. "You treated me differently than everyone else. You

2

were friendly. Open. I thought it would be nice to take the same classes you did."

"Wait a second," Camilla said. "Are you saying the only reason you chose anthropology was because of me?"

"What's wrong with that? One profession is as good as any other, as far as I'm concerned. I have no regrets. You've turned out to be the best friend I've ever had. The past seven years have been the happiest years of my life."

Camilla's eyes widened. "Oh my!" she declared. Then, more softly, "Harry, you shouldn't have. A person's life's work should be something they're passionate about, something they're interested in above all else."

"I'm interested in you above all else," Harry said. Catching himself, he said much too quickly, "I mean, interested in anthropology. Maybe I don't have your exaggerated appreciation of Indians, but I still find their cultures fascinating." He gestured at the high weeds they were diligently scouting. "If we can find the proof you're after, think of the publicity. We'll be famous."

"Oh, I wouldn't go that far," Camilla responded.

"Your father will have to eat his words," Harry said, grinning. "And I want to be there when that happens. After how shabbily he's treated you, it's long overdue."

Camilla was going to say something, but just then she noticed a swarthy figure striding purposefully toward them. "What is it, Tonekotay?"

The Delaware's angular face was impassive, as always. He rarely showed emotion. Of medium height he had a stocky build and was superbly muscled. In keeping with Delaware custom, his torso was streaked with red ocher and bright bloodroot. A deerskin breechclout and moccasins were all he wore. On his right hip hung a knife. A quiver and long bow rested on a slant across his barrel chest. "I not like the quiet," he announced in his clipped English. "It is better we go back."

"To the base camp?" Harry said before Camilla could reply. "Not on your life. It took us five hours to get here, and we've only just begun. If we go back we'll have lost the whole day."

Tonekotay fixed his dark eyes on Baxter. Eyes that glittered with vitality and intelligence—and something more. "Better to lose day than lose life." Red ocher also streaked his face, from the tip of his chin to the crown of his head. The streaks were widest on the shaven skin on either side of the cock's crest that ran down the middle. He didn't appear to be much over thirty, yet Camilla knew he was pushing fifty.

"What do you think the quiet means?" she asked, motioning sharply at Harry to hold his tongue.

"Not sure," Tonekotay said, and it was plain his uncertainty bothered him. "Could be enemy. Could be *them*."

Harry indulged in one of his habitual snorts. "Oh, please. Quit filling her head with needless worry. They don't exist anymore. By all accounts they were completely wiped out long ago. The best we can hope for is to find the remains of one of their villages. To assert the contrary is childish."

"Please, Harry," Camilla said sternly. "Be civil."

"I can't help it," Harry snapped. "I'm tired of his superstitious nonsense. So what if we've gone farther than any previous expeditions? So what if we're deeper in these woods than any white man has been since the days of the voyagers? For all our so-called guide here knows, if there are Indians out there, they're as friendly as he is."

"Could be," Tonekotay patiently conceded. "But could be hostile, too. What if they do not like strangers in their lands?" He scanned the surrounding forest. "They watch us work. I feel their eyes."

Camilla gazed into the murky woodland and couldn't suppress a faint shudder. Across the clearing, the three graduate students who had volunteered to come along were earnestly rooting through the grass, oblivious to the possible danger. Two were women scarcely younger than she. Their instructor, and hers at one time, was over by the stream, treating himself to a sip of water. "I'll ask Professor Petticord what to do," she suggested. "He's been on more of these than we have."

"But it's our expedition, not his," Harry objected. "He's here at your invitation. The decision should be ours."

"It won't hurt to ask," Camilla insisted.

The professor had removed his floppy hat and was about to dip his whole head in the stream. Several years over sixty, he was as spry as a man half his age.

"Professor, a word if I may," Camilla said, coming up behind him.

"What is it?" Petticord rose, his knees popping loudly. He had a birdlike build and a hooked nose that resembled an oversized beak. "What has put a scowl on the pretty face of the best student I ever had?"

Camilla took the compliment in stride. "Tonekotay thinks we should head back to our base camp. He says we're being watched."

"Do tell." Professor Petticord shoved his hat onto his balding pate. "This might be just the stroke of luck we needed. If there are friendly Indians about, they could prove immensely helpful in our quest."

"But what if they're not friendly?" Camilla brought up.

"That's highly unlikely," the professor said. "The Iroquois Confederacy was shattered over two centuries ago, and most other tribes, even our allies, were either exterminated or driven westward. The Delawares are a case in point." He paused. "No, my dear.

5

The era of the woodland warrior is long over. If there truly is a tribe living in this vicinity, I'd wager a year's salary they're peaceful."

Tonekotay materialized at Camilla's side. He had overheard, and said in clear disapproval, "You not go back then?"

"No. Not unless you can offer definite proof we're in danger," Professor Petticord answered. "My students and I are under a time constraint, remember? We have another week to help Miss Kemp and Mr. Baxter, then we must return to Durnell University." Reaching out, he patted Camilla's hand. "I must thank you again for inviting us along. It's done me a world of good to get out in the field. Reminds me of the old days."

Tonekotay was unslinging his bow. "You make a mistake, Petticord. Before the day is done, you see."

"See what? Hostiles? Need I remind you that Mr. Baxter and myself are armed with Colt's latest side-arm?" The professor patted a revolver in a flapped holster on his left hip. "A few well-placed shots should suffice to discourage anyone with un-friendly intent."

"What do you say?" Tonekotay asked Camilla.

Camilla glanced from one to the other. "I respect both your opinions," she said diplomatically, "but I have to side with the professor. I'd hate to lose an entire afternoon unless there's a compelling reason to do so."

The search continued. Half an hour went by without any result. Camilla was about to suggest they forge northward when one of the anthropology students, a brunette by the name of Heather, gave a shout and commenced flapping her arms as if trying to take wing. Everyone rushed over. She was holding part of a pow-der horn. Cracked and pitted from the ravages of time, it bore several faint etchings or symbols.

6

"Permit me," Professor Petticord said, and examined the artifact carefully.

"Well?" Harry anxiously goaded. "Are we on the right track? Was our informant correct? Or has this whole thing been a wild-goose chase?"

The professor wagged their find. "I'd say this is quite promising. These marks tell me it was manufactured in France. Judging by its age, it was last held by human hands during the French and Indians wars."

"So a French trapper might have lost it," Harry said in disgust.

"Don't be so quick to jump to conclusions, young man. Very little trapping was done in this region by whites. It could just as well have belonged to an Indian. The French had a monopoly on the fur trade at one point, and gave hundreds of powder horns like these in trade for hides."

"You're speculating," Harry griped.

Camilla, exasperated, poked him. "Must you always look at the worst side of things?" She took the horn from her mentor. "This could well be proof a warrior culture existed in this area."

"Never forget," Professor Petticord said. "The tribe we're researching was reputed to be the most warlike of all. They didn't get along with anyone. The Iroquois, the Hurons, the Micmac, all hated and feared them."

"I've read the accounts," Harry said. "I know all about their dark secret. All about how they—"

Camilla pressed a finger against his lips. "That's enough out of you," she cautioned. But the harm had been done.

"What secret is he referring to?" asked Heather. "No one ever said anything to us."

Before Camilla or Harry could respond, Tonekotay shouted, "They come!" and abruptly sprang forward. "Run! I will try to hold them!" Planting himself midway to the trees, he notched an arrow to the sinew string on his ash bow.

"Is he serious?" Professor Petticord said. Hardly were the words out of his mouth than he was jerked backward by a feathered shaft that transfixed his right shoulder from front to back.

One of the students screamed.

Camilla leaped to the professor's side. Tonekotay's bow string twanged, followed by the sounds of unearthly howls coming from the woods. Petticord staggered, as much from shock as from agony, and would have fallen had she not wrapped an arm around him. Wheeling, she glimpsed darkling shapes bounding toward them. "We must get out of here!" she hollered, and sped as rapidly as she was able toward the south end of the clearing. "Can you move on your own?"

The professor's chin bobbed, but his very next step belied his claim. His knees buckled and he almost pitched onto his face.

The rest were running, Harry well in the lead and fumbling at the flap to his holster as if his fingers were coated with wax.

Camilla glanced back and saw Tonekotay unleash three arrows in swift succession, firing so swiftly his movements were a blur. She saw him reach for a fourth, saw him jolted by a shaft that caught him low in the ribs. He stayed on his feet, never so much as flinching. Backpedaling, he let loose with two more arrows, his noble self-sacrifice buying them precious moments. "Faster!" she shouted to the others. "Flee for your lives!"

Harry produced his Colt. Awkwardly thumbing back the hammer, he banged off a pair of wild shots. It was a wonder he didn't hit one of his own party.

Camilla realized she couldn't reach the south end of the clearing before their attackers overtook her. The trees to the west were closer. Veering to the right, she plunged into the vegetation, the professor slumped against her side. He didn't weigh much but it was enough to impede her as she skirted a wide thicket and wove through packed pines.

"Hang on, Professor," Camilla coaxed. She had lost sight of the onrushing figures and she assumed they had lost sight of her. "I'll head south in a bit and we'll be at the base camp before sundown."

"Did you see?" the professor asked weakly. "After all out effort! We were right, my dear. We were right!"

Here he was, an arrow in his shoulder, a scarlet stain spreading across his shirt, and all he could think of was the legend. "Crow about it later," Camilla said. "For now, you need to save your breath. We have a lot of ground to cover."

They rounded another thicket and Camilla came to a lurching halt. Blocking their way were more dark shapes. "How—?" she blurted.

"Look at them!" Professor Petticord marveled.

Camilla did. She looked at their faces, their terrible, savage faces, and in the depths of her soul felt the icy grip of mortal terror.

1

A lone rider arrived at the Imperial Inn long after sunset, a tall man in buckskins caked with the dust of many miles of hard travel. He brought his weary pinto stallion to a stop and bent his head back to survey the ornate three-story structure. Most of the gilded windows were ablaze with light. Shadows swirled within. Entrance was gained through a pair of polished oak doors, on either side of which hung bronze lanterns. Near the doors was a small sign painted in gold letters.

"The most expensive rooms this side of anywhere but well worth the price," Skye Fargo read aloud. "Sumptuous dining included." Underneath, in small print, was the warning, "Riffraff not welcome."

Stiffly dismounting, Fargo stretched to relieve a kink in his back. It had been a long day in the saddle and he could do with a hot meal and a good night's sleep. "This is the place," he said, giving the Ovaro a pat. "I'll see about bedding you down."

Merry laughter wafted from one of the rooms. Fargo let the reins dangle and climbed a short flight of steps to the double doors, and on through. He squinted against the bright glare in the lobby, his lake-blue eyes taking everything in. It was lavishly furnished, with wine-red carpet, landscape paintings on the walls, and plush easy chairs and sofas, half of which were occupied. Men in tailored suits glanced up from the newspapers they were reading. Women in dresses that cost more than most people earned in a

11

month stopped chattering like chipmunks to view him with detached interest. Heedless of their stares, Fargo strode to a mahogany counter and cleared his throat.

A portly desk clerk had his bulbous nose buried in a potboiler, a dime novel entitled, *Maleska: The Indian Wife Of The White Hunter,* by Ann Sophia Stevens. He jumped when Fargo slapped the counter, nearly dropping the book. "My apologies, sir. I didn't notice you come up." The man blinked, studying Fargo's attire. His gaze fastened on the gunbelt around Fargo's waist. "Oh my."

"You're supposed to have a room reserved in my name."

"We are?" the clerk responded skeptically. Setting the dime novel down, he stepped to the register. "It's not often we have someone of your—" Catching himself, he said, "I mean, we tend to cater to a rather wealthy clientele. Our rooms run three times as much as those in other inns. You might be better off staying at the Wayfarer down the road. It's probably more in your price range." When Fargo didn't respond, he nervously ran a pudgy finger down a page. "I don't see your name listed."

"You don't even know what it is."

"Oh. That's right." Swallowing hard, the clerk timidly asked, "Whom do I have the honor of addressing?"

Fargo told him, adding, "The reservation was supposed to have been made over a week ago by Lucius Kemp."

The clerk's eyes widened. "*The* Lucius Kemp? Of the New York Kemps? People say he's one of the richest men alive. He stays here on rare occasions, although I've never been fortunate enough to be on duty when—"

Fargo tapped the register. "Is my name there or not?"

The clerk started flipping pages. "Over a week ago, you said? Then it should be right about here." He

12

stopped and bent low. "My word. Here it is. With a checkmark, no less."

"A checkmark?"

"Yes sir. It means the owner has left special instructions. I'll be right back." Rotating on his heel, the man hustled into an office. There was the sound of a desk drawer being opened, and loud rustling.

The next thing Fargo knew, the clerk hurtled back out as if his britches were aflame. He had gone deathly pale and beads of perspiration dotted his forehead. Snatching a small bell from a shelf, he raised it overhead and began shaking it in a frenzy of agitation. Everyone in the lobby turned.

A pair of young men in starched uniforms came from a side room and snapped to attention like military cadets awaiting orders.

"This gentleman is staying in the Royal Suite," the clerk informed them. "He is to be afforded special treatment during the remainder of his stay. Jeffers, run on up and ensure the Suite is as it should be. Fresh fruit and flowers and all the rest. Thompson, you'll go out and fetch the gentleman's bags." The clerk bestowed an oily smile on Fargo. "How did you arrive, might I ask? By stage? By carriage? By phaeton, perhaps?"

"By horse."

"You *rode*?" Recovering his composure, the clerk barked at Thompson, "You heard our guest. Take his mount around to the livery and have it tended, then bring his personal effects up to the suite—"

"Just my saddlebags and rifle will do," Fargo said.

"Rifle? How extraordinary." The clerk wriggled his fingers and the pair dashed off. Leaning on the counter, he whispered so no one else could overhear, "Far be it for me to tell you how to conduct yourself, sir. But I would hate for a friend of Mr. Kemp's to run afoul of the local constabulary. This is Pennsylvania, not the Western frontier. There are laws dealing with firearms and the like. I'm afraid it's not entirely legal to go around wearing a gun."

"I plan to take mine off as soon as I'm in my room," Fargo set the man at ease. His stomach chose that moment to growl, reminding him he hadn't had a bite to eat since the day before. "Where's your dining room? I'm hungry enough to eat a bull buffalo."

"You are? The dining room stopped serving half an hour ago." The clerk glanced down at the register, at the checkmark next to Fargo's name. "But in your case we can certainly make an exception. Most of the staff is still here, cleaning up. Give me a quarter of an hour to arrange things."

Fargo extended a hand. "My key?"

With a grand flourish the man slid one from a box. "Here you are. The Royal Suite. If you'll permit me, I'll see you up to the top floor."

"I think I can find it on my own," Fargo said dryly. He made for the stairs, his spurs jangling, and had only taken a few strides when the clerk overtook him.

"Please, sir. We show the same courtesy to all our special guests." Scooting ahead, he graciously beckoned. "Right this way."

The carpet was so thick that Fargo's boots sank half an inch with each step. At the first landing the stairs angled to the right. He was about to start up the next flight when a raven-haired vision of beauty in a lacy blue dress and a matching hat rushed out of the adjoining hallway and collided with him. He had a fleeting impression of soft breasts pressed against his arm, then she stepped back, appalled.

"Oh, my! How clumsy of me! Please forgive me."

"No harm done," Fargo said, inhaling the tantalizing fragrance of musky perfume. In her early twenties, the woman had exquisite hazel eyes, full lips, and a luscious body with curves in all the right places. "Do it again if you want."

She laughed gayly. "Aren't you the brazen rake? If

14

I were the prim and proper lady my mother always wanted me to be, I'd take offense."

The desk clerk descended. "It was all my fault, Miss Wingate. I should have seen you coming." To Fargo, he said, "This is Bethany Wingate, of the Philadelphia Wingates. She's been with us several days now, waiting for someone."

"Honestly, Mr. Gardner," Bethany said in annoyance. "I don't see where that is anyone's affair but my own."

"Maybe you'd like to join me in the dining room in a bit?" Fargo said, offering his hand.

Bethany Wingate smiled. "I thank you for the offer, kind sir, but I must decline. Again, please forgive me." She pivoted to depart.

"Come along, Mr. Fargo," Gardner urged.

Bethany Wingate paused and glanced over a slender shoulder, her eyes narrowed quizzically. "Then again, perhaps I've been too hasty. Although I've eaten, I suppose a cup of tea or coffee wouldn't hurt. How soon should I be there?"

"Twenty minutes," Fargo said, which should be more than enough. The dark-haired lovely's cherry lips quirked upward and she continued on down the stairs in a swirl of silk. Turning, he found the desk clerk hadn't budged. "Something on your mind?"

"Congratulations, sir. You're not the first guest to take a fancy to her, but you're the first one she's given the time of day. Just this morning a handsome fellow invited her to go for an afternoon stroll in the garden and she about bit his head off. You must be special."

"And hungry. Let's get this over with."

The Royal Suite was identified by a silver plaque on the door. Fargo expected one or two rooms, but there were four. Like the lobby, they dripped of luxury; mahogany furniture, a fireplace, French doors that opened onto a balcony, a bedroom fit for a king, and a canopy bed large enough for the Ovaro to lie in.

Vases of fresh flowers added a dash of color, and a plate of fresh fruit decorated a small table.

"As you can see, we spare no expense where our best guests are concerned," Gardner bragged. "All you need do is pull on this cord—" He pointed at one next to the bed, "and a member of our fine staff will be both at your door and at your service."

Fargo wasn't accustomed to being waited on hand and foot, and he wasn't sure he liked the notion. "I can manage on my own."

"Of course you can, sir," Gardner agreed much too readily, "but it doesn't hurt to have us lend a helping hand, as it were. It's what we're paid to do." Excusing himself, he went to prepare the dining room.

An immaculate bathroom drew Fargo's interest. A china basin had been filled to the brim, and beside it were several folded towels and wash cloths. He removed his hat, stripped to the waist, and washed up. His saddlebags and Henry repeater arrived as he was finishing. Donning his spare shirt, he fished out a red bandanna, used the bedspread to wipe dust and dirt from his boots, and was ready to go. Or almost. Reluctantly, he unbuckled his gunbelt and laid it on the bed. He was loathe to go abroad without it but the clerk had been right. He wasn't west of the Mississippi anymore. He was among civilized folk now. Most every town and city had an ordnance against going around heeled.

Fargo thought longingly of the far-distant Rockies and the sea of amber prairie he called home. He'd preferred the wilderness to the densely populated East. New York, his destination, had the dubious distinction of having more inhabitants than any other state, with almost four million. New York City was the largest in the country, bigger than Denver and St. Louis combined.

For the umpteenth time since he'd received the telegram that had lured him from his usual haunts, Fargo questioned whether he was doing the right thing. The fee he was being paid, ten thousand dollars, was nothing to sneeze at. But to earn it he had to tolerate civilization for longer than he ordinarily liked. He reminded himself there was more at stake than the money. If the information in the telegram held true, only someone with his particular skills could do what needed to be done.

Fargo ensured the door was locked, pocketed the key, and ambled downstairs. The dining room was past the lobby, along a short hall. A candelabra had been placed in the center of a table close to the door, and three employees in white jackets were flitting about, setting out plates and silverware.

"Mr. Fargo!" Gardner said grandly. "Welcome. Have a seat, if you wish. We're just about done."

Another man in white shoved through a door at the rear, pushing a cart laden with bottles of wine.

"This is Claude," Gardner said. "He'll take over from here. If I can be of any further service, I'll be at the front desk." He scurried off.

Claude brought the cart to a stop and courteously bowed. "Good evening, monsieur. How about a bottle of vintage wine to start things off?"

"How about some coffin varnish?" Fargo said, easing into a chair.

"Monsieur?"

"Rotgut. Bug juice. Red-eye."

"I am not sure—" Claude began.

"Whiskey," Fargo said. "And leave the bottle."

Bethany Wingate picked that moment to breeze into the room. "I hope I haven't kept you waiting." Her hat was gone, and she had done up her hair in a bun that was held in place by a large gold barrette. She had also touched up her lips and added a splash of rouge to her cheeks. By any standard she was breathtakingly gorgeous. One of the staff dutifully held out a chair for her.

17

"I was just getting set to order," Fargo said. He couldn't help but admire her more-than-ample bosom. Covered as they were by thin white lace, her mounds were clearly defined. He imagined what it would be like to lather them with his tongue.

"Coffee for me," Bethany said, "spiced with a healthy dollop of brandy." She giggled girlishly. "For my circulation, you understand."

A menu was placed in front of Fargo but he didn't bother reading it. "Steak," he told Claude. "An inch thick, with all the trimmings. Potatoes, corn, half a loaf of bread, and plenty of butter. Can you manage all that?"

"Oui, monsieur," Claude said. "Might I suggest a plate of oysters or mushrooms for your appetizer?"

"Put the mushrooms on the steak," Fargo directed. "The oysters you can forget. Unless the lady would rather have some?"

Bethany had a hand over her mouth, hiding a grin. "Thank you, but no. I never ingest anything that looks as if it came from someone else's stomach."

Fargo laughed, and the kitchen staff dashed away to do their bidding. His dinner companion arched a delicate eyebrow, giving him the sort of scrutiny he would give an unknown animal.

"Forgive my boldness in accepting your invitation, but you intrigue me. It isn't often I meet someone in buckskins." Bethany's eyes lingered on his broad chest and wide shoulders. "I take it you're a frontiersman?"

"That's as good a description as any," Fargo acknowledged. Scout, plainsman, tracker, he had been called many things.

"How marvelous. I've read about the frontier, of course, in dime novels and the newspapers. What's it like? The wilds, I mean? All those Indians always on the warpath. It must be positively horrid."

Fargo wasn't a talkative man by nature, but for her

sake he went into considerable detail, concluding with, "Indians are no different than whites. Some will treat you as decent as a Quaker. Others will lift your scalp just because they don't like the color of your skin."

"You have a colorful way with words," Bethany said. "But what about the terrible beasts I've heard of? Grizzlies the size of wagons. Wolves that travel in huge packs. Don't they scare you the least little bit?"

"Unless wolves are rabid or starving, they shy away from humans," Fargo said. "Grizzlies are another matter. To them, we're food on the hoof. But they're unpredictable. Half the time they'll run off. The other half, they'll rip a person to shreds."

"Goodness." Bethany shuddered. "You wouldn't catch me living out West for all the jade in China. Why anyone would ever want to eludes me."

Fargo's estimation of her dropped a few notches. "Most move west for the freedom. Being able to do what they want, when they want, with no one looking over their shoulders telling them how to do it."

"That makes no sense. Here in the States we're just as free."

Were they? Fargo mused. Or was she fooling herself? Either way, he wasn't in the mood for a long-winded discussion. He wanted to fill his belly, wet his throat, and maybe, the lady willing, indulge in a vastly more pleasurable act later on. "Tell me about you," he said to change the subject. He had yet to meet a woman who didn't like talking about herself, and Bethany Wingate proved no exception. She chattered on and on about her upbringing in Philadelphia, where her father owned a string of businesses, and about how she was on her way to visit a dear aunt in Pittsburgh.

His meal arrived, and Fargo ate with relish. The steak was done to perfection; the potatoes melted in his mouth. After dabbing his plate clean with the last slice of bread, he washed it all down with whiskey, chugging straight from the bottle, then sat back and patted his stomach.

Bethany watched in amusement. "I must say, you're different from any man I've ever met. I doubt my parents would approve. You're too primitive for their tastes." She winked playfully. "But not for mine."

Fargo knew an invite when he heard one. "Is that a fact? I'd like to hear more. Maybe you'd like to go for a stroll?"

"Outdoors? It's much too chill. Why don't we go up to my room instead?"

Happy to oblige, Fargo rose and came around the table to slide out her chair. As Bethany rose she coyly contrived to brush her arm against his.

Claude hurried from the kitchen, wiping his hands on an apron. "You are leaving, monsieur? Isn't there anything more you desire? Dessert, perhaps? We have chocolate cake, the most delicious pudding, and a selection of fresh pies to choose from."

"What I want isn't on the menu," Fargo quipped. Taking Beth's arm, he walked her out, and as soon as the door closed behind them, she burst into laughter and impulsively hugged him.

"I was joking when I called you a rake earlier, but I see now you're positively scandalous."

The hallway was deserted. Fargo pulled Bethany into the shadows, into a recessed doorway, and molded his mouth to hers. He was delighted when her lips parted to admit his tongue. Their tongues entwined in a velvet swirl of sensation, and a new hunger came over him. A hunger that had nothing to do with more food. Cupping her firm bottom, he ground his hardening manhood against her inner thighs and was rewarded with a low gasp and a throaty moan.

Bethany stepped back. "My, my," she said huskily. "Right out here in the open? Are you trying to ruin my reputation?" She tugged, leading him toward the lobby. "I can be naughty now and then, but I'm not an exhibitionist. I prefer more privacy, if you don't mind."

"Not at all." Fargo liked how her hips swayed as she walked, and the sultry pout to her full lips.

Very few guests were left in the lobby. It was past ten, and most everyone else had turned in. An elderly matron bestowed a disapproving glare as they went by. The matron's male companion, though, grinned knowingly.

Fargo gazed past them, toward a large window adjacent to the entrance, and spied two men standing just outside, bathed in the glow of the bronze lanterns. Beefy, gruff-seeming men dressed in woolen caps and thick coats. They weren't the sort of clientele the inn preferred. He assumed they were looking for a place to stay for the night, and he was about to turn away when the shorter of the pair suddenly spotted him, stiffened, and gripped the other man's arm. Surprise registered. Then they spun and raced off into the night.

Fargo didn't know what to make of it. Any other time, he would have gone out to investigate. But at the moment he had one thing and one thing only on his mind.

"Miss Wingate! There you are!" Gardner was at the front desk, waving a small yellow envelope. "I have something for you. A most unsavory character dropped it off a few minutes ago with express instructions for me to deliver it into your hands."

"Unsavory?" Bethany said.

"He was rude, Miss Wingate. Rude and uncouth. He claimed it's a message from your father, although why your father would use the services of a ruffian like him is beyond me. He had the audacity to grab me by the front of the shirt and threaten me with physical violence if I failed to carry out his instructions."

"My word. My father would never hire someone like that. Maybe there's been a mix-up of some kind." Accepting the envelope, Bethany excused herself and walked a dozen feet away to read the contents in private.

"A marvelous woman, is she not?" Gardner said in envy.

Fargo didn't reply. He would be better able to answer that question in the morning.

"I must remember to talk to Mr. Arthur Adams, a regular of ours, the next time he stays with us," Gardner rambled blithely on. "I recall him saying last year he knew the Wingates quite well, and that Bethany Wingate was a stunning blonde. Obviously, his memory isn't what it used to be."

"Maybe she dyed her hair," Fargo suggested. "Women are fond of changing their appearance."

"True," the desk clerk said. "They're also sensitive about having it brought up. I'm not about to go over and ask if that's her natural color. She's liable to slap my face for my impertinence."

Bethany's back was to them. Fargo couldn't see her expression but he noticed her stiffen and slowly lower a yellow sheet of paper she had been reading. She looked toward the front of the inn, then replaced the letter in the yellow envelope and shoved both into her leather handbag. When she turned a subtle change had come over her. Fargo couldn't peg it down, exactly, but she had a slightly harder cast to the set of her jaw and her eyes had lost their impish allure. "Is everything all right?"

"My younger brother has taken ill," Bethany said. "It's not life-threatening, but my father wants me back in Philadelphia as soon as I can get there."

"I'm sorry to hear that, Miss Wingate," Gardner said. "Someone once told me you were an only child."

"Not so." Smiling, Bethany looped an arm around Fargo's. "Now what say you escort me to my room?

I need to get to bed if I'm to start back early tomorrow morning."

Fargo couldn't tell if she was sincere or putting on a show for the clerk's benefit. He found out when they reached the landing and weren't visible to those below. Her hands hooked behind his neck and she sculpted her lush body to his. "I thought maybe the news had spoiled your mood," he remarked.

"My brother will be fine. My father is a worrywart, is all." Bethany kissed him, her passion undeniable.

Fargo returned the favor, his hands rising to her shoulders, to her hair. Unexpectedly, she drew away, grasped both his hands, and hastened down the hall.

"What was I thinking?" Beth said. "Privacy, remember?" At number 16 she rummaged in her handbag and produced the key. "We'll have to keep the noise down," she whispered. "Both rooms on either side are occupied."

A globe lamp had been left on. Bethany deposited her bag on a dresser and reached for the lamp's base. "I like it dark."

"Not me," Fargo said, slipping in front of her so she couldn't turn it off. He never had understood why anyone in their right mind would prefer to make love in inky blackness. Half his enjoyment came from seeing what he was touching.

Bethany hesitated, then melted into his arms and kissed him with renewed ardor. The feel of her breasts on his chest set his groin to twitching. She didn't let the kiss linger, though. Pushing him back, she pointed at a darkened doorway.

"Why don't you turn back the quilt while I get undressed?" Beth raised her hands to the barrette to undo her hair.

Fargo would rather undress her himself, but he didn't argue. Grinning in anticipation, he moved toward the bedroom. Why he glanced back he would never know, but it was well he did. For the gold object

23

in Bethany Wingate's hair wasn't a barrette, after all. It was a double-edged, pencil-thin dagger, and it gleamed brightly as she raised it to bury the blade in his back.

2

Astonishment rooted Skye Fargo in place as Bethany Wingate flew at him with her face contorted in raw bloodlust and the dagger poised to stab. Instinctively, he swept up his arms to protect himself, and the blow meant for his unprotected back glanced off his wrist. Fargo lunged, seeking to grab her, but Bethany shifted, evading him, and lanced her blade at his neck. He threw himself backward, narrowly sparing himself a grave wound, or worse, and demanded, "Drop that thing or else!"

It fell on deaf ears. Hissing, Bethany came at him again, swinging the dagger from side to side.

Fargo retreated, his mind a tangle of confusion. He had never set eyes on the woman before, yet here she was trying to do him in. It made no sense. But one thing was for sure. He wasn't about to stand there and let her do it. Avoiding a thrust to the chest, he swung on the ball of his foot and clipped her on the chin with a right cross. He wasn't able to brace himself or he would have sent her reeling. As it was, she stumbled against the dresser, vigorously shook her head to clear it, and hiked her weapon again.

"Enough is enough," Fargo growled, swooping his right hand to his hip. But the Colt wasn't there. He'd forgotten his gunbelt was in the Royal Suite. He darted toward the door to the hallway but Wingate cut him off, her dagger weaving a glittering promise of imminent death.

"No you don't! You've got to die! No matter what!"

25

Her shrill cries filled the room, provoking a muffled shout from the next. Hearing it, and evidently fearing someone might see fit to come see what all the commotion was about, Bethany drove herself at him like a woman gone berserk, determined to end their clash quickly. She slashed, she hacked, she repeatedly speared the dagger at his heart and his neck.

Fargo was hard-pressed to stay out of her reach. He twisted, he ducked, he kicked a small table at her legs, but she deftly sidestepped. Risking a glance, he spotted a chair to his left and rushed to grab hold. Bethany was on him before he could. Cold steel missed his hand by a cat's whisker. A second swipe nicked his forearm, shearing through the buckskin and drawing a trickle of blood.

"We'll never let you!" Bethany railed. "Do you hear me? I'm the first, but I won't be the last!"

Fargo had no idea what she was talking about. He tried for the chair again, expecting her to go for his hands. When she did, he dropped straight down, onto his side, and lashed out with both legs. His boots slammed into her abdomen, smashing her backward.

Arms pinwheeling, Bethany kept her balance. The man in the next room was pounding on the wall, demanding to know what all the noise was about. She glanced at it, then at Fargo, and snarled, "This isn't over yet." With that, she sped to the door, snagging her handbag as she dashed by, and fled in a whirl of silk and lace and flying raven hair.

"Damn!" Fargo heaved to his feet and gave chase. He raced into the hallway, took three more steps, and stopped in consternation. There hadn't been time for Bethany to reach the landing yet the hallway was empty. He looked both ways, wondering if she had darted into another room.

Just then the door to 17 opened and a middle-aged man in an ankle-length nightshirt stormed out. "What the devil is going on? Some of us are trying to sleep! I have half a mind to complain to the management."

"Be my guest," Fargo said, and went back in. Throwing the bolt, he opened the dresser drawers one by one, after clues as to why he had almost been murdered. He thought he would find them filled with clothes and other articles. Women were notorious for packing twice as much as they needed. But except for the top one, they had gone unused. And all he found in the top one was a frilly bathrobe.

Growing more puzzled by the moment, Fargo explored every nook and cranny, but he came up empty-handed. Or so he thought until he sorted through her cosmetics. There was the usual assortment of creams, powders, and whatnot, as well as a sterling silver compact engraved with flowers. He tossed it back onto the vanity and the compact flipped over. Engraved on the bottom was an inscription, *'To my beloved P. K.'*

On a whim Fargo slipped the compact into a pocket. He checked the corridor before showing himself. The inn was as still as a cemetery at midnight, so still he heard the occasional creak of floorboards under the carpet as he made a beeline for the Royal Suite. The instant he was across the threshold he strapped on his gunbelt, confirmed the Colt was fully loaded, and marched right back out.

Other than Gardner, the lobby was now deserted. Unnoticed, Fargo stepped up to the counter and thumped on it to get his attention.

The clerk was engrossed in a dime novel while idly munching on a cookie. Startled, he bit clean through the cookie and half of it fell to the floor. "Mr. Fargo! Why do you keep doing that? A simple 'hi' would suffice." Gardner's eyes flicked right and left. "You're alone? Frankly, I didn't count on seeing you again before my shift was over."

"Can you prove to me Bethany Wingate is who she claimed to be?"

"I beg your pardon?"

Fargo was playing a hunch. "How do we know the woman claiming to be Wingate really is who she says?" There were too many inconsistencies; the compact, the dark hair, the fact she was supposed to be an only child.

Gardener snickered. "How much whiskey did you imbibe tonight? That's the most preposterous accusation I've ever heard."

"Has Wingate paid her bill yet?"

"In cash, in advance, the day she arrived. She booked a room through tomorrow." Gardner set down the dime novel. "Why are you making an issue of her identity?"

"Because she just tried to kill me."

Slapping his leg, Gardner cackled in near-hysterics. As it gradually dawned on him Fargo wasn't joking, his mirth trickled to a strangled gurgle punctuated by a confused bleat. "You're not pulling my leg?"

"How did she reserve the room?" Fargo asked.

"How? By letter. The manager showed it to me but I didn't pay much attention. Last I knew it was still in his office."

"Show it to me."

Once more perspiration broke out on the clerk's brow. "I'm afraid that's not possible. All correspondence is held in the strictest of confidence. If I showed it to you I could be fired. It's against the rules."

"The rules be damned." Fargo moved toward the gap between the front desk and the wall.

"Wait! Please!" Gardner pleaded. "Give me a minute, and I'll let you look at it on one condition. You must give it right back. Promise?"

"Why would I bother to keep it?" Fargo hedged.

True to his word, the clerk emerged from the office

with a yellow envelope. "This is the one. Lord, I hope we don't get caught."

Fargo remembered the envelope Bethany Wingate received earlier. It, too, had been yellow. The postmark was New York City, not Philadelphia where the Wingates were from. There was no return address. Opening it, he unfolded a yellow sheet of stationary identical to the one Wingate had been reading. The letter had been dated ten days ago, two days after he received his telegram from Lucius Kemp. Written in a distinctly feminine hand, it was short and to the point, requesting a room be reserved for Bethany Wingate on the dates specified. Folding it, Fargo pretended to slide it back into the envelope, but instead he slipped it up his right sleeve, tucked the envelope's flap under, and gave the envelope back to Gardner.

"Where is Miss Wingate now?" the desk clerk inquired.

"I was hoping you could tell me," Fargo said. "Did you see her go running by?"

Gardner shook his head. "I sure didn't."

Fargo gazed up the stairs. Odds were, she was still in the inn. But he couldn't very well go barging from room to room searching for her, not at that hour.

"Do you want me to send someone for the sheriff?" Gardner asked. "It will take half the night to reach Harrisburg, but it might be best under the circumstances."

The last thing Fargo wanted was a long delay. The sheriff would spend most of the day poking around and asking questions. He might not get out of there until the following morning, and he needed to reach New York City as quickly as possible.

Fargo had been in St. Louis when the telegram was delivered. The very next morning he had set off along the old National Road, riding from first light until well past dusk. And so it went day after day. A couple of times he stopped at inns for the night, but usually he made camp in secluded spots, a few pieces of pemmican his supper. He'd left the National Road at an appropriate point to head overland by a more direct route and now he was in Pennsylvania between Pittsburgh and Harrisburg, nearing the latter. He still had another two hundred miles to go.

"Forget the law," Fargo told the desk clerk. From his pocket he took the money that had been sent with the telegram and peeled a twenty from the wad of four hundred. "This is for the trouble I've put you to." He peeled off another. "This is to keep your mouth shut."

Gardner had missed his calling. He should have been a magician. The bills were whisked under his jacket. "Never fear!" he beamed. "I'm the model of discretion when I need to be. My lips are sealed."

Not entirely convinced, Fargo bounded up the stairs to the Royal Suite. He bolted the door, propped a chair against it as added insurance, and lay on the canopy bed, fully clothed, mulling over his encounter. Was it possible the woman had mistaken him for somebody else? He recalled Gardner saying how she had been waiting around for someone. And how she had changed her mind about dining with him after the clerk mentioned his name. It would seem, then, that *he* was the one she had been waiting for, and that her attempt on his life was no accident.

What was he getting himself into? Fargo wondered. Who wanted to stop him from reaching New York? Why hadn't Lucius Kemp mentioned his life might be in danger? More important, should he forget the whole thing and head back to the frontier? The four hundred dollars was his to keep no matter what he did. He was tempted, strongly tempted. He didn't like being a walking target. But his life wasn't the only one at risk. There was someone else to think of.

Sitting up, Fargo pulled the telegram from his pocket and read it again.

WESTERN UNION

From: Lucius Kemp
      114 Kensington Place
      New York, NY

To: Skye Fargo
    The Sarasota Hotel
    St. Louis, Missouri

Mr. Fargo,
      Your presence is requested at my residence at
      your earliest convenience. I am in dire need of
      your help. My favorite niece has disappeared in a
      remote region along the U.S./Canadian border.
      I want you to find her.
      In return for the services I am willing to pay
      you ten thousand dollars.
      Enclosed is a four hundred dollar advance to
      use as expense money until you arrive, and is
      yours to keep however you decide.
      Please respond with your intent as soon as
      practical.
                  Desperately Yours,
                  Lucius Kemp

    The patriarch's signature was an uneven scrawl, as
if written by a man who could barely hold a quill pen.
It was common knowledge Kemp was getting on in
years. He was over eighty by most accounts, and not
in the best of health.

    Fargo sighed, and replaced the telegram. Sometimes
he was too damn high-principled for his own damn
good. He didn't know Kemp's niece. She meant nothing to him. Yet the thought of her lost amid the dense
woods of the deep north had spurred him into leaving
the earthy comforts of the Sarasota Hotel—and the
arms of a friendly fallen dove—and hurrying East.

    Fargo blamed it on his never-ending urge to help
folks in need. Again and again he had put his life in

peril for total strangers, and all for what? It was foolish. Hell, it was stupid. But he couldn't help himself.

"I'm an idiot," Fargo said, and closed his eyes. Sleep claimed him almost instantly but he slept fitfully, awakening at the slightest of sounds.

As was Fargo's custom he was up before sunrise. No one was in the lobby. No one saw him leave. Gardner was dozing at the front desk and Fargo didn't bother to wake him up. Stepping out in the crisp predawn cold, he saw low banks of gray clouds scuttling across the sky, obscuring the stars.

The doors to the livery were closed. Fargo had to pound for over a minute before a disheveled stableman in hastily donned overalls removed the bar to admit him.

"Who the devil are you?" the man sullenly asked. "Why in blazes did you get me out of bed so early? I could have slept another half hour yet."

"I'm here for my horse."

The man yawned and scratched the stubble on his chin. "Which horse would that be, mister?" he asked irritably.

"An Ovaro. Maybe you were asleep when they brought it in." Fargo shouldered past and strode down the aisle to the third stall on the right. The stallion nuzzled him as he opened it. He saddled up, strapped on his saddlebags, slid the Henry into the saddle scabbard, and stepped into the stirrups. Kneeing the stallion to the double doors, he reined up. "Well?"

"Well what?" The liveryman had made no attempt to open them and was standing with his hands stuffed down his overalls.

"Are your arms broken?" Fargo asked. "Or should I climb down and break them for you?"

Muttering under his breath, the liveryman swung the right-hand door out. As soon as the pinto moved past, he closed it again, swearing luridly.

"Easterners," Fargo said, and trotted down the gravel lane that linked the inn to the main highway. The road was deserted, but it wouldn't be for long. He held to a brisk walk, the pinto's shod hooves ringing hollowly on the stone surface. Before long a faint tinge framed the horizon, a harbinger of the new day. The sky was still totally overcast, and a stiff wind had picked up from the northwest, bringing with it the scent of moisture.

Fargo liked Pennsylvania. Despite all the people, vast tracts were covered by verdant forest. Oaks, maples, and elms were common. In the lowland valleys weeping willows grew in profusion. So did ash trees, which were rare in the West, so rare that tribes sometimes fought for control of the regions where they grew because ash bows were rated superior to every other. Poplars and sycamores were also present in great numbers. He saw few cottonwoods, though, which were as abundant as rabbits out West.

Fargo had to chuckle at the Pennsylvanian mountains. Compared to the Rockies they hardly deserved the title. They weren't much higher than foothills. The tallest, he'd heard tell, was three thousand feet high, whereas the Rocky Mountains boasted scores of peaks four times that high.

Still, the state had its charms, and Fargo could see why people were content to live there. Most were farmers. Harvested fields of wheat, oats, barley, and corn crisscrossed the landscape, sprinkled here and there by white farmhouses and red barns. Well-fed cattle grazed amid green pastures, but the grassland wouldn't be green for long. Winter wasn't far off, and the majority of trees had already changed color. A picturesque tapestry of leafy boughs in hues of red, orange, and yellow cloaked the mountains, their colors dulled by the overcast heavens.

Presently a wagon hove into sight. A farmer was

rattling eastward on his way to Harrisburg, the bed of his wagon laden with bales of hay. Fargo overtook it and nodded as he went by.

Grinning, the man removed a corncob pipe from his mouth. "Greetings, neighbor! God be with thee." He was dressed all in black except for a white shirt, and wore square-toed black boots.

An Amish farmer, Fargo guessed. Whole communities called Pennsylvania home, peaceable men and women who had forsaken worldly goods and tried their utmost to live by the Golden Rule. They refused to lift a hand against their fellow man, even to defend themselves. Admirable convictions, Fargo reflected, but not very practical west of the Mississippi where outlaws and hostiles were as thick as fleas on a coon dog and had no qualms about gunning down innocents for the clothes on their backs or the hair on their heads.

The traffic grew heavier the closer Fargo drew to the capital. An hour elapsed, and then, for no particular reason, he shifted in the saddle and glanced back. A quarter mile away, matching his gait, was a solitary rider on a black horse. He wouldn't have thought much of it except the man appeared to be wearing a woolen cap and blue coat—exactly like the two men outside the Imperial Inn the night before.

Was he being followed? Fargo decided to put it to the test by bringing the pinto to a trot. Thirty seconds later when he looked back, the man on the black horse had done the same. He slowed, and the rider did likewise. "You don't know it yet, mister," Fargo said, "but you and I are about to get acquainted."

A sign announced Harrisburg was ten miles off.

Fargo had to make his move before they reached the city limits. Once there, the Colt had to go into his saddlebags or he risked arrest.

A tree-lined country lane, branching off to the south, offered Fargo the opportunity he needed. Two freight wagons were about to pass it. Applying his spurs, Fargo cantered on by them, looked back to be sure the rider couldn't see him, and veered off the road into the lane. Drawing rein at the base of a majestic maple, he waited for the man in the woolen cap to catch up. He didn't have to wait long.

Furiously lashing his mount, the rider galloped past. He had risen in the stirrups and was scanning the road ahead. Judging by his expression he was extremely upset.

Fargo moved into the open and gave chase. In no time the Ovaro trailed the bay by only a few yards. But the rough character in the woolen cap was so intent on spotting him that the man didn't think to look back.

They neared a sharp bend. Fargo noticed traffic had briefly thinned, and he took advantage of the situation by pulling abreast of his unsuspecting pursuer. "Looking for someone?" he casually asked.

For a few seconds the rider was too stupefied to react. Then his right hand darted under his heavy blue coat.

Fargo was faster. He streaked the Colt up and out, clubbing the man across the temple.

Limbs flying, the rider tumbled from the saddle and on down a grassy embankment into a thicket bordering a field. He tried to rise but collapsed.

It happened so swiftly, no one had seen. Fargo shoved the Colt into its holster, seized the bay's reins, and slowed to a walk. Wheeling over the embankment, he rode toward where the rider lay.

The man was on his belly, unconscious. His woolen cap had come off, exposing close-cropped sandy hair and a left ear that resembled mashed cauliflower.

Dismounting, Fargo nudged the prone form with the tip of his boot, and when nothing happened he sank onto one knee and rolled the man over. Under the fellow's coat, tucked under his belt, was a nickel-plated Smith and Wesson double-action revolver, a newer model ideal for carrying concealed because it was hammerless and wouldn't snag on clothing when drawn. Fargo wedged it under his own belt, uncurled, and nudged the man again. A groan rose on the wind.

As luck would have it, the rain Fargo had predicted began to fall, a light sprinkle that dampened the rider's thick-boned face. The man stirred, his fingers twitching, and Fargo nudged him a third time.

Beady bloodshot eyes snapped open, fixing on Fargo in baffled hatred. The man started to sit up, then saw Fargo's hand was resting on the butt of the Colt. "Damn you, mister. You had no call to do that."

"Who are you and why are you following me?"

The man gingerly touched a growing goose egg on his temple. "I don't know what you're talking about. You can go to hell for all I care."

"Wrong answer." Greased lightning in motion, Fargo palmed the Colt and struck the rider on the other temple. The man sagged, out to the world again, with a new welt to match the first. "Some people are too stupid for their own good," Fargo commented. Twirling the Colt into its holster, he went through the man's pockets. All he found were a few coins and a small folding knife.

Fargo stepped to the black horse. Easterners typically didn't use saddlebags, but there was a bedroll. Removing it, he spread it out on the ground. Cached inside were a spare shirt and extra trousers, a pair of gloves that had seen better days, several socks, and a scuffed wallet. A wallet that bulged with bills. Fargo counted them. Two hundred and ten dollars in small denominations, all new bills not long in circulation.

Tucked behind them was a slip of paper. Written on it, in the same feminine hand as that on the letter he had taken from the Imperial Inn, was the inn's address and instructions. *Be there two days before he is due to arrive, just to be safe. Contact me immediately after the job is done and the rest of your money will be sent."* In the front of the wallet was a card that identified the bearer as one Martin Stevens, a long-shoreman from New York City, which explained the woolen cap and the heavy blue coat, attire longshore-men were partial to.

Fargo stuck the card into his pocket with the letter, rolled up the bedroll, and tied it onto the bay. A steady drizzle fell by now, and water rolled off the brim of his hat as he turned.

Martin Stevens groaned anew, and shortly opened his eyes.

"Let's try this again, Martin," Fargo said.

Befuddled by the two blows, Stevens struggled up onto his elbows. "How do you know who I am?" he gruffly demanded.

"I know a lot of things," Fargo fibbed. "The woman who hired you is going to be mighty disappointed."

"The woman?" Stevens said, and glanced at his mount, at his bedroll. "So that's it. I'm not as dumb as you think, mister. You can beat on me until dooms-day and I still won't tell you a thing."

Fargo's bluff had failed. "I doubt it will take that long," he said, and slowly drew the Colt.

Martin Stevens recoiled. "Hold on there, damn you! You can't go around pistol-whipping people for no reason."

"I have the best reason in the world." Fargo hefted the Colt. "Someone hired you to kill me and I want to know why."

"It's not the why that should concern you, it's who," Stevens said. "As sure as I'm lying here, you're a walking dead man. And there's not a damn thing you can do it about it. Not when you're up against the likes of—" Stopping, he chuckled. "Well, let's just say if I were in your shoes, I'd set sail on the next ship out of the country and never come back."

"Who sicced you on me, Martin?"

"If I say, I might as well dig my own grave and let you shoot me." Fear etched Stevens, but not fear of Fargo. "It would all come out the same. People with that kind of power can do whatever they want."

"Does this have some connection to Lucius Kemp?" Fargo probed.

"You'll have to find out for yourself." Stevens glanced up the embankment and, just like that, his whole attitude changed. "But I might be persuaded to give you more information for some hard cash. A hundred dollars, say?"

A tiny voice in Fargo's mind screamed a warning. Something wasn't right. The longshoreman was giving in too easily. Suspecting the truth, he spun, and there, midway down the rain-slicked bank, was Stevens's partner, taking aim with an identical nickel-plated Smith and Wesson revolver.

3

Everything happened so fast.

Skye Fargo flung himself to the left at the exact split second the second longshoreman fired and a slug meant for his chest cleaved the space where he had just stood. He landed on his shoulder, drawing the Colt as he did, but before he could squeeze off a shot the clouds unleashed a deluge. Sheets of rain blotted out everything beyond arm's reach, shrouding the world in watery gloom. He couldn't see the killers, couldn't see the horses.

Another shot cracked, but it went wide. Fargo heard the man he had pistol-whipped yell, heard an answering shout from the other man on the grassy bank. He reared upright and moved toward where he thought the first man should be, but the would-be assassin had vanished into the rain.

A horse nickered stridently.

Fearing the pair might try to steal the Ovaro, Fargo barreled in its direction. He had the cocked Colt in his right hand. Stretching out his left, he groped at the cascading water like a blind man, wary of blundering into Stevens or the second assassin.

Fargo's fingertips brushed slicked hairs. Stepping closer, he discovered he had hold of the pinto's mane. Finding the reins was easy. To fork leather, he had to locate a stirrup, hold it steady so he could insert his boot, then swing astride the hurricane deck. He reined toward the bank, then promptly changed his mind.

Finding the pair in the downpour was impossible. He was better off sitting tight until it ended. Remembering a small tract of trees only a few dozen yards to the southwest, he goaded the pinto toward where he hoped they would be. All the while, cold, heavy drops battered him mercilessly, drenching his buckskins and soaking him to the skin.

Another shout pierced the pounding rain, from farther off.

Fargo plodded on until a vague mass rose in front of him. He had located the trees. Once under them, their overspreading limbs shielded him from the brunt of Nature's tantrum. He stayed in the saddle, eager to give chase, but the deluge continued unabated for the next ten minutes. When it finally tapered off, it did so as abruptly as it had started, dwindling to a fine misty sprinkle in a span of heartbeats.

Spurring the Ovaro to the highway, Fargo rode eastward. He reasoned the killers had done the same and were somewhere up ahead. But although he held to a trot until he was less than a mile from Harrisburg, he didn't spot them.

Fargo had a decision to make. Initially he'd intended to skirt Harrisburg to the north, but now it seemed wiser to push straight on through to save time. Accordingly, he cautiously crossed over the Susquehanna River and entered Pennsylvania's capital. Few residents were abroad. The rain had driven most indoors. Wagons, buggies, and carriages lined the shoulders, their owners either in dry havens or preparing to get underway. No one caught sight of the Colt or the Smith and Wesson. Or if they did, they had the good sense not to confront him.

Now and then the breeze bore the scent of food. It was almost noon, but Fargo forged on, steeling himself to do without until nightfall. On the other side of the city another decision had to be made. To the best of Fargo's recollection, he could either take the Lancas-

40

ter Turnpike into Philadelphia and then swing north-ward to New York, or he could strike off directly overland.

Better roads lay to the east, and better roads meant a shorter trip. Since avoiding delays was crucial, Fargo opted to shave hours by sticking to the major thoroughfares.

A mile beyond Harrisburg Fargo removed his gun-belt, wrapped it around the holstered Colt, and placed it in a saddlebag. He left the Smith and Wesson tucked under the front of his pants but took the precaution of covering it with his buckskin shirt.

Although the rain had ceased, the clouds lingered. It was the middle of the afternoon before stray rays of sunshine broke through. They did little to dry Fargo out, and by early evening the dampness was taking an unwelcome toll. Fargo started to shiver, to feel hot and flushed. He was coming down with something. Exactly what was uncertain, but he had a hunch he'd get a lot worse before he got better.

Fargo couldn't remember the last time he'd had a cold or the flu. So it was doubly ironic that his body chose this day of all days, when time was so critical, to succumb. A hot bath and a warm bed were called for. Spending the night outdoors under damp blankets would only make things worse.

At sunset Fargo came to a series of hills and wound through them into a secluded valley. Situated at the center was a small hamlet, no more than twenty build-ings scattered along a single muddy street. One was a general store. Another was a blacksmith's. A third was a farm house converted into an eatery for travelers, and on a post by the gate was a small sign that adver-tised, *Rooms For Rent, By The Day Or The Week*.

Fargo reined up at a hitch rail. On the front porch were two rocking chairs and an old mongrel that wagged its spindly tail but couldn't muster the energy to rise. At Fargo's knock, someone called out for him to wait a moment. Shoes clomped on a hardwood floor, and the outer door opened to reveal a tall brunette in a homespun dress.

"Howdy, stranger. You look as if you can use a hot meal. The dining room is around to the side. Follow the footpath and let yourself in."

"I'm more interested in renting a room for the night," Fargo said, and his teeth chattered uncontrollably.

The woman opened the screen door. She had brown eyes, an aquiline nose, and a nice body. "You're awful pale. Are you feeling poorly?"

"A little," Fargo conceded. "I could use a hot bath. I'm willing to pay extra."

She pursed her lips, then pressed a palm to his forehead. "Mercy. You're burning up. I've heard there's something going around. A lot of folks lately have been bedridden. You need doctoring, and I guess I'm elected. But don't get any funny notions. I might be a widow, but that doesn't give anyone the right to take liberties."

"All I want is a good night's rest," Fargo stressed. He motioned toward the hitch rail. "I have a horse—"

"Leave him to me. I'll take him around back in a while and bed him down proper. Right now the important thing is to get you warm." The brunette stepped aside so he could enter. "Go down the hall and into the last room on the right. I'll put water on to boil."

"Thank you," Fargo said. Gritting his teeth, he did as she had directed. In the middle of the room was a waist-high tub. A sink graced one of the walls, a towel rack and a mirror graced another. He hung his hat and bandanna on a peg but held off undressing so as not to offend his host.

The woman didn't leave him alone all that long. Carrying a striped towel and a bar of lye soap, she came over and felt his forehead again. "No doubt about it. If we don't nip this in the bud you'll be too sick to get out of bed by morning." She hung the towel on the rack. "I'm Cheryl Taylor."

"Pleased to meet you," Fargo said, shivering, and introduced himself.

"You're the only fool on the road tonight, so it looks as if you can have my undivided attention." Cheryl gave the tub a whack. "It'll take a good half an hour to fill, even with four pots on the stove at once. I'll fetch you one of my husband's robes so you can shuck those wet buckskins while you're waiting."

"What happened to him?" Fargo asked.

"My husband? A tree fell on him. Can you believe it? He was clearing acreage and an old elm fell the wrong way. A neighbor found him, and they had the body covered in canvas when I got there. They said it was too terrible for me to see."

"I'm sorry."

Cheryl glanced sharply at him, then softened. "That's nice of you, but there's no need. It was a year ago this month. I'm over it by now."

Fargo had his doubts but he held his tongue. He sank onto a stool and rested his head in his arms. It had been one hell of a day. There had been two attempts on his life, his body was on fire, and he felt as weak as a proverbial kitten. To top it off, somewhere out there lurked a pair of hired cutthroats who wouldn't hesitate to earn their dirty money by finishing him off while he was too weak to fight.

Footsteps brought Fargo's head up. Cheryl had the robe, along with a flannel shirt and overalls.

"While you're soaking I'll hang your buckskins over the fireplace to dry, and you can wear these when you get out."

"I'm grateful for all you're doing," Fargo said.

Cheryl smiled for the first time. "You sure are a polite cuss. My husband, God rest his hardworking soul, never thanked me for anything in twelve years of marriage." She motioned. "Shed your duds and put on the robe I brought while I check the water."

Fargo's fingers felt as thick as railroad spikes. They wouldn't work as he wanted them to, and he had to pry and tug at his boots to get them off. Strapped to his right ankle in a slim sheath was his Arkansas toothpick. He hid it in his left boot and slid the Smith and Wesson into the right one. Next he removed his shirt. It clung to him like a second skin, and hiking it over his head required a monumental effort that left him exhausted.

"Is that all the further you've gotten?" Cheryl had entered without him noticing. "Let me help you with the rest."

"That's all right," Fargo said, surprised she had offered.

"I'm a grown woman. I've seen naked men before and wasn't struck deaf and dumb." Cheryl unfastened his belt and began to peel his pants down. "If it embarrasses you, just close your eyes."

Fargo laughed, and kept his eyes open.

"So you do have a sense of humor?" Cheryl said. "There's hope for you yet." Calmly, methodically, she stripped off his pants and wrung them out over the sink. She also wrung out his shirt and red bandanna. "You were downright waterlogged. Why in the name of all that's holy were you traveling on a day like today?"

"I had no choice."

"Nonsense. We always have a choice. My husband didn't need to go out clearing timber the day he died. I'd asked him to do work around the house. But he made the choice to chop down trees, and paid for it with his life."

Fargo was colder than ever. Goosebumps erupted all over him, and he clasped his arms to his chest.

"You're freezing, aren't you?" Cheryl said. "Hang on. The first four pots should be hot enough soon."

Fargo hoped so. His cheek on a knee, he closed his eyes and felt himself drifting off. The loud swish of water being poured into the tub awakened him.

"It takes twelve to fill it," Cheryl mentioned out of the blue, "but you can climb in as soon as I'm done with this batch. Give yourself a good scrubbing." She dropped the soap in and departed.

Fargo shuffled over, his legs as wobbly as twigs. He lifted his right foot, carefully placed it flat so he wouldn't slip, and eased down. The water was wonderfully hot. He leaned back, his knees against his chest, and reveled in the warmth spreading through him. He wanted to stay awake, but his traitor body had other ideas. Before he knew it, he had fallen back asleep.

Fargo was vaguely aware of more water being poured in, of Cheryl's soft voice. The level rose until it was inches below his chin. Fingers on his shoulder motivated him into sitting up. "Sorry. I can't keep my eyes open."

"No need to apologize, Skye," Cheryl said, her voice seeming to float to him from a great distance. "It's plain you're too weak to scrub yourself so I'll do the honors."

"I can do it," Fargo said.

"Why are men so pigheaded?" Cheryl asked. "Here you are, barely able to lift a finger, and you quibble over being washed. I'd expect it from a five-year-old but not a grown man."

Fargo felt the soap slide across his shoulders and down his back. His manhood, which always had a mind of its own, grew stiff and hard.

Cheryl moved the soap in tiny circles. "I liked to wash my husband, but the only times he let me was when he had too much to drink. He didn't think it was right. Which is ridiculous, if you ask me, given that we live in Fornication."

45

"Fornication?" Fargo couldn't have heard correctly.

"Our little community." Cheryl's hand glided along his ribs to his chest. "Don't be shocked. Pennsylvania is famous for outrageous names. Haven't you heard of Intercourse? Or Blue Balls?"

"I must be delirious." Fargo was slipping in and out of consciousness, with more out than in. He dreamed Cheryl's hands roamed over every square inch of his body. He could have sworn he felt her fingers on his pole, stroking him. But when he opened his eyes she was in front of the mirror, staring at her own reflection.

"Feeling any better?"

"Not really," Fargo admitted. Truth was, he was feeling worse. His head hurt, and his body was so much mush. He tried to sit up, to no avail.

"Sleep is what you need now," Cheryl said. "Plenty of it. Followed by some chicken soup and medicinal tea." She touched the mirror. "After that, who knows? Loneliness is like acid. It eats at us until there's nothing there."

"Ma'am?" Fargo said, perplexed.

"Nothing. Forget it."

Fargo shut his eyes and was sucked into a twilight realm where he couldn't distinguish between what was real and what wasn't. Cheryl somehow raising him out of the tub, that seemed real. And Cheryl helping him into the robe. But the impression he had of her lavishing kisses on his face and neck had to be a fever-induced delusion. The same with the moist sensation of lips on his earlobe.

Someone moaned, and Fargo was sure it wasn't him. Then a vortex sucked him into its benighted depths and time lost all meaning. He slept, slept blissfully until a sound restored him to the land of the living. He was flat on his back on a down mattress, covered to his chin by a sheet and blanket. Sunlight bathed the panes of a window that faced the foot of the bed.

Cheryl had just opened the curtains. "I didn't mean to disturb your sleep," she said, and roosted near his pillow. She was wearing a different dress, a tighter one that displayed more cleavage. She had also washed and brushed her hair to a lustrous sheen. "I've paid you a visit every hour on the hour, all night long. I can't tell you how happy I was when your fever broke about eleven this morning."

"What time is it now?" Fargo's head no longer hurt. Nor was he afflicted with the chills. He sat up and the blanket drooped about his waist.

"Two in the afternoon. You were out for over seventeen hours." Cheryl's eyes drifted to his chest. "You talked some in your sleep. I didn't catch much of it. Names, mostly. Susie. Lavender. Janet. Kin of yours?"

"Good friends," Fargo said, and let it go at that. She might not like it if she knew they were the names of doves he had frolicked with.

"Care for that soup and tea?"

"And a roast ox if you have one," Fargo bantered.

Cheryl smirked. "Overdo it and you'll suffer a relapse. The soup will have to suffice. If you keep it down, for supper I'll whip up something special." She raised the blanket to his chin, and coughed. "Your buckskins are dry, so I guess you won't need my husband's duds after all. I'll bring them up after you've eaten."

Fargo watched her walk from the room. Memories resurfaced, bits and pieces of the bath and its aftermath, but whether they were real or a fantasy or a patchwork of both, he couldn't say. He did know that the thought of her fondling his pole aroused him considerably, a condition he sought to conceal by bunching the blanket over his redwood.

Cheryl returned bearing a wooden tray. On it was a steaming bowl of soup, a cup of tea, and crackers. "Don't gulp this down," she advised. "Slow and easy does it until you're back on your feet."

"Yes, mother," Fargo said, and she chortled. He took a sip of tea and almost yipped. Any hotter and it would scald his mouth.

"You're welcome to stay another night," Cheryl brought up as he dipped a spoon into the soup. "The extra rest wouldn't hurt, especially if you have a long journey ahead of you."

"I just might take you up on that," Fargo said. By morning he would be raring to go, and the stallion would be fully rested. They could cover twice as much ground as usual. "How much do you charge a night?"

"In your case, not one cent."

The room, Fargo observed, was sparsely furnished. Like many women trying to make a go of it on their own, Cheryl was barely scraping by. She needed money but was too proud to admit it.

The meal was delicious. Soft chunks of fresh chicken and thinly sliced potatoes in a thick milky broth. Honey spiced the tea. Fargo had an urge to wolf down both, but did as she had suggested and took his sweet time. As his belly warmed, a sense of lethargy filled his veins and his eyelids grew leaden. He stifled yawn after yawn.

Cheryl moved to a chair by the window and sat staring out, lost in thought. She didn't speak again until he was almost done. "My grandmother used to say that sleep is the best cure for every ailment under the sun. After you're done, tuck yourself in and enjoy a nap. By tonight you'll be fully restored to your old self."

"Have you seen anything of two men in blue coats?" Fargo thought to ask. "They might have stopped here looking for me."

"No one else has been by all day," Cheryl said. "You're still my only boarder. Some weeks are slower than most. Summer is generally busy, but so are Thanksgiving and Christmas." She glanced around. "I don't mean to pry, but I found the gun under your

48

shirt. I thought it would be best to put it in your saddlebags, and lo and behold, there was another one." She stood. "Then there was the knife under your pant leg and the rifle in your saddle. Do you make a habit of being a walking armory?"

"I can explain."

"I hope so. I like you, Skye. I like you a lot. I'd hate to think I've taken a highwayman under my roof."

Fargo told Cheryl a little about what he did for a living, and the telegram that had brought him East. After he related the bare essentials of his run-in with the two toughs, she came to the same conclusion he had.

"Someone doesn't want you to reach New York City. Have any idea why?"

"Not yet," Fargo admitted. But one way or another he aimed to unravel the mystery, and those responsible would regret it.

"Well, you're safe enough here," Cheryl said. "I have a sign that says all my rooms are taken. I'll go put it up so no one else will bother to stop." She stepped to the door.

"I don't want to put you to any bother," Fargo said. Or to have her lose money on his account.

"It's no bother at all." Cheryl smiled warmly. "With just the two of us, I can give you the attention you deserve." She started to walk out, then realized what she had said. "I mean, the attention you need, what with the condition you're in." Averting her face, she whisked away.

Grinning, Fargo polished off the last cracker, sipped the remaining spoonful of tea, and pushed the tray to the edge of the bed. Lying flat, he slid a hand behind his head and listened to faint sounds issue from below. He had a feeling that before the night was done, he was in for a pleasant treat.

Sleep claimed him within minutes. Fargo slept soundly, and when next he opened his eyes the room was mired in gloom. Night had fallen. Through a gap in the curtains he glimpsed stars. It was a constellation, the Big Dipper, and by its position in the sky he deduced he had slept another six or seven hours. It was well past eight. He sat up and stretched.

A rosy glow filled the hallway and a soft tread heralded Cheryl, who was carrying a lamp. "So you're finally up? Last I stopped in, you were sawing logs louder than my husband used to. How do you feel?"

"Fit enough to wrestle a grizzly," Fargo exaggerated. "Fetch my clothes and I'll get up."

"Are you sure?" Cheryl acted disappointed. "I don't mind feeding you in bed. I'm even baking a cherry pie for dessert."

Fargo wasn't fooled. What she really wanted had nothing to do with food, which was fine by him. Then she said something that changed everything.

"While I was out putting up my sign, Mrs. Dixon came by. She works over to the general store. We were talking about some new bolts of cloth when she mentioned that a couple of strangers showed up this morning. Crude men in blue coats and wool caps. They used a lot of foul language and kept ogling a couple of young girls. One of them looked as if he'd been stomped by a mule."

"Did she say what they wanted?" Fargo asked, sitting bolt upright.

"They bought coffee and sugar. And the one who was all black-and-blue wanted to know if anyone in buckskins had gone by in the past day or so."

"Where are the two men now?"

"Gone. They rode on east and must be halfway to Philadelphia. So you have nothing to worry about."

If there was one lesson living in the wild had taught Fargo, it was to never take anything for granted. "My clothes," he insisted. He would do some scouting around and ensure the would-be killers were really long gone.

To her credit Cheryl didn't object. She was gone a short while, and she brought back not only his clothes, but his saddlebags and rifle, too. "I washed and dried your buckskins, underwear, and socks while you slept. I also cleaned your hat and polished your boots." Placing everything on the bed, she immediately left again. "I'll be in the sitting room if you want me."

Fargo hopped out of bed and swiftly dressed. Instead of strapping on his gunbelt, he jammed the Colt under his belt so it would be less conspicuous, as he had done with the Smith and Wesson the day before. He left the hammerless revolver in his saddlebags. Likewise his spurs, which he had no use for at the moment.

Fargo skipped down a short flight of narrow stairs to the room with the wash tub. Past it was the kitchen, filled with the mouth-watering aroma of the pie in the oven. He slipped out the back door and closed it. Cheryl's old dog was tied to a nearby post but all it did was raise its head and stare a second, then go back to sleep. In a large three-sided shed at the rear of the lot stood the Ovaro, munching on hay. The stallion shared the shed with a pile of firewood and a few garden implements.

Fargo stood for a few minutes letting his eyes and ears adjust. When they had, he conducted a quick circuit of the house. The valley lay tranquil under a celestial canopy, the serenity broken now and again by the barking of farm dogs and the occasional lowing of a cow. Scattered farmhouses broke the blackness of night, their windows ablaze. Moving to the middle of the road, Fargo looked in both directions. It was empty for as far as he could see. A sweep of the surrounding hills failed to turn up any trace of a campfire.

Fargo stepped to the hitch rail, gave the road a last scrutiny, and was pivoting toward the side of the house when a faint noise to the east gave him pause. Hooves clomped dully, growing slowly louder as the animal approached at a walk. He melted into the shadows.

Soon the rider materialized, an older man wearing mostly black, mounted bareback on a plow horse.

Another Amish farmer, Fargo reckoned.

"Good evening, friend," the man called out, waving a brawny hand. "What are you doing there? Playing at hide-and-seek?" Hearty laughter rumbled from his barrel chest.

Fargo stepped into the open and watched until the farmer was swallowed by darkness. No one else appeared, and he ambled to the shed and spent a few minutes with the pinto. A shadow flickered across the kitchen window as he hurried up the path. Cheryl preparing supper, he thought, and opened the door.

Cheryl was there, sure enough, but she wasn't cooking food. She was over by the kitchen table, dressed in a thin nightgown, the cherry pie beside her. Looking him square in the eyes, she leaned back so her breasts thrust against her gown, smiled nervously, and asked, "Which would you like more?"

4

Another lesson Skye Fargo had learned was that women, by and large, were as unpredictable as high-country weather. A man never knew from one minute to the next what they were thinking, or from one day to the next what kind of mood they would be in. Any man who claimed otherwise was either the biggest liar in all creation or the most self-deluded yak this side of a sanitarium.

Most men liked to complain that women were the most cantankerous creatures ever born, and many sincerely believed they were put on earth specifically to make men miserable. A drinking acquaintance of Fargo's once told him, in all earnestness, that females were natural-born nags, and by the time they reached marrying age the majority had perfected their talent to a fine art.

Fargo was willing to acknowledge some women had the dispositions of cactus-stuck mules. But so did some men. And for all their contrariness, it had been his experience that women were more a source of delight than they were aggravation—provided the men they were with treated them halfway decent. He liked women, liked them a lot. Maybe that explained why most took a shine to him and did things they wouldn't ordinarily think of doing with other men.

Cheryl Taylor was a good example. She didn't impress Fargo as the sort to throw herself at every male boarder who stayed overnight. She was too timid, too unsure of herself, too afraid to uncork the feelings she bottled up inside. Yet here she was, practically throwing herself at him, her brave smile belying the fear in her eyes. Fear he might not find her attractive. Fear she had made an idiot of herself.

Fargo gained a few moments to think by throwing the bolt and slowly crossing the room. As flattered as he was, he had never been one to take advantage of vulnerable women. Tricking them into climbing under the sheets wasn't his way. So now he placed a hand on Cheryl's shoulder and said, "I'd have to be loco to pick the pie. But you've got to understand something. Come morning I'm leaving, and odds are we'll never—"

Cheryl covered his mouth with a warm palm that bore a musky scent. "Do you think I don't know that? I'm not making any demands. I won't go into hysterics when you're gone." Removing her hand, she bestowed a feather-light kiss. "If the parson were to waltz in on us, he'd brand me a shameless hussy in front of the whole congregation. But he's never been married. He's never known the thrill of—"

"There's no need to explain," Fargo interrupted, and bent forward. But she stopped him by putting both hands against her chest.

"Yes, there is. If for no other reason than my own peace of mind. I haven't lain with anyone since my husband died. A year it's been. A whole year. More loneliness than any one person should have to abide. Endless nights of crying myself to sleep, of hugging his pillow as if it were him. Remembering." Tears glistened, and a tiny drop trickled down her left cheek.

Fargo waited. She would let him know when the moment was right.

"I'm tired of being alone. Tired of pining for what I once had. Lord help me, but for a while I'd like to forget the past, forget all the heartache I've been through. I'd like to feel the thrill again. I'd like to feel what it's like to be a woman." Cheryl cupped his chin. "Don't ask me to explain why I picked you. Maybe it's because you remind me a little of my husband. Maybe it's because you've treated me more decently than most and didn't try to shove a hand up my dress the minute you learned I was a widow. Or maybe—" Cheryl pressed herself against him, "maybe it's because I can't deny my needs any longer."

Fargo was going to say that whatever her reason, he was all for it so long as she didn't expect more than he was willing to give. She never gave him the chance. Her delectable lips glued themselves to his in a searing kiss of raw hunger. Her satiny tongue inserted itself into his mouth and swirled around his own. Fingernails bit deep into his shoulders, so deep he flinched. His own hands drifted to her hips, molding them like clay, and from the depths of her throat came a tiny mew.

The kiss lasted forever. Cheryl sucked on his tongue, rimmed his gums with the tip of her tongue, then nibbled on both his lips from end to end. Her breath grew hot enough to melt wax, her eyes became hooded with carnal lust. Locking her hands behind his neck, she ground her hips against him in abandon.

"I want you so much."

Fargo felt his hat fall to the floor. He caressed Cheryl's silky hair, her soft neck. He sucked on her ripe lower lip as if it were a strawberry. She imitated his every act, squirming the whole while. He started to steer her toward the door so they could go upstairs, but she dug in her heels.

"Don't. Please."

"You've changed your mind?" Fargo said.

Cheryl's answer was to devour his mouth, then say huskily, "No. Not on your life. I want to do it here."

Fargo gazed around. "In the *kitchen*?" He could think of half a dozen more comfortable spots.

"A bed would remind me too much of my husband," Cheryl said. "We never did it anywhere but the bedroom. I wanted to. But whenever I suggested a change of pace, he said I was too wanton for my own good."

"I like wanton," Fargo said, and cupped her breasts. Cheryl went rigid as an ironing board, but only for a few seconds. Uttering a tiny cry, she oozed against him. Her fingers roamed across his shoulders, his neck, his face. His fingers kneaded and squeezed her twin melons, stoking the flame of passion that had been kindled deep inside her into a rapidly rising inferno.

Cheryl grew more animated, more uninhibited, with each passing minute. She was starved for affection, starved for the pure ecstasy that resulted from the union of a man and a woman. Now that she had an outlet for her long-suppressed desires, she gave rein to them in unreserved abandon. Her kisses were molten pools of need. Her nipples became as hard as tacks. The junction of her thighs was a furnace, radiating heat like the sun. She was eager for release, eager for him to match her ardor.

Fargo had other ideas. He was in no particular rush, not when they had all night. He paced himself, taking forever to caress her breasts. Taking longer to rove over the rest of her body, from her globes to her nether mound. But not lower, not yet, not until she was so aroused she couldn't stand it.

"Mmmmmm," Cheryl moaned when he tweaked a nipple. She wriggled in anticipation as his right hand roved down the length of her spine to the small of her back. "Now," she cooed. "Please take me now." Arching forward, she splayed her legs wide, as inviting as a woman could be.

Fastening his lips to her throat, Fargo lathered her neck from jaw to collarbone, then devoted his attention to her earlobes, first the left, then the right. Concomitantly, his right hand squeezed the two halves of her pert posterior. He delved his middle finger be-

56

tween them and she rose up onto her toes, her mouth agape.

"Yes! There! Again!"

Instead, Fargo forked an arm around her waist and gently pushed her around the table and up against the kitchen wall. She looked at him quizzically, confused by his intent until he pulled at her cotton nightgown, raising the hem to her hips. At the same time he plucked at the buttons that would grant him access to her breasts. When the last button came undone, the nightgown parted, exposing the tops of both her creamy hills. He licked them, kissed them, parted the gown even more and inhaled one, rolling it on the end of his tongue.

"Ahhhhh. You have no idea what you're doing to me," Cheryl breathed.

Fargo most certainly did. Her nipples were extremely sensitive. Every flick of his tongue elicited a gasp or groan. Lower down, his fingers played over her smooth inner thighs, running up and down and around and around, straying close to her womanly core but never touching it. It had the effect he had foreseen.

"What are you waiting for?" Cheryl complained, thrusting her bottom against him. "I want you in me! I want you in me *now*!"

Fargo continued to titillate her nipples and to caress her legs and thighs, but he didn't touch her womanhood. He intended to hold off until she was thoroughly aroused and couldn't stand the suspense any longer.

Cheryl squirmed and wriggled, impatient for him to do so, and finally, in a gambit to incite him into taking the final step, she cupped his manhood. "Oh, my! You're as hard as iron."

So hard, in fact, it hurt. Fargo's pole throbbed as she stroked him with one hand and cupped him underneath with the other. Turnabout was fair play, and now she did to him as he had been doing to her. She wasn't as adept as a fallen dove would be, though. Her squeezes were much too rough, her strokes much too forceful, as if she were striving to rip open his pants and haul his manhood out into the light. Once, when she cupped him, she closed her fingers too tightly, causing him to wince.

"I can't wait much longer!" Cheryl protested.

Fargo raised his head from her heaving breasts and slowly sank to his knees. She stared down in confusion, plainly unaware of what he was up to. Fargo pushed her nightgown up above her hips. She wasn't wearing anything under it.

"What—?" Cheryl began, her eyes growing wide as saucers. "Mercy! My husband never did that. I—"

The moment Fargo's mouth made contact with her molten center, Cheryl let out a cry of joy and astonishment. Flinging her arms against the wall, she bent her head all the way back and rose into the air. Fargo had to grab her legs to hold her in place as his tongue lapped at her sugary juices.

"Oh, Skye! I never! Oh! Oh! Oh!" Cheryl spurted, a violent release made doubly so because it was her first in ages. She bucked like a mustang, panting wildly, her hot body churning and writhing.

It was all Fargo could do to hold on. Her drenched thighs quaked like aspens in a thunderstorm and her knees would have buckled if he hadn't braced them. She moaned nonstop now, tossing her head from side to side, overcome by sheer bliss and loving every second. He devoured her until she was limp as a wet rag. Then he rose, lifted her in both arms, and carefully placed her on the kitchen table.

Dazed by multiple orgasms, Cheryl said weakly, "I never knew it could be like this."

Fargo wasn't anywhere near done. He positioned her legs with her feet at the edge, lowered his pants, set the Colt on the table, and aligned the tip of his member with her moist opening. Cheryl quivered as he rubbed himself up and down. He only inserted a quarter of an inch or so, teasing her with what was to come.

"Ohhhhhhhhhhhhhh." Cheryl suddenly scooted her bottom toward him, seeking to draw him up into herself.

Pulling back, Fargo smiled, then slowly started to insert his pole, inch by gradual inch. When he was half inside, he held perfectly still, savoring the sensation of her rippling walls. She was a magnificent sight, red in the cheeks, her lips as full as ripe strawberries, her mounds twice their normal size, her nipples pointed toward the ceiling. Lightly pinching one, he tweaked and pulled.

"Please," Cheryl begged. "For the love of God, please!"

Placing his hands on her hips, Fargo held fast and abruptly lanced up into her, burying his throbbing sword to the hilt. Cheryl screeched and surged partway up off the table. Her dilated eyes fixed on him in wonder a moment. She cried out again as Fargo commenced a rocking motion. Again and again he speared into her. Pacing herself, he settled into a steady rhythm, as much to prolong her pleasure as his own.

Cheryl's eyelids fluttered and she filled the kitchen with coos and gasps and tiny whines. Her fingers locked onto his forearms and her nails bit into his flesh. She didn't do it on purpose. She was adrift in a sensual sea, so lost in rapture she was unaware of what she was doing.

Fargo's tempo increased. He could feel his explosion building, but he refused to let himself go. Not yet. Not until Cheryl gushed once more. A constriction formed in the base of his throat. His vision blurred. He swore he could hear the blood rushing through his veins.

"Ah! Ah!" Cheryl's hands slid onto the table and she clenched the edge so hard, her knuckles were pale. "I'm close again! So very close!"

Fargo hoped so. He couldn't hold out much longer. His manhood was fit to erupt and it wouldn't take much to trigger his release. He thought of his rifle, his saddle, the Ovaro. He thought of anything and everything that would take his mind off what he was doing and enable him to keep the dam from bursting.

Cheryl suddenly ground her bottom against him. "I'm there!" she screamed. "Oh, Skye! I'm there!"

Fargo could tell. Her inner walls had closed around his member and sheathed him like a calfskin glove. The next moment she spurted, soaking him. It was all that was needed to send him over the brink. Pinpoints of bright lights exploded before his eyes at the selfsame instant a keg of dynamite went off between his legs. This time he was the one who virtually lifted her up off the table. He rammed his pole into her like a battering ram pounding at the gates of a city. The slap of their bodies was loud in the kitchen's confines, but nearly drowned out by her throaty cries. He lost all sense of time, of place. Pure pleasure coursed through him, pleasure so potent it was intoxicating.

Fargo took forever coasting to a stop. Cheryl was still, her eyes shut, tiny tears in the corners of each. She stirred when he pulled out, tucked himself into his pants, and lowered her to the floor. He left the Colt lying on the table.

"Thank you."

"Anytime," Fargo joked, lying beside her and cradling her head on his shoulder. By rights he should carry her up to a bedroom, but he didn't have the energy.

"I mean it," Cheryl said, and embraced him, fiercely hugging him to her bosom. "It meant more to me than you'll ever know. You've reminded me of all the things I've been missing. Maybe it's high time I cast off my widow's grief and found myself a new husband. There's bound to be a man somewhere who might find me appealing."

"Any man would," Fargo said, and for his flattery he received a warm, grateful kiss and another hug. He pulled up his pants and buckled his belt.

"You're the most remarkable man I've ever met," Cheryl said. "It's a pity there aren't more like you."

"If you say so." All Fargo craved now was rest. Later, over supper, she could talk his ear off.

"Did you just feel a draft?" Cheryl asked, and tugged her rumpled nightgown down around her knees.

"No."

"It must be this cold floor. I've got goosebumps all over. Would you mind if I ran upstairs for my heavy robe? I won't be gone long."

Fargo didn't mind at all, just so she quit jabbering and let him enjoy a short nap. "Take as long as you want," he responded, on the verge of drifting off.

Cheryl sat up. "Say! Who are you? How did you get in here? Didn't you see the sign out front? I don't have any vacancies."

Belatedly, Fargo realized someone else was there. Willing his sluggish body to move, he rose onto an elbow and started to turn. The click of a gun hammer froze him in place.

Framed in the hall doorway was Martin Stevens, his woolen cap low over his brow. In his left hand was a Lindsay two-shot belt pocket pistol. "We meet again, mister," he said coldly, "and this time the boot is on the other foot, eh?"

Fargo slowly rose, his hands out from his sides, and glanced at the Colt.

"Don't even think it," Stevens warned, striding into the kitchen. "At this range I can't miss." He warily came up to the side of the table and snatched the Colt off it. "Where's my own revolver?"

"Upstairs," Fargo said.

"I'll get it after I'm done here," Stevens stated, and sidled to the right so he had a clear shot at the two of them. "As for your question, lady," he addressed Cheryl, "I climbed in through a front window. You ought to know better than to leave it unlatched."

"No one hereabouts locks their windows or doors," Cheryl replied. "We're trusting souls."

"You're stupid souls," Stevenss said in contempt, "and your stupidity is my gain. Now I get to finish your boyfriend off and earn a heap of cash. Enough to let me live comfortably the rest of my born days."

"You'd kill someone in cold blood?" Cheryl asked, aghast.

"For a hundred thousand dollars I'd kill my own mother and not lose a night of sleep afterward," Stevens informed her, and turned his attention to Fargo. "You're probably wondering how I found you." He chuckled. "It was child's play. Ever since you gave us the slip, my friend and I have asked everyone we ran into if they'd seen you. Now and then we'd find someone who had. Until we passed here, that is. Over in the next valley there wasn't anyone who remembered you. So we figured you were holed up somewhere."

Fargo should have realized they might backtrack, and chided himself for being unforgivably careless.

Stevens was cocky now that he had the upper hand. "I remembered an old bag at the general store here saying there was a local gal who rented out rooms, but to her knowledge no one was staying there at the time. I decided it would be best to come back and make sure." He chortled. "Damned smart of me, no?"

Cheryl was angry. Putting her hands on her hips, she said defiantly, "You've gone to a lot of trouble for nothing. You can't kill him."

"Why not?" Stevens humored her.

"Because you have a witness. I'll report you to the

sheriff and you'll spend the rest of your life behind bars."

The killer looked her up and down as if he couldn't believe his own ears. "We meet idiots in all walks of life, don't we?" he said more to himself than to them. "Tell her how it is, mister. Tell her why I won't spend one day in jail."

"He's going to kill you, too," Fargo enlightened Cheryl. "He'll murder anyone who stands in his way."

The longshoreman nodded. "After I dispose of you two, I'll set the house on fire. The authorities will find a couple of charred bodies, and with any luck, they'll never suspect foul play. I'll be free to enjoy my new-found wealth wherever and however I choose."

Cheryl took a step toward him. "You would do that? You'd kill an unarmed, defenseless woman?"

"Lady, you just don't get it, do you?" Stevens said. "I don't give a damn whether you're a woman or not. I don't give a damn if you're unarmed. Hell, for all I care, you could be a brat in diapers and I'd still blow out your wick."

"You're a fiend," Cheryl Taylor said, and shocked both Fargo and the assassin by screeching like a bob-cat and hurling herself at Stevens with her fingernails hooked to rip and rend.

Stevens was caught flat-footed. He had the Lindsay in one hand, the Colt in the other, but both were trained on Fargo, not on Cheryl. He shifted toward her but she was on him before he could squeeze either trigger. Her nails raked his face, tearing him open from his forehead to his chin, and he howled in com-mingled agony and rage.

Fargo was only two steps behind her. He saw the Colt sweep up, heard a thud as the barrel connected with Cheryl's head. She folded like an accordion at Stevens's feet and Stevens pointed the Lindsay at her. She was a heartbeat away from receiving a slug to the brain when Fargo lowered a shoulder and slammed into the longshoreman with the force of an onrushing steam engine. Stevens was bowled backward, into a cabinet. Dishes rattled as Fargo waded in with both fists flying. He landed a right, a left, a right. The Colt smacked to the floor and skittered off under the table.

"Not this time!" Stevens railed, fighting back. He swung the Lindsay at Fargo's face but Fargo ducked, executed a right-cross that rocked Stevens sideways, and followed through with an uppercut that snapped Stevens onto his heels. In desperation, Stevens threw his arms around him and lunged toward the center of the room.

Suddenly letting go, Stevens jammed the Lindsay's muzzle against Fargo's midriff. Fargo wrenched aside as the gun went off. Other than a slight stinging sensation and powder burns on his buckskins, he was unharmed. Clamping his hands onto the killer's gun arm, Fargo whipped his knee into Stevens's elbow.

The longshoreman yelped and dropped the pocket pistol. "You about busted it, you son of a bitch!"

Fargo aimed to do more than that. His left fist sank knuckle-deep into the other man's gut. Stevens doubled over, but promptly unleashed a backhand to Fargo's face that drove Fargo against the stove. In reaching down to brace himself, Fargo brushed his hand against the oven, still hot from the cherry pie. His skin hissed and blistered. Jerking his hand away, he sidestepped—straight into a looping right thrown by Stevens. It glanced off his ribs, not doing any real damage, but spiking him with torment.

Martin Stevens glanced frantically around, spotted the Lindsay, and dove for it with his good arm outstretched.

Fargo leaped. He reached Stevens as the killer heaved erect with the Lindsay cocked, and a kick sent the man stumbling. The pistol discharged, the slug digging a furrow in the floorboards.

"Die, damn you!"

Stevens was bringing the gun up again, but this time Fargo didn't try to kick it loose. He flung himself at the table, at the Colt lying underneath. The kitchen resounded to the boom of the Lindsay and a fist-sized chunk of table dissolved in a rain of wooden slivers. Some stung Fargo's cheek as he wrapped his fingers around the Colt and twisted.

Martin Stevens transformed to ice. Blanching, he tossed the pocket pistol aside and bleated, "No! Don't! My gun is empty! I'm unarmed!"

"That wasn't going to stop you from killing this woman," Fargo said, nodding at the unconscious Cheryl. "Why should I let it stop me?" With every fiber of his being he yearned to squeeze the trigger, but if he did he was no better than the vermin in front of him.

Stevens grasped at a straw. "You wanted more information, remember? You wanted to know who sicced me on you, and why."

"I'm listening," Fargo said, moving to Cheryl's side. A nasty gash above her ear was trickling blood.

"You don't know what you're getting yourself into. You're riding into a war, a war that can only have one outcome."

"What the hell are you babbling about?" Fargo said brusquely. "Lucius Kemp needs help finding a lost niece and wants me to track her down. That's all there is to it."

"Hardly. I know about Camilla. But she's not what really matters. The old man hasn't been keeping up with current events. He can't see the forest for the trees, and soon they're all going to come crashing down on top of him."

"You'll have to speak plainer than that," Fargo commanded. "I want names. I want details."

"What do I get in return?"

"Your life." It suddenly struck Fargo that Stevens was deliberately being evasive, just as he had been on the road during their previous encounter. Stevens was stalling, keeping him occupied. There could only be one reason.

Fargo pivoted toward the hallway but no one was there. Thinking he had overreacted, he started to turn back toward Stevens—and spied the other longshoreman at the kitchen window, a rifle pressed to his shoulder.

5

Years ago, when Skye Fargo was still in his teens, he had been given his first revolver. It had been his most cherished possession. For hours each day he had practiced drawing, practiced hitting targets, practiced twirling it and flipping it and performing a dozen other tricks. He had practiced to the point where the six-shooter became an extension of his hand and arm. To where he could draw in the blink of an eye and squeeze off six shots so swiftly they sounded like one.

Time and again, Fargo's skill had proven invaluable. In the wilderness a man's life often depended on his speed at unlimbering his hardware, and countless outlaws and hostiles had found out to their regret that Fargo was second to none in that regard.

Now, as Fargo whirled and saw the other assassin at the kitchen window, about to put a bullet into him, his hands moved of their own accord. His right hand flashed the Colt up and out even as his left slashed at the hammer. With remarkable rapidity he fanned the pistol three times, and at each shot a slug smashed through the pane and into the skulker outside, punching the killer backward a step at each blast.

The man's rifle barrel drooped. The longshoreman blinked a few times, the spark of life fading from his eyes a bit more with each blink. After the third he did a slow pirouette to the ground and disappeared below the sill.

A hint of movement galvanized Fargo into pivoting

toward Martin Stevens. Stevens had risen, snatched a butcher knife off the counter, and was almost on top of him. Fargo fired, but the butcher knife was already descending and the blade struck the Colt's barrel, deflecting it and sending the shot into the floor.

Fargo tried to level the Colt, but Stevens seized his wrist. Simultaneously, Stevens thrust the butcher knife at his chest. To save himself, Fargo grabbed Stevens's wrist. For a moment they were face-to-face, eye to eye. Then Stevens snarled like the coyote he was and pushed with all his might in an effort to shove Fargo against the kitchen table and upend him.

Fargo stood firm. Digging in his boot heels, he resisted with all the strength in his corded sinews. Inch by inch he began to force the knife back.

Stevens grunted. He growled. He snorted like a mad bull, his nostrils flared. His face grew beet-red and his veins bulged. "Damn you!" he raged. "I will kill you yet! Do you hear me? I *will*!"

Not if Fargo could help it. Suddenly sliding a boot behind the longshoreman's legs, he shoved and sent Stevens sprawling. But in falling, Stevens held onto Fargo's wrist. Fargo was pulled off-balance and fell to his knees.

Like a striking rattler, Stevens arced the butcher knife at Fargo's throat. Fargo jerked to one side and the razor tip missed him by a fraction. He sought to tear his gun arm free but Stevens clung tight and arched the knife again.

Ducking, Fargo threw himself onto his back. He had to break loose, and break loose quickly. Sooner or later the blade would connect. Tucking his right leg to his chest, he slammed it into the longshoreman's sternum.

Stevens was knocked back, lost his hold on Fargo's wrist, and slid four or five feet across the floor. Almost instantly he lunged to his feet. Near him was a chair, and as he rose he grabbed hold and hurled it.

Fargo rolled to the right. The chair skittered by crashing into the table. He expected Stevens to close in for the kill and straightened, the Colt out and ready. But the wily assassin was racing toward the hallway. Another couple of strides and he would reach it.

Taking quick aim, Fargo started to curl his finger around the trigger. He was a hairsbreadth from firing when Cheryl Taylor rose up into his sights. She had a hand pressed to her head and was tottering unsteadily. Fargo stepped to the right for a clear shot but by then Stevens had bolted from the room.

"Stay put," Fargo instructed her, and sped through the doorway. If he let the killer escape, if he didn't end it right then and there, Stevens would try again sometime, and would go on trying until one of them was dead.

A gust of cool wind fanned Fargo as he drew abreast of the sitting room. The window on the far side was open, and a leg was just sliding from view. Veering toward it, Fargo swept the curtains aside. Stevens was dashing across the yard toward a picket fence. Beyond the fence was a stand of trees where Fargo suspected the two killers had hidden their mounts.

Sliding over the sill, Fargo sprinted for all he was worth. He saw Stevens reach the fence, pause to glance back, and spring to the other side. Without breaking stride he came to the same spot and hurtled over. The trees were thirty feet away. Caution dictated he go slowly, but he couldn't afford to be cautious, not with so much at stake. He plunged recklessly into the vegetation, heedless of the risk, casting about right and left for the horses he was certain must be there.

A whinny confirmed it. Under a weeping willow stood two saddled mounts. But Martin Stevens was nowhere to be seen.

Baffled, cautious of a trick, Fargo moved toward them. He probed the shadows, scanned the boles, looking everywhere. A few yards from the horses he stopped, stumped as to where to look next. Then he saw the bay raise its head and gaze into the willow above him just as a limb rustled.

Fargo dived forward, into a tuck and roll. There was a muffled curse, and the sound of Stevens thudding to the ground. Fargo pushed onto a knee as the long-shoreman came at him like a man possessed, swinging the butcher knife in a frenzy. Fargo fired. Stevens was jarred by the impact but didn't go down. A long spring carried the killer forward and, the next thing Fargo knew, they were grappling as they had in the kitchen.

Stevens kneed Fargo in the ribs, wrenched fiercely, and speared cold steel at Fargo's jugular. Only a last-instant flick of Fargo's arm saved him, blocking the blow and inciting Stevens to new heights of savagery. The man was virtually beside himself. Suddenly planting a boot in Fargo's stomach, he reared for the coup de grace.

"I've got you now!"

The killer's gloat was premature. Fargo levered his body in a half-circle and his shins caught Stevens just behind both knees.

Stevens folded, landing askew with one arm partly under himself. He uttered a low cry, levered onto his left knee, and glanced down at himself in astonishment. His right arm rose from behind his back. He still held the butcher knife, only now the ten-inch blade was stained with blood—his own. He had fallen on it. Touching his other hand low to his back, he stared at a dark smear on his palm and fingers. "No! It can't be!"

Fargo stood and leveled the Colt. "It's over. Drop the knife."

The longshoreman gawked at him. "It wasn't sup-posed to be like this. A hundred thousand dollars would set me up for life."

"Drop the knife," Fargo repeated.

Stevens pressed an arm to his forehead. "I feel weak. You've got to help me. You've got to fetch a doctor."

"Like hell." Fargo didn't trust the man any further than he could throw one of the horses. Stevens might be shamming to lure him in close. "Last warning. Either drop the knife or I'll drop you."

Stevens swayed, then slumped and lowered the butcher knife toward the grass. "All right, all right. I'm doing it. See?"

Fargo was watching the blade, waiting for it to hit the ground. But it never did. Martin Stevens had no intention of giving up, and with an inarticulate howl he pumped upward, the knife shearing at Fargo's heart. Fargo fired once. A hole blossomed in the center of the killer's forehead and he was flipped onto his back in a disjointed heap.

The echo of the shot rolled off across the valley. Dogs began to bark, and one vented an unearthly howl.

Fargo nudged the body, kicked the knife into the grass, and let himself relax. Tension drained from him like water from a sieve as he walked to the fence and hopped over. Disposing of the bodies could wait. He went in through the window, lowered and latched it, and was almost to the hallway when Cheryl appeared, a wet towel pressed to the gash above her left ear.

"I heard a shot!" she declared, distraught. "I thought maybe—" Her eyes moistened and she threw herself into his arms.

"They're both dead," Fargo revealed after a while.

"Thank God." Cheryl kissed him on the cheek. "But it's not the end of it. You know that, don't you? Whoever sent those men will send more."

Shouts punctured the night, coming closer to her house. Fargo led her down the hall to the front door. Through the living room window he could see torches and lanterns bobbing like fireflies out on the road.

Heavy footsteps approached her porch, and heavy knuckles drummed forcefully on the door.

"Mrs. Taylor? Are you in there?"

Cheryl gave the towel to Fargo, smoothed her hair, and opened the door a crack. "Mr. Dixon? What's all the fuss about?" Past her stood a bearded man in overalls and a sweater, holding a lantern.

"I'm sorry to disturb you, ma'am, but didn't you hear the gunfire? It sounded as if it came from this direction."

"I've been napping," Cheryl fibbed. "I was dead to the world."

"There was gunfire," Dixon elaborated. "Four or five shots, the last louder than the rest." He surveyed her yard. "I can't believe you didn't hear them."

"Maybe it was a hunter off in the hills and you only thought the shots were closer. Everything is fine here. Now, if you'll excuse me, it's late and I'm not feeling all that well."

Dixon apologized again for intruding, and Cheryl bid him good night and closed the door. Fargo glided to a window, cracked a curtain, and peered out. Dixon rejoined seven or eight people out in the road and a discussion ensued. One of the men, apparently, was all for conducting a search of the area and kept gesturing at adjacent lots. But when the others bent their steps homeward, so did he.

Fargo didn't waste another moment. It was a good thing the two horses in the willows hadn't acted up, or the good citizens of Fornication would have found Martin Stevens and launched a house-to-house search for his killer. He headed for the sitting room.

"Where are you going?" Cheryl asked, tagging along.

"To get rid of the bodies." As a precaution, Fargo blew out the lamp in the sitting room before he eased over the sill.

Cheryl's hand fell on his wrist. "Be careful. These

72

are decent folk, but they won't take kindly to gunplay in their community. They're liable to hold you in custody until they can send for the sheriff." She smiled. "I wouldn't want that to happen."

"Makes two of us." Fargo crouched and cat-footed along the house to the kitchen window. The body of Stevens's partner lay in shadow under it. Hoisting the dead man over his shoulder, Fargo picked up the man's rifle, a new Spencer, and hastened to the stand of trees.

The horses were munching on grass a few feet from Stevens's body, unfazed by the scent of blood. "Easy fella," Fargo said to the sorrel, and draped the second killer over the saddle. He draped Stevens over the big bay, then ushered both animals to the edge of the road.

No one was out and about, but a lot of windows were lit and the slightest noise was bound to draw attention.

Fargo paralleled the road until he came to a field bordering the hamlet to the north. From there he bore to the northeast toward the low hills a quarter mile distant. The night was clear and cold, the stars uncommonly bright. Out of habit he listened for the yips of coyotes and the wavering howl of wolves but the latter no longer roamed Pennsylvania and in this part of the state neither did coyotes although there were some further west.

Except for an isolated farm that glowed like a lighthouse in a sea of darkness, Fargo had the night to himself. He used the occasion to review all that had happened and tried in vain to make sense of the few clues he had. Stevens's comment about a "war", if true, might be the key.

When Fargo reached New York, his first order of business would be to find the woman who had reserved a room at the Imperial Inn posing as Bethany Wingate, and to learn all he could about Stevens and his accomplice. He reached into his pocket to satisfy himself that the letter and the identification card were still there and was stunned to find the pocket was empty. He wondered if he had accidentally lost them during his fight with Stevens, or if perhaps Cheryl Taylor had removed them when she washed and dried his buckskins. He would ask her later.

A line of trees appeared. Deciduous trees, for the most part, oaks and walnuts and maples. Fargo hiked fifty yards into the woods and stopped at a small clearing. Lying the bodies side-by-side, he went through their clothes. Stevens had nothing new to offer. The second longshoreman wasn't carrying an identification card, but Fargo did find a scrap of paper with the words "Joe's Shanty" written on it, and an address. He also found another Smith and Wesson hammerless revolver, a dagger with an ivory handle, and a derringer, all of which he stuffed into the bedroll on the bay, along with the Spencer.

Fargo ventured into the trees. A short sweep turned up a suitable downed limb. One end tapered to a point, ideal for his purpose. Returning to the clearing, he began to dig. Fortunately for him, Pennsylvanian soil was famed for being soft and fertile. Quite a contrast from the Rockies where the ground was perpetually as hard as metal. The grass came away in large clods. Once he had the outline of a hole six feet long and four feet wide, he dug straight down, loosening the dirt enough so he could fling it with his hands. Half an hour of constant labor later, he had a suitable double grave.

Fargo lowered the bodies to the bottom, folding their arms across their chests. He untied the sorrel's bedroll, unrolled a blanket, and spread it over the two men, then filled in the hole. Gathering leaves and fallen twigs and branches, he covered the grave, camouflaging the spot so it resembled the surrounding area.

Taking the sorrel's reins in his left hand, Fargo

climbed onto the bay, wheeled toward the hamlet, and clucked the horses into a brisk walk. He considered leaving them with Cheryl so she could sell them and earn some money. But if anyone ever came looking for the longshoremen, the mounts might be traced back to her. She would have a lot of explaining to do. He decided instead to put them to better use.

To Fargo's surprise, she was waiting for him out near the back of her lot. Bundled in a robe and a heavy coat, she opened the gate to admit him and helped him unsaddle the horses and place them with the Ovaro. Fargo carried the bedrolls indoors. Tossing them on the kitchen table, he said. "Thanks for your help. But you should have stayed inside where it's nice and warm."

"Can I help it if I'm a worrywart?" Smiling, Cheryl snuggled against him. She roamed a hand over his abdomen, and glanced down. "What's this hole? And powder burns? You've been shot!"

"It's nothing," Fargo said. Had it been, he wouldn't be standing there.

"So you say," Cheryl retorted, and hitched at his shirt. "Look at this! You were wounded and you didn't even say anything!"

Fargo looked. The slug had creased him, barely breaking the skin. "I've been hurt a lot worse," he mentioned.

"Men! Always having to act so tough." Cheryl stepped to a cupboard. "I have some salve that will help you mend." A lot of jars were lined up in neat rows on a high shelf. Most contained preserved food. A few were for medicinal use, including a sticky salve that smelled like the west end of an eastbound ox.

"I made this myself out of beeswax and a few secret ingredients," Cheryl revealed as she rubbed it on. "It's an old family remedy, brought over from the Old Country a hundred and fifty years ago by my great-great-great grandmother."

"Secret ingredients?" Fargo said, scrunching up his nose. "Was one of them a dead cow?"

"How did you know?" Cheryl said, pretending to be shocked. Then she laughed and hugged him and peppered his lips and cheeks with warm kisses. "You haven't changed your mind about staying the night, have you?"

"No." Fargo needed the extra rest.

"Good." Cheryl rubbed her chin against his. "Because I was hoping that you and I—" Her mouth curled in sultry hunger. "Well, you know. I promise not to keep you up too late. I'd just like for you to have a few pleasant memories to remember me by."

"What about the holes in your kitchen window?" Fargo brought up. "I should patch them to keep the cold out until you can buy a new pane."

Cheryl glanced at them, and shrugged. "They're small holes. I'll patch them myself tomorrow." Clasping his hand, she headed for the stairs. "We have to keep our priorities straight," she added, grinning.

"Your husband was right," Fargo kidded her. "You're too wanton for your own good."

"Trust me. You'll love every minute of it."

Cheryl insisted on undressing Fargo herself, then had him lie buck naked on the bed while she shucked her nightgown and climbed in beside him. Fargo reached for her, but Cheryl pushed his arms down. Then, kneeling, she kissed him over every square inch of his body. Soft, tender, little kisses that slowly aroused his sexual hunger. He burned with desire before she was done, and his pole was at full attention. Again he reached for her, again she wasn't ready. Shifting to the foot of the bed, she began licking him. She started at his ankles and licked a wet path up the inside of each leg to his inner thighs. It set his whole body to tingling. He was squirming with need when she rose and sculpted her mouth to his manhood.

A groan escaped him. Fargo closed his eyes and let

her give free rein to her craving. He was cast adrift from himself, lost amid a pillowy cloud of sensual sensation. His own craving climbed until he was close to bursting at the seams. When he couldn't stand it any longer, he bent and gripped Cheryl's shoulders and pulled her higher.

Her eyelids were hooded, her lips puffy and slick. She smiled languidly as she straddled him and reached down to guide him into her innermost recesses. "Ohhhhhhhhhhh. What you do to me."

Fargo was enveloped by satiny warmth. Above him dangled her pendulous breasts, her rosy nipples as inviting as candy. He sucked one into his mouth and rolled it with his tongue, and Cheryl exhaled loudly and moved her hips in a rocking motion.

"Yes! Like that. Oh, yes!"

Fargo cupped both ripe melons and molded them with his fingers as if they were clay. Cheryl panted lustily, her eyes fully closed. Their hips were moving in unison, pumping ever so slowly though as they let their mutual pleasure build toward its inevitable climax. Fargo's hand drifted across her right shoulder and down the length of her spine, at which point she arched her back and the pink tip of her tongue rimmed her lips. He caressed her firm bottom, kneading each in turn, and her hips rose a little higher.

"What you do to me!" Cheryl declared, lowering her mouth to his. Her breath was red-hot, her tongue insatiable. Their kiss went on and on, seemingly forever, and when they parted, she kissed his cheeks, his ears, his chin, his neck.

The bed under them creaked as Fargo thrust harder up into her. He was trying to pace himself, but it was harder to do than the last time. Fatigue was to blame. His body vibrated with the building urgency of release, and his usual trick of thinking about something else was only partly effective.

It didn't help that Cheryl Taylor couldn't get

enough of him. Her passion had been so long denied that having let herself go once, she yearned to make up for all those months of self-denial by experiencing lovemaking to its fullest. She had cast off every inhibition she possessed. She truly was wanton in every sense of the word. Her mouth, her hands, were everywhere, tireless in their carnal quest.

Fargo didn't mind when a woman was the aggressor. Any man who did was an idiot. Sometimes women just had to be. Sometimes they had to let down their hair and do all the things they'd always wanted to do but were too timid or too restrained to carry out.

Cheryl's lips fastened onto his left earlobe and her fiery breath fanned his neck. Her fingers plied the hard muscles on his chest and shoulders.

Fargo thought of how well she had handled herself when her home was invaded, and how quickly she had recovered and put it behind her. She was a strong, intelligent woman. He had a hunch that before another year was out she would latch onto a suitable suitor and walk down the aisle a second time. Only she would do it differently. She wouldn't choose someone who would brand her a hussy for being lively in bed. Next time she would pick someone who would appreciate her for the treasure she was, a man who would let her frolic under the sheets to her heart's content.

Cheryl's nails dug into Fargo's arm, ending his musing. He raised his mouth to the soft base of her throat and lathered it, then focused on her bobbing mounds. Their hips were grinding together without cease, and Cheryl's husky breathing was like a bellows.

"Ah! Ah! I'm close, lover. I'm very close."

So was Fargo. He pinched one nipple, then the other. He lightly bit her shoulder. He cupped her bottom to hold her steady and rammed upward.

Cheryl tossed her head from side to side, stiffened, and stared down into his eyes as if striving to stare into his very soul. Her hair hung over her flushed face in a chaotic wild mane. "No one has ever made me feel the way you make me feel. I want you to know that."

Fargo grunted, and rammed into her again.

"You've shown me things. Taught me I shouldn't be so prudish. That my life is far from over." Cheryl bestowed a wet kiss that lasted minutes, then whispered in his ear, "This is for you."

Fargo stiffened as she ground herself against him with renewed vigor. Her inner walls contracted, sheathing him in rapture, heightening the bliss tenfold. He nearly exploded. Gripping her shoulders, he matched her rhythm, bucking up off the mattress each time she levered downward. The entire bed lifted off the floor, bouncing like a ball. It was just as well no other boarders were staying there because the pounding of the bedposts would have woken everyone up.

Cheryl arched her back, and spurted. Her body quivering uncontrollably, she clamped her thighs to her hips. "Now!" she screeched. "I can't hold back any longer!"

Nor could Fargo. His release was as violent as hers. Heaving upward, he drove his pulsing rod into her yielding tunnel, his left arm locked around her waist, his right arm around her neck. Their mouths met and locked. He pumped and pumped, and pumped some more. Immersed in a boiling cauldron of bubbling pleasure, they both cried out, and cried out again.

When, after an eternity, they sailed over the crest and coasted down to earth, Fargo released her and sagged back, exhausted, caked with sweat, and supremely satisfied. She had drained him dry.

Cheryl collapsed on top of him, her cheek on his shoulder. Tiny breaths fluttered across his chest. "I almost passed out! You're unbelievable." She ran a finger down his chest to the flat of his stomach. "Thank you."

Fargo closed his eyes. "Anytime."

Giggling, Cheryl pecked his chin. "I'll never forget you. Not as long as I live. If you're ever back this way . . ." She left the thought unfinished.

Fargo didn't say anything. It was highly unlikely he would be. To hint otherwise would only give her false hope. She had to get on with her life just as he had to get on with his. He hugged her close, then settled down to sleep. He needed a lot of rest. Tomorrow he would push on to New York and look up Lucius Kemp. With someone out to kill him, he'd need all his wits about him.

And then some.

6

Skye Fargo had heard a lot of stories about New York City. Most everyone who had been there claimed it was a madhouse. Small wonder. It was the largest in the country, and the most congested. He had heard tell that people were packed together like sardines, and that most lived in apartments no bigger than a breadbasket. He'd always taken the accounts with a grain of salt, but now, riding through the heart of the bustling metropolis, he saw for himself the tales weren't exaggerated. If anything, they were vastly understated.

New York City was bedlam unleashed. Close to three-quarters of a million people crammed into an area not fit for an eighth that number. For some reason, in defiance of all logic, instead of spreading outward the city was spreading *upward*. Five and six story buildings were common, and there was talk that before the century was out ten stories would be the norm.

To Fargo, it was like riding along endless stone-walled canyons. Canyons crammed with passers-by and the many conveyances that carried them about the city.

Every street was packed wheel-to-wheel. There were carriages, coaches, phaetons, and broughams. There were shays, coupes, gigs, and rockaways. Omnibuses were everywhere, public modes of transportation that made Fargo think of extremely long stagecoaches, with four rows of seats that held three passengers each. They were driven by madmen. Fargo lost count of the number of omnibuses barreling along thoroughfares as if the drivers owned them, forcing smaller wagons and buggies to get out of their way or be run down.

The unending throng of traffic resulted in enormous jams. A dozen times Fargo had to skirt twisted grids of wagons, buses, carriages, and carts. Brawny policemen always plunged into the thick of the mess and got everyone going again. Anyone who argued regretted it. The police weren't loathe to use their fists and clubs as incentive.

As bad as the wheeled traffic was, the number of pedestrians was even worse. A seething river of humanity ebbed and flowed like a high-country waterway swollen by Spring rains. They pushed, they shoved, they cursed one another. And the amazing thing was, they accepted the state of affairs as perfectly natural.

Fargo hadn't been in the city thirty minutes and already he wished he was back in the Rocky Mountains. He had Kemp's address but no directions on how to get there, so he was obliged to ask for help. New Yorkers, though, weren't the friendliest folks on the planet. Most bustled by without so much as a sidelong glance, refusing to give him the time of day. At first he thought his buckskins were to blame since he didn't see anyone else wearing them. But after a bit it dawned on him he wasn't being singled out. New Yorkers were rude to everyone, including other New Yorkers.

Rounding a congested corner, Fargo beheld a burly policeman with ruddy checks and long sideburns standing on the left side of the street. Reining the Ovaro over, he said loud enough to be heard above the constant racket, "I can use some help."

"Can you now, laddie?" The policeman had a thick

Irish brogue. He was twirling a short club that was hooked to his wrist by a leather thong. "What's with the getup? Are you with one of those touring theatrical troupes?"

"I'm just in from St. Louis," Fargo said. "Here to see a gent named Lucius Kemp."

"Sure you are," the policeman said, his jowls shaking with mirth. "And tomorrow I've got an appointment to see the President. I hope the little woman remembers to iron my best blues."

Fargo leaned down, his arm across the saddle horn. He wasn't wearing his gunbelt. Carrying a firearm in the city limits was against the law, so he had stuffed his Colt into a saddlebag. The Henry was concealed in his bedroll. "What's your handle?" he asked.

The Irishman straightened. "My handle? Do you mean my name? Why do you want to know?"

"So when Lucius Kemp asks why I got there late, I can tell him you were to blame." Fishing out the telegram, Fargo unfolded it and held it so the policeman could see it. "Is this proof enough for you?"

The policeman's mouth moved as he scanned the lines. His brown eyes widened, and his next glance contained newfound respect. "You were serious!"

"I'm here to help Kemp find his niece. I'm a tracker."

"I read about her in the newspaper," the policeman said. "She went missing way off in the woods somewhere." Assuming an air of importance, he pointed with his club. "I'll give you directions to Mr. Kemp's front door. You take Third Avenue, here, down to—"

Out of nowhere, a coal-box buggy bore down on the pinto. Fargo tried to move aside but there was nowhere to go. He was hemmed by pedestrians on the left and heavy traffic on the right.

Hauling furiously on the reins, the driver brought the buggy to a stop a yard away and swore like a sailor. "Move that nag, you damned country bumpkin! Don't you know that wheeled vehicles have the right of way?"

The policeman glowered. "That'll be enough out of you. Can't you see I'm helping this man?" He gestured for the buggy to go around. "Be on about your business."

A typical New Yorker, the driver did no such thing. "Who do you think you're talking to? I'll have you know my cousin is a good friend of the mayor's. You're an officer of the law. Enforce it! Move this lout out of our way or I'll report you to your superiors." Two men in the buggy with him nodded their approval.

"Will you indeed?" The policeman smiled at Fargo. "Excuse me a moment, sir. One of our good citizens has too much wax in his ears." Continuing to smile, he walked over to the buggy. "Now then. Your sister knows the mayor's sister, is that it?"

"No, you lunkhead," the driver snapped. "My cousin knows the mayor. And I'll have him report you if you don't do as I told you."

The Irishman was a portrait of innocence. "Would that be a cousin on your father's side or on your sainted mother's side?"

"What the hell difference does that make?" the irate driver demanded.

"Not a bit," the policeman admitted, and just like that walloped the malcontent across the head. The driver buckled and started to fall out, but the passenger beside him grabbed his arm. "Now then," the Irishman said, wagging the club, "when he comes around, tell him my name is O'Malley, and I don't give a damn if he's the mayor's twin, no one tells a policeman what to do." He stepped back. "Get this rig out of here before I clap irons on all three of you and run you in for making a public nuisance of yourselves."

The driver's two friends were more level-headed than he was. They meekly swung the buggy past the Ovaro and blended into the frenetic flow.

"Now then," the Irishman said, "where were we?"

Fargo should have known that Lucius Kemp would live in one of richest, most prestigious areas in the city. Kensington Place was located in Kensington Heights, where every home was a mansion and every mansion dripped wealth. Entering the Heights was like entering a whole new world. Gone were the bustling people, the stifling traffic. Here there were wonderfully quiet tree-lined streets. Spacious yards replaced the brick and stone, and the warbling of mockingbirds and robins replaced the hubbub of voices and the din of clattering conveyances.

Kensington Heights earned its name by virtue of the low hill it was situated on. A hill that, by Fargo's reckoning, wasn't more than a hundred feet high. 114 Kensington Place turned out to be a mansion on the crest, the biggest mansion of all, with more acreage and trees and flower gardens than any other. A wrought-iron fence surrounded the grounds. Entry to the estate was through a burnished bronze gate that gleamed in the sunlight like polished gold. A gate that was closed and manned by two guards in a small shack just inside.

Fargo brought the tired stallion to a stop and pulled out the telegram. He figured they would want to read it before they would let him in, but when they stepped from the shack and saw him, they dashed to the gate to open it.

"You can go right up, Mr. Fargo," the shorter of the pair said. "Mr. Kemp instructed us to admit you the moment you arrived."

Fargo kneed the pinto forward. "I guess you don't get many visitors in buckskin." He imagined that was how they knew who he was.

"Your clothes have nothing to do with it, sir," the

short guard said. "If you had shown up in a suit and bowler we'd still recognize you."

The other guard chimed in with, "Mr. Kemp gave us a detailed description, sir. Your height, your weight, everything down to the color of your eyes."

"Even how you wear your hair," said the short one, and pointed up the drive. "Follow this around to the front and someone will be there to greet you."

Nodding, Fargo rode on. Towering maples plunged him in shade, splendid trees hundreds of years old. An elderly man in overalls was raking leaves, and smiled as he went by. Further on a gardener was poking around in the earth with a trowel. He, too, smiled.

A lot had been written about Lucius Kemp. By some accounts he was a heartless shark who put business before everything else and ran roughshod over those under him. But based on what Fargo had seen so far, those accounts had to be mistaken.

Kemp was an immigrant. He'd arrived in the United States from Poland at the tender age of three. His father had opened a wholesale seafood business on the docks of New York and it prospered into a chain of Kemp Fisheries all along the East Coast. When Lucius came of age, his father took him on as a full partner, and that's when things really heated up.

Lucius came up with a brainstorm. He ordered a whole fleet of special ice wagons built to transport seafood inland, wagons he designed himself. They enabled him to do what no one else could; supply fresh seafood to every city and town in the interior. In less than a year the family's income quadrupled.

Lucius invested the profits, diversifying in various industries. He had a natural flair for business, and within ten years was the wealthiest man in New York. Within twenty he was the wealthiest in America. His palatial home, the newspaper reported, cost five million dollars, a staggering sum. It was said he had a legion of servants to wait on him hand and foot, and that in his later years he had become a recluse.

Fargo passed the last of the maples. Ahead was a wide marble portico, and parked at the bottom of the wide steps leading up to it was a luxurious golden town coach with gold striping, attached to a team of four white horses. Behind it was an elegant olive-green brougham. Behind that, a cobalt-blue carriage that boasted decorative scroll work done in gold-leaf etching. Perched on the high seats of all three were coachmen in immaculate uniforms that included long-tailed coats and gloves.

Fargo reined up and swung down. There was no hitch rail. Before he could take a step, a grey-haired man in a black suit came rushing down to meet him.

"You're Mr. Fargo, are you not, sir?" the man asked with a deferential bow.

"Is there anyone here who doesn't know who I am?" Fargo rejoined, grinning.

"I'm Webster, sir. Mr. Kemp's butler." The man indicated the portico. "If you'll be so kind as to precede me, I've been instructed to take you to his study. Don't worry about your horse. The stable staff will attend to it."

"Not so fast." Fargo turned to his saddlebags and bedroll and began to untie them. "What kind of man is your boss? I've heard a lot of different stories."

"I would imagine you have, sir," Webster said. "The newspapers print the most outlandish tales. But you can't believe everything you read."

"How do you feel about him?" Fargo quizzed. He noticed the curtains to a second-floor window part, and a man and woman stared down at him, their features in shadow.

"I've been in Mr. Kemp's employ for thirty-one years," Webster said proudly. "That should tell you plenty."

"You think highly of him, I take it?"

"Mr. Kemp is the salt of the earth, sir. Oh, he's made a few enemies over the years. A man in his position can't help that. But he always treats his staff with respect and courtesy. In all the decades I've worked for him, he's never once been cross with me, never once raised his voice in anger."

Fargo shouldered his saddlebags. The bedroll went under his left arm.

"I can carry those for you, sir," Webster volunteered, automatically reaching out. "It's expected of me."

"Not this time," Fargo said. With someone out to do him in, he wanted a gun near him at all times. He hadn't run into any trouble since leaving Fornication, although once, a few miles outside of New York City, he'd had the distinct feeling he was being followed. The road had overflowed with traffic, though, and he couldn't spot anyone remotely suspicious. The one person he thought it might be, a pug-nosed character in grungy clothes, had darted on among other pedestrians.

Fargo passed between gleaming marble columns and through a mahogany door. An elfin woman in a maid's uniform and a younger man in a suit identical to Webster's were waiting just inside, standing crisply at attention in a hallway distinguished by wine-red carpet, polished paneling, an arched ceiling, and paintings by European masters. Life-sized sculptures decorated alcoves trimmed in gold.

"Allow me to introduce Jeffrey and Marta," Webster said. "They will wait on your every need during the remainder of your stay."

"Your belongings, sir?" Jeffrey offered, reaching out as Webster had done.

"Leave them to me," Fargo replied more curtly than he intended, and all three exchanged glances.

"Out where I come from," he said to allay suspicion, "a man does things for himself."

"As you wish, sir," Webster said courteously. "Mr. Kemp isn't a stickler for convention, either. I suspect the two of you will hit it off."

That remains to be seen, Fargo reflected. "Where's the study?"

"I'll escort you," Webster said.

Marta gave a tiny cough. "Excuse me, sir. Before you go, is there anything special you require in your room?"

Smiling, Fargo gave her the sort of hungry look he gave lusty saloon girls, and she blushed from chin to hairline.

"I meant of a hygienic nature, sir," Marta said softly. "Or perhaps you would like a snack or a drink brought up before supper?"

"A bottle of the best whiskey in the house will do me just fine," Fargo said. "Leave it on my dresser." He had a lot of trail dust to wash down.

"As you wish, sir."

Webster had stopped several yards away to wait. He moved on when Fargo did, and when they came to a junction, the butler bore to the right.

"Tell me more about those enemies you mentioned," Fargo said offhandedly.

The butler's eyebrows pinched together. "A rather unusual request, if you don't mind my saying so, sir. But it would be remiss of me to go into detail. I would violate the long-standing trust Mr. Kemp has placed in me. As a matter of discretion, I hold such information in the strictest confidence."

"Has anyone ever tried to kill him?"

Webster stopped so abruptly, Fargo almost ran into him. "How extraordinary. If you'll pardon my presumption, sir, your questions are best directed toward Mr. Kemp himself." He seemed to want to say more, but was reluctant.

"Spit it out," Fargo goaded.

"Might I inquire exactly why you posed such a re-markable query, sir?"

Fargo was fishing for information that might shed some light on the attempts on his life. The butler impressed him as being an honorable man, so he had no qualms in answering, "Because someone tried to plant me six feet under on my way here. One of your boss's enemies, maybe."

"My word!" Webster was genuinely horrified. "Do you mean someone attempted to murder you? I never expected it would come to that."

"What would?" Fargo said.

Webster looked both ways and his voice dropped to a whisper. "I'm afraid I'm not at liberty to say just this moment. Perhaps later this evening I can pay you a short visit and elaborate." Suddenly Webster turned and locked eyes with Fargo. Gripping his wrist the butler slipped into an urgent tone and said, "Whatever you do, don't let your guard down. You're no safer here than you were en route. There is much more to this whole affair than you were told in the telegram you were sent."

"Kemp let you read it?"

"I wrote it, sir, at Mr. Kemp's direction, of course. I also function as his personal secretary and manservant." Webster resumed talking in a normal tone. "Now, if you'll be so kind as to follow me to the end of this hall."

Every room they passed was a monument to wealth, to the absolute best money could purchase. The furnishings made those at the Imperial Inn seem shabby by comparison. Literally no expense had been spared, and the result was a magnificent home worthy of royalty, a residence fit for a monarch. Or for someone just as rich and powerful.

"Have a seat in the study," Webster said, stepping aside at the doorway.

"Don't you mean the library?" Fargo jested. In all his life he had never seen so many books in one place, shelf after twelve-foot-high shelf arranged in long row after long row, filling a room five times as spacious as the Imperial's lobby. Old books, for the most part, musty with age, some of the titles too faded to read.

"Mr. Kemp is something of a collector," Webster said. "He prides himself on owning some of the rarest volumes known to man. Many come from monasteries. His Shakespeare collection alone is priceless."

To the right of the doorway was a small area reserved for reading. It contained a couple of chairs and a small table.

"Please wait here, sir," Webster said. "I'll return shortly with Mr. Kemp."

The moment the butler was gone, Fargo placed his saddlebags and bedroll on the table, partially unrolled the bedroll, and slipped the Colt from its holster. Verifying the chambers were loaded except for the one under the hammer, Fargo pulled his buckskin shirt out, tucked the Colt under his belt, and lowered the shirt over it. No one would suspect the pistol was there unless they bumped against him. He rolled the bedroll back up and tied it.

Kemp had yet to appear. Pushing his hat back on his head, Fargo strolled along a bookcase, reading some of the titles. There was a multi-volume set of *The Decline and Fall of the Roman Empire,* a tome entitled *Plutarch's Lives,* and beside it, leather-bound, gold-embossed editions of *The iliad* and *The odyssey*.

A whiff of strong perfume brought Fargo to a halt a second before a sultry female voice addressed him.

"Can you imagine anything more boring than wasting your life reading all these stuffy words?"

Fargo turned.

Beside the table lounged a sandy-haired vixen in a print dress that clung to her hourglass figure as if it were painted on. She sashayed nearer, her hazel eyes regarding him with lively interest. She had high cheeks, even white teeth, and lips formed into a perpetual pout. "Don't tell me that my uncle has put you in charge of his silly old collection? I'll have to rethink my lifelong aversion to visiting the study."

Chuckling, Fargo leaned on a shelf. "Afraid not. I'm here to help your uncle with something else."

The woman stopped cold. "Oh my God. It just hit me. You're him, aren't you? Skye Fargo? The scout Uncle Lucius sent for? The one they say can track an insect over solid rock?"

"If that's what your uncle thinks, he's been reading too many dime novels," Fargo responded.

"Are you kidding? My uncle wouldn't be caught dead reading that 'trash', as he calls it." She held out a hand capped by raspberry-red fingernails. "I'm Beda Kemp, by the way. The youngest of his three nieces."

"How many does he have?" Fargo inquired, liking the warmth of her palm and the suggestion of a different warmth deep in her eyes.

"You're not familiar with the family tree? Then let me break it down for you." Beda swiped at a stray bang. "Uncle Lucius has two brothers, Dalbert and Berton. Berton has two children, Camilla and her brother Laurel—"

"Camilla is the one who went missing?" Fargo broke in.

"That's her. She's always been adventurous, always going off into the middle of nowhere after moldy old bones and relics." Beda shook her head. "I ask you, is that any way for an intelligent person to spend their life? She was asking for trouble and she found it. Her and her merry band of incompetents got themselves lost in the deep woods."

"You said there were three nieces," Fargo reminded her when she paused.

"Oh. Then there's me and my older sister. We have

92

a brother, Ronald, who's sulking around here, somewhere. Our father, Dalbert, was born twenty years after Lucius and Berton, so they were never very close to him. Which is why Uncle Lucius has always favored Camilla and Laurel over my sister, Ronnie and I."

From the doorway came a ragged cough that caused Beda to tense up slightly. Forcing a smile, she pivoted.

"I've done no such thing, child," disagreed the family patriarch. Lucius Kemp was bundled in a heavy red sweater and baggy pants three times his size. Hunched over in a wheelchair, he had the aspect of a man on his last legs. Wispy strands of white hair crowned a scarecrow face ravaged by a network of blue veins and sickly yellow splotches. Gnarled fingers rose and pointed at Beda Kemp, and when he spoke, his vocal chords crackled like brittle bones. "Give me credit where credit is due. I've never played favorites and you know it."

"Then why is it you picked Camilla over the rest of us?" Beda challenged. "I'd call that favoritism, plain and simple."

The wheelchair creaked into the study, pushed by Webster. The seat, arms, and backrest were padded, and it had wooden stirrups for Kemp's feet. He pointed at the reading area and Webster pushed the wheelchair over to the table.

Beda was on her way out, her nose in the air, her dress jiggling delightfully. "I won't bandy words with you, Uncle. We've been all through this a dozen times. You've made your choice. But don't blame the rest of us if we don't like it."

Lucius Kemp gazed sorrowfully after his youngest niece, then sighed and ran his crooked fingers through his whisker-thin hair. "Were ignorance gold, she would be wealthier than I. How ironic that we don't acquire true wisdom until our waning years. We need it most when we're young, but we're too young to realize it." His grey eyes focused on Fargo as Fargo approached. "So here you are. My last and best hope."

"I came as quickly as I could."

"For which I'm eternally grateful." Lucius coughed. "Tonight you will dine with us and I'll explain the crisis in detail. Tomorrow you'll leave for the border and strive your utmost to locate Camilla."

"I haven't agreed to work for you yet," Fargo said. "And I won't until I've learned everything there is to know."

"All that matters is my niece is missing," Lucius rebutted. "The most decent, noble girl you would ever want to meet. She's everything to me, Mr. Fargo. The daughter I never had." His lower lip quivered. "My dear wife, Sally, couldn't conceive. We tried and tried, but it was no use. She went to her reward about fifteen years ago, and I've been on my own ever since. Sweet Camilla is my sunshine, my life."

"What about your other nieces? And your two nephews?" Fargo began to think Beda's criticism of her uncle might be justified.

"I love them dearly. But they lack the one quality that sets Camilla apart. That makes her special."

"What would that be?" Fargo asked.

Lucius Kemp smiled. Half his upper teeth were gone, and those on his lower gum were yellowing with age. "Camilla is a virgin."

7

Two hours later Skye Fargo stood in front of a full-length mirror in the second-floor room he had been given and adjusted his red bandanna. In a few minutes he was due to join the Kemp clan for supper. He had on his cleanest buckskins, and his hair was neatly combed. Supper was a "formal affair", as Lucius Kemp described it, and everyone dressed up for the occasion.

Fargo was puzzled by his prospective employer. After Kemp's comment about Camilla, he'd wanted to learn more. But Kemp had excused himself, saying he had important business to attend to.

"We'll talk again at supper. All your questions will be answered then. Or most of them," the aged patriarch amended with a peculiar smirk.

At a snap of Webster's fingers, Jeffrey the apprentice butler, and Marta the petite maid seemed to pop out of the walls. They had guided Fargo to his room and hovered over him as if he were a two year old until he tired of their silliness and whisked them out. Fifteen minutes later Marta had shown up to inform him a hot bath had been drawn.

Marta had scented the water with lavender and added tiny bubbles. Despite that, Fargo soaked a good long while. Luxuriating in the comfort, he dozed off. Later, as he began to wash, Jeffrey marched up to the silver tub holding a long-handled brush. "What do you think you're doing?" Fargo demanded.

"I'm ready to scrub your back."

"Like hell you are." Fargo nodded at the door. "Make yourself scarce."

Crestfallen, the servant had responded, "I'm only trying to do what is required of me. I scrub the backs of Laurel and Ronald all the time."

"Are they too lazy to scrub their own?" Fargo asked, and was dumbfounded when the young man burst into tears and fled the bathroom. His amazement grew when, moments afterward, Marta strolled in as innocently as could be, holding the same brush.

"Forgive my boldness, sir, but you should be ashamed of yourself. Jeffrey is an extremely sensitive soul."

Fargo was beginning to wonder if all New Yorkers were born with a few bolts loose. "Is it a crime in this city for a man to wash himself?"

Marta's slanted green eyes danced with amusement. "You miss the point, sir. I might be overstepping my bounds, but it wouldn't have hurt for you to be civil. Now he'll be an emotional wreck the rest of the day."

"And that's my fault?" Fargo said, snatching the brush.

"To be perfectly blunt, yes," Marta said, demurely clasping her hands in front of her. "You're in polite society now, and we have certain rules we adhere to."

Fargo resented the implication he was an uncouth bumpkin. "Do you have someone scrub your back when you take baths?"

"Well, no, but—" the maid started to reply.

"I didn't think so." Fargo sank lower into the tub. "Don't let the door hit you on your pretty little fanny on the way out."

"Sir!" Marta exclaimed, her cheeks twin peaches. In a huff, she spun and flounced to the doorway, where she paused to glance back and remark, "Do you really find my posterior attractive?"

"It beats a buffalo's all hollow," Fargo said, and laughed when she stomped out and slammed the door.

That had been an hour ago. Now, Fargo donned his hat and turned from the mirror. He had been given a large key, which he pocketed once he was positive his door was securely locked. The Colt was nestled under his shirt, the Arkansas toothpick was in its ankle sheath. He hadn't gone three steps when he acquired a shadow in a staff uniform.

"I'm to escort you downstairs, sir," Jeffrey said.

"I thought you were going to spend the rest of the day blubbering," Fargo mentioned. "Just give me directions and I'll find the dining room alone."

Jeffrey was a marvelous pouter. "Honestly, sir. That was uncalled for. Has anyone ever told you that you have a cruel streak?"

"Has anyone ever told you that you can't go through life bawling every time somebody hurts your feelings?" Fargo rejoined. "West of the Mississippi a man isn't considered much of a man if he acts like a baby."

"You're not west of the Mississippi anymore."

"So everyone keeps reminding me," Fargo said. And the longer he was there, the more he missed the mountains and the prairie and the unfettered life he cherished.

The dining room was on the ground floor. Five times as long as it was wide, it boasted four sparkling chandeliers and a table able to seat two dozen people in high-backed chairs. Only seven were present and they were at the near end, as moody a bunch as Fargo ever laid eyes on. At the head, in his wheelchair, was Lucius Kemp. On the elder Kemp's right sat a man equally as old but with a full head of white hair, far fewer wrinkles, and dark bags under his eyes. It had to be Berton Kemp, Fargo guessed, Camilla's father. On Lucius's left sat the other brother, the younger one. Dalbert Kemp was taller and thinner and had a hooked nose that lent him a hawkish countenance. He wore a gold ring on each hand, a gold pin in his tie, and a fob watch, its thick gold chain dangling from a vest pocket.

Next to Berton had to be his son, Laurel. In his early thirties, Laurel was the mirror image of his father, only much more heavyset. He had his chin in one hand and was glumly munching on a dinner roll.

Next to Dalbert sat his daughter, Beda, wearing a fine gown, and her brother, Ronald. It was Ronnie who interested Fargo most. His general build was a lot like his father's, only he was taller and thinner. Where his father wore two rings, Ronnie wore six. Where Dalbert wore a thin stick pin, Ronnie wore a pin a quarter of an inch thick. And while Ronnie, like Dalbert, had a single gold chain hanging from his vest, Ronnie's was twice the size. He wore enough gold to feed a thousand starving people for a year.

Jeffrey stopped and clicked his heels. "Ladies and gentlemen, your indulgence please. Announcing your honored guest, Mr. Skye Fargo."

All eyes swiveled as Fargo sauntered over. Berton and Laurel registered curiosity. Beda was amused. Dalbert acted bored. Ronnie, though, betrayed fleeting hostility, hostility he immediately concealed behind a ferret-like smile.

"Mr. Fargo!" Lucius Kemp declared. "We've been waiting for you with keen anticipation. Permit me to introduce everyone."

All of Fargo's guesses were proven right. He nodded at each of them in turn. Berton smiled warmly. Laurel nodded back. Dalbert gave a little wave, Beda merely chuckled, and Ronnie simply sat there.

Berton then rose and said, "I can't tell you how much this means. For the first time in days I have real hope my daughter will be found." He pumped Fargo's hand with sincere vigor. "Whatever you need, you have only to ask. The full resources of the Kemp family are yours to command."

"To a degree," Dalbert corrected him. "I don't extend my trust lightly. He must prove himself worthy before I'll regard him as highly as Lucius does."

Lucius smacked the arm of his wheelchair in irritation. "How can you be so critical when Camilla's life is at stake? Bert is nearly beside himself with anguish. He deserves your full support, not your typical carping."

Dalbert smiled thinly. "There you go again, older brother. Assigning blame without just cause. I didn't say I wouldn't support Bert. I merely stressed I'm not as enthusiastic about your scout's abilities as you are. The proof is in the pudding, as the common rabble have it."

Lucius jabbed a bony finger at his sibling. "I'll have you know, Dal, that Mr. Fargo comes highly recommended. Every military commander I contacted assured me he's the best tracker alive. If anyone can find Camilla and the others, he's our man."

"Frankly, one scout is as good as another, as far as I'm concerned," Dal said airily. "You can defend him to high heaven but it won't change my opinion."

Fargo stepped between them. "The scout can defend himself. If it's humanly possible, I'll find Camilla and the others." He glared at Dalbert. "And I won't need your help or anyone else's to do it."

Ronnie came up out of his chair with his fists clenched. "Have a care, mister! No one uses that tone with my father. Do so again and I'll soundly thrash you."

"You're welcome to try," Fargo said. He was in a perfect mood to pound on someone, and it might as well be the arrogant dandy.

Ronnie started forward, but stopped when Beda grabbed his wrist and shook her head. Lightning bolts shot from Ronnie's eyes as he reluctantly sat back down.

"Please forgive their attitude," Lucius said. "The family has been under a lot of strain since I made an important announcement several months ago. Camilla's disappearance has compounded the situation."

"I'm listening," Fargo said. Before he agreed to help, he needed to find out what he was getting himself into.

"All in good time," Lucius said, and gestured at an empty chair. "Have a seat. We'll discuss everything over supper."

Webster took that as a cue to arrive on the scene pushing a solid silver cart lined with alcoholic beverages. Fargo had his choice from the best on the market; whiskey, brandy, Scotch, rum, bourbon, wine, ale, and more. It reminded him Marta had yet to provide the bottle of whiskey he had requested for his room. Filling his glass, he tipped it to his mouth and relished the warmth that spread rapidly down his throat and into his gut.

Ronnie was sizing him up like a hawk sizing up prey. "Perhaps we should dispense with food altogether. Our scout seems much more fond of liquid refreshment."

"That will be enough," Lucius said sternly. "Unless you want to be completely cut from my will, you'll show proper respect."

"Cut me off more than I already am?" Ronnie asked sarcastically. "Why, I could qualify for pauper status. My friends would laugh me to scorn."

Fargo's dislike of the man was rising by leaps and bounds. "You have friends?" he asked, and faced Lucius, who had turned to Webster and was instructing the butler to have the staff begin serving the meal. "Forget the food. I want answers and I want them now. I've traveled halfway across the country to get here. It's the least I deserve."

"Very well," Lucius Kemp said. "Where do you want me to start?"

"What happened to your niece?" Fargo asked. It was as good a place as any.

"As my telegram explained, she went missing somewhere along the U.S.–Canadian border. Foul play is suspected. The region they were in is very remote. There isn't a town within eighty miles."

"What was your niece doing there?"

"Her work. Camilla is an anthropologist by trade. It's a new field having to do with the science of human beings, as Professor Petticord likes to refer to it."

"Who?" Fargo said.

"Sorry. Her mentor at Durnell University. He went along on the expedition. So did several of his students and a long-time associate of hers, Harry Baxter. They were doing research on a lost tribe, the Killamak."

Fargo had never heard of them and commented to that effect.

"I shouldn't be surprised," Lucius said. "The Killamak were reputedly wiped out two centuries ago." He nodded at Bert. "Perhaps my brother should do the honors. He's much more conversant with the facts."

"Only because I had to listen to my daughter go on and on about them day and night," Bert said with a halfhearted grin. "The Killamak were the most feared tribe of their day. They held their own against the likes of the Iroquois Confederacy and the Hurons, and they resisted white encroachment long after all the other tribes in the region had given up."

"Yet they were wiped out?" Fargo interjected.

"So history has it," Bert said. "Disease was to blame. Smallpox, most likely, although it could have been any white disease to which they had no natural resistance. Other tribes have suffered just as grievously, if not more."

Fargo was familiar with the stories. The Mandans were the most spectacular example. Onetime lords of the upper Missouri River country, they had welcomed white trappers and explorers to their villages and been repaid for their kindness with smallpox. Out of a total population of over nine thousand, only one hundred and twenty-four survived the devastating epidemic that resulted.

"My daughter was fascinated by the Killamak, by their culture, their customs," Bert was saying.

"Some would call it an obsession," Ronnie said.

Bert ignored him. "She was tremendously intrigued when she received a report that some Killamak artifacts had been found along the Canadian border. So she contacted her mentor and set the wheels in motion to pay the area a visit."

"Did they have a guide?" Fargo inquired. It would be just like a group of Easterners to traipse off into the deep woods without taking adequate precautions.

"Did I neglect to mention the Delaware my daughter hired?" Bert said. "I can't recall his name but he's an experienced woodsman. Camilla had every confidence in him."

"Misplaced confidence, evidently," Ronnie commented. "Or she would be here with us now."

Fargo had encountered a few Delawares in his travels. Once a powerful Eastern tribe, they had been driven from their lands and pushed relentlessly westward by white expansion. First into the Appalachians, then into eastern Ohio, then into Missouri. A pattern that repeated itself over and over. Yet strange to relate, they never developed a deep hatred for whites as many other tribes had. Even though mistreated, they maintained peaceful relations.

The Delawares became a tribe without a home, but they never lost their tribal identity. In order to support their families, Delaware warriors hired themselves out as trappers, hunters, and guides, and they were highly respected for their skill. Those Fargo had met impressed him greatly. Camilla Kemp was to be complimented for her decision. But it added an extra element of mystery to the disappearance. It was unthinkable a Delaware would get lost. And if Camilla's group had run into trouble, the Delaware would have hastened back for help.

Unless he were dead.

"How soon were search parties sent out?" Fargo asked.

"As soon as it became apparent my niece was overdue," Lucius answered. "I put an advertisement in every major newspaper in the state requesting the services of every woodsman worthy of the name. We've had over a hundred men scouring the woods of northern New York for the past two weeks and they haven't turned up a clue."

"It's as if my daughter and her friends walked off the ends of the earth," Bert said forlornly.

The mention of two weeks gave Fargo added cause for concern. "How long has Camilla been missing?"

Lucius pondered a moment. "Tomorrow it will be exactly twenty-one days since a runner arrived from their base camp. I put ads in the newspapers that very afternoon. I also hired a prestigious detective firm to locate you as quickly as possible." He sipped some brandy. "You see, I'd read about you last year in the *New York Post*. How you saved those settlers in the Sierra Nevadas."

"How long was Camilla overdue when the runner was sent?" Fargo quizzed them.

"Three days," Lucius said. "The last time anyone saw them was when they struck off from their base camp to investigate a promising site."

Fargo performed a few mental calculations and didn't like what he came up with. "So, all told, no one can account for the expedition's whereabouts for almost a whole month?"

"I know what you're thinking," Lucius said. "But they had plenty of provisions, and the Delaware was a competent hunter. If they strayed into Canada there's every chance they're still alive and well."

That wasn't how Fargo saw it. The longer they were gone, the less likely it was they were still breathing. If he assumed, for the sake of argument, that they were alive, in three weeks time they could have wandered hundreds of miles deep into Canada's formidable wilderness, into a region where few whites had ever set foot. "Other than the Delaware, how many of your niece's party were skilled at living off the land?"

"None that I'm aware of," Lucius replied, and glanced at his brother for confirmation.

"Professor Petticord had been on seven or eight similar treks," Bert said. "Once he spent a whole month in the pine forests of New Jersey."

Fargo didn't regard that as much of a feat. The pine forests of New Jersey were nowhere near as rugged or inhospitable as the vast untamed tracts of Canadian northland. Few Americans realized just how sparsely populated Canada was, or how much of it had yet to be fully explored. Grizzlies, mountain lions, and wolves were everywhere.

Then there was another factor, a factor no one had mentioned yet. Winter wasn't far off. In another month, possibly sooner, cold weather would set in. Plummeting temperatures would add to the problems the expedition faced. Heavy snow was also a threat. All it would take was one blizzard and they were as good as dead.

"You're very quiet," Lucius said. "Are you contemplating their prospects?"

"Among other things," Fargo said.

"Be honest with us," Bert said. "What are my daughter's chances?"

"Slim," Fargo conceded. There was one ray of hope, though. Horses left deep tracks, and although weeks had gone by, some vestiges should remain. Once he found a few, he would stick to their trail like a bloodhound. He was surprised none of the woodsmen Lucius had hired hadn't done the same, and he said so.

Lucius and Bert looked at one another. Then Lucius cleared his throat and said, "They didn't take horses."

"What?" Fargo's ray faded to a sliver.

"They went in on foot," Bert detailed, "packing in their tents and provisions on their backs. My daughter felt horses were unnecessary. An added burden they could do without. Besides which, she doesn't have much experience on horseback. Neither do most of the others."

Now Fargo understood why the woodsmen hadn't found anything. Human tracks were easily obliterated by rain, by the wind, by falling leaves and pine needles. Finding whatever sign the expedition left would be akin to looking for a needle in a haystack.

Ronnie sat up. "I can tell by your expression, scout, that the enormity of your task is beginning to sink in. I'm no expert, but even I know a lost cause when I hear one. How can you track if there aren't any tracks?"

Laurel stirred, breaking his silence. "Leave it to you to stress the worst aspect of things. Just once in your life, why don't you think of someone other than yourself? Granted, my sister and you haven't gotten along very well in ages. But some people at this table think highly of her."

"Now, now, cousin," Ronnie said, grinning, "Your sister has always been near and dear to me. Didn't we play together all the time when we were younger? Remember the games? The fun?"

"That was then," Laurel said. "You've changed since we were kids. You're not the same person."

"I grew up," Ronnie said. "I suggest you do the same." He gazed out a nearby window at the gathering twilight. "Life isn't a fairy tale, cousin. Sooner or later we must cast off our childhood delusions. Sooner or later we must come to terms with the bleak reality of it all."

Beda raised her glass of rum in a mock salute. "To

my beloved brother, the ultimate cynic. To him, money matters more than morals, and riches are thicker than blood."

Ronnie shifted toward her. "That will be quite enough out of you," he warned. "I refuse to be criticized for having our family's best interests at heart."

"What are you two talking about?" Dalbert asked his offspring.

Neither answered. The timely arrival of the food spared them from further questioning as a bevy of smartly uniformed men and woman brought tray after steaming tray to the grand table, an assortment of dishes the likes of which would do justice to the best restaurants in New York City.

Fargo didn't know where to begin. He had his choice of sterling silver trays piled with beef, fish, pork, and venison. Of platters heaping with mashed potatoes, scalloped potatoes, and potatoes sauteed in a thick cheese sauce. There were platters of corn, of green beans, of lima beans. Platters of wheat bread, rye bread, and barley bread. As if that weren't enough, he was offered bowls filled with butter and honey and a selection of jellies and jams. He hadn't eaten a decent meal since Cheryl Taylor's place, and he was famished. Grabbing a large fork from one of the trays, he speared slabs of meat and piled them inches-high in the center of his plate. Around them he ladled portions of potatoes and corn and string beans. He ended up with a small mountain of food, enough to feed two or three men. About to dig in, he sensed the movement in the room had stopped, and he glanced up.

Everyone was staring at him in wonderment, even the servants. Beda was grinning. Ronnie smirked in that smugly superior manner of his and asked, "Are you sure that's enough? We can have the chef slaughter an ox for you. If one happens by, that is."

Lucius Kemp had a small strip of fish and a small

baked potato on his plate, that was all. "Pay no attention to him, Mr. Fargo. Most of us haven't had much of an appetite since Camilla disappeared. But don't let that stop you from eating your fill."

Fargo didn't. In the wilderness a man had to eat what he could, when he could. Game didn't fall into a hunter's lap. Feast and famine were the normal cycle, and frontiersmen learned to adapt. Weeks might go by before he had another meal half as good. So he finished every last morsel on his plate and had second helpings of beef and corn. He ate until his stomach felt fit to rupture and he thought that he couldn't possibly swallow another mouthful. That was when they brought out the pies and cakes.

It was over dessert that the conversation resumed, Dalbert taking up where they had left off by turning to his son and daughter and saying, "Now what was that you were talking about a while ago? About riches being thicker than blood?"

"Perhaps you should direct your question to Uncle Lucius," Ronnie said. "He's the one who decided only one of us is worthy of his affection."

"That's not true." Lucius put down his spoon. "All of you know my days on this earth are numbered. The doctors tell me I'll be lucky to live out the year. I had to choose an heir now, while I still could."

"And you picked Camilla," Ronnie stated resentfully.

"She'll receive the bulk of my fortune, yes," Lucius said. "But I've made provisions for the rest of you, haven't I?"

"Oh, yes." Ronnie's laugh tinkled like shattered glass. "Half a million dollars for each of us. Half a million paltry dollars."

"Paltry?" Fargo repeated. To him it was an astronomical sum, more money than he had earned in his entire lifetime.

Ronnie nodded. "Compared to fifty million, half a

million is a pittance. In case you haven't heard, money is power. Whoever inherits my uncle's fortune will become one of the most powerful people in the country. But a measly half-million?" His sneer was masterly. "It might as well be two cents."

"That can always be arranged," Lucius said.

"Spare me your idle threats, uncle," Ronnie said. "You've made your sentiments crystal clear. Camilla is your favorite and always has been. So you selected her. But don't expect me to stand up and cheer. I would do anything to be in her shoes." Ronnie fixed a smoldering gaze on Fargo. "Anything at all."

8

The biggest surprise of the evening came when the meal was over. Webster brought cigars for the men, and Dalbert was lighting his when he mentioned, "I'm sorry Pan didn't make it here tonight, Lucius. She went to visit a friend in Pennsylvania. In Harrisburg, I believe. She hasn't made it back yet."

Skye Fargo had just asked Webster for another whiskey. "Pan?" he said, thinking of the compact that belonged to the woman who had tried to kill him at the Imperial Inn. The compact inscribed with, *"To my beloved P.K."*

"Short for Pandora, my oldest daughter," Dalbert said, puffing like a chimney. "She's always been the independent sort. I asked her to stick around until you arrived, but she couldn't be bothered."

"That's my big sister for you," Ronnie said in admiration. "She does what she wants, and everyone else be hanged. When we were little we had to play the way she wanted to play or she clawed our eyes out."

"You're exaggerating, son," Dalbert said. "Your sister was never as violent as all that."

In his mind's eye Fargo relived those harrowing moments when the madwoman came at him with her glittering dagger. "Does she have black hair, by any chance?"

"Why in the world would you think that?" Dalbert said. "No, her hair is the same color as Beda's. Both are the spitting image of their mother."

Fargo scrutinized Beda closely, comparing her features to the woman at the inn. There was a resemblance, but not enough of one to prove it had been Pandora. "When do you expect her to show up?"

Dalbert blew a smoke ring. "With Pan there's no predicting. She's like a butterfly. She flits all over the place as her whims dictate."

Bert dismissed the topic with a wave of his hand. "We have more important things to discuss. Namely, how best to go about finding my daughter and restoring her safely to the loving bosom of her family." He leaned toward Fargo. "You must bring my baby back to me at any cost. I don't care what it takes.

Lucius stirred in his wheelchair. "That reminds me. We haven't talked over the terms I offered you, Mr. Fargo. I can double the amount if it's not enough."

"It's not the money that matters," Fargo said. It was finding out who wanted him dead. He had his suspicions, but voicing them without proof would accomplish nothing but put whoever was to blame on their guard.

"Money doesn't matter?" Ronnie snickered. "There's an infantile concept if ever I've heard one. Didn't you hear me a while ago? In this world all that *counts* is money. It buys influence, position, prestige. It's the great arbiter, the barrier that separates the makers and breakers from the downtrodden and broken. Only a complete simpleton would be inane enough to say money is of no consequence."

"I agree," Dalbert said. "Without money what does life have to offer? The finer things don't come cheap."

Lucius muttered something under his breath, then said out loud, "Listen to the two of you. Need I remind you that ninety-nine percent of the money you have came from me? Were it not for my generosity, Dal would still be working as a house painter. And you, Ronald, would still be breaking your back lifting boxes down on the docks."

Fargo inwardly smiled. So Ronald Kemp had once

been a longshoreman? How very interesting. "I'll agree to help find Camilla on one condition," he informed them.

"What would that be?" This from her father, Berton.

"I do it my way," Fargo said. "I don't take orders from anyone. I search at my own pace, and I won't be interfered with."

"That sounds like four conditions to me," Beda noted. "Want us to put them in writing and have my uncle notarize them?"

"Hush, child," Lucius scolded her. To Fargo he said, "Imposing conditions isn't necessary. You'll have free rein to do as you see fit. I will provide a written document to that effect, prepared by my lawyer, placing the entire resources of my business empire at your complete disposal."

"All I need is someone to guide me to where your daughter and her friends were last seen," Fargo said.

Ronnie pushed back his chair and stretched. "You'll need more than that, scout. Or hasn't my dear uncle filled you in yet on the complexities of the situation?" He glanced at Lucius, whose thin lips were pressed tight. "No? Perhaps I should do the honors then. You see, you won't be the only one out there looking for sweet Camilla."

"The search parties are still out searching?" Fargo figured.

"Not only them," Ronnie said, "but every tramp and deadbeat from Florida to Connecticut. Word has gotten out. Newspapers all along the Eastern Seaboard have reported the story. Scores of hopefuls have flocked to northern New York thinking they'll be the one to find her and reap a rich reward from the wealthiest man alive."

Fargo shifted. "Is this true?" he asked Lucius.

The patriarch was tapping his fingers on the arm of his chair. "Regrettably, yes. I'd have gotten around to filling you in soon enough."

"That's not all," Ronnie crowed. "I'll bet Uncle Lucius hasn't told you about the Indian problem, has he? Or about Camilla's not-so-secret secret."

Tired of the runaround, Fargo snapped, "I want to know everything and I want to know it now or I'm walking out the door." He was bluffing. He wouldn't do any such thing with the life of a young woman at stake. But they didn't know that.

Ronnie pushed his chair back and propped his shoes on the table. "With your permission, Uncle Lucius? Uncle Bert?" When neither objected, he continued. "Reports have reached us from the search parties. It seems there's been Indian trouble. One man took an arrow in the thigh. Another was beaten within an inch of his life."

"Does anyone know which tribe is to blame?" Fargo probed.

"Tribe?" Ronnie chuckled. "You've misunderstood. When I called it an Indian problem, I meant just that. *One* Indian, and only one, has been going around telling every white he meets to get out of there, or else. When they balk, he becomes violent. He's driven dozens off. Judging by the accounts, he has the rest trembling in their boots at the mere mention of his nickname. Redface, they call him."

"One Indian has done all that?"

"Entertaining, is it not?" Ronnie said cheerfully. "But now we get to the best part of all. You see, Camilla didn't go up to the border on a lark. She received a report that Killamak artifacts had been found." Ronnie paused for effect. "Recently made artifacts."

"Recent?" Fargo must have missed something. "I thought the tribe died out centuries ago."

"So it's been claimed. If true, it's probably just as well they were. Because the Killamak were reputed to be the fiercest tribe in the Northeast. They were so savage, even the Iroquois and the Hurons were scared of them." He paused again. "Do you have any idea what the word Killamak means?"

Fargo shook his head.

"Loosely translated, 'Brain Eaters'", Ronnie revealed. "Like the Iroquois and others, the Killamak were notorious for torturing their enemies Not only that, it was rumored they engaged in a sacred ritual where they cracked open the skulls of some of those they caught and ate the brains."

"Must you go into such gory detail?" Berton criticized.

As Fargo had learned the hard way, some tribes were partial to inflictinr pain and suffering. Down in Arizona he once came upon a grisly scene where six Mexican freighters had been ambushed, tied upside-down to the wheels of their wagons, and then had fires lit under them by their Apache captors. Elsewhere in his travels he'd witnessed sights as bad or worse.

Ronnie was enjoying himself. "To my silly cousin, finding the lost tribe was her Holy Grail. She couldn't stop talking about it. How it would be the discovery of the century. How it would make her famous." He sucked on his cigar. "She overlooked one trifling detail, though. How it might also make her dead."

Berton was becoming angry and Fargo didn't blame him. "Damn, but you're a cold fish. We don't know what has befallen her yet, so I'll thank you to refrain from talking about my daughter as if she's deceased until we establish beyond a shadow of a doubt that she is."

"My apologies, uncle," Ronnie said. "We wouldn't want the reports of her demise to be premature, would we?" He smirked at Fargo. "So now that you know what you're getting yourself into, have you changed your mind?"

The opposite had occurred. Fargo was more determined than ever to save the young woman and her friends, and in the process see that those who tried to murder him reaped their just desserts. "I'm going to do my best to find Camilla and the rest of the expedition."

Lucius and Berton were profoundly relieved and thanked him over and over. Laurel sat glum and silent. Beda's brow was knit in thought. Dalbert showed no interest whatsoever.

Ronald, on the other hand, didn't like it one bit. Clenching his fists, he said angrily, "So be it, scout. I've tried to persuade you of the folly of your undertaking, but you refuse to listen to reason. When they find your bleached bones five years from now, I'll be sure to remember to have a drink in memory of your stupidity."

Fargo was up out of his chair and around the table in four long bounds. Before Ronnie could think to resist, Fargo clamped his right hand onto the dandy's throat and squeezed. Ronnie bleated like a terror-struck sheep and sought to tear his hand loose but couldn't. Slowly applying pressure, Fargo said matter-of-factly, "I'm tired of your insults. I'm tired of your sneers. But most of all, I'm tired of being a target." Leaning closer, he whispered, "I know you're behind the attacks. Make one more attempt and it will be your last."

Ronnie was the color of a beet. Sputtering and thrashing, he wriggled like a worm on a hook, his lower lip slick with spittle.

"Here, now!" Dalbert protested, rising. "How dare you manhandle my son! Release him this instant!"

Lucius was trying not to show his glee and failing miserably. Berton was stunned. Laurel looked as if he had just been given the present he always wanted. Beda, oddly enough, was unruffled, and calmly sipped her drink.

Fargo pivoted, and shoved Ronnie, spilling him and his chair in an undignified heap. Several servants moved to help but stopped at a gesture from Webster, who made no effort to hide how pleased he was.

Scrambling onto his knees, Ronnie rubbed his throat and snarled, "How dare you! I don't know what the hell you were prattling on about, but I promise you haven't heard the last of this! No one abuses me like you just did! No one!"

Fargo started to turn away. The man's threats were so much hot air as far as he was concerned.

"Damn your impertinence!" Ronnie roared. Lunging at the table, he gripped the hilt of a carving knife and whirled.

"Ronald, no!" Lucius cried.

It wasn't the shout that stopped the hothead. It was Fargo's right hand, sweeping out from under his buckskin shirt with the Colt level and the hammer thumbed back. Fargo curled his finger around the trigger, but at the last split-instant stopped himself from firing. Ronnie had frozen, and was standing only a foot or two from Beda. The slug might pass through him and hit her.

"A gun!" Dalbert exclaimed. "The man has a gun!"

The tableau had frozen, the servants horrified, Berton and Laurel agape. Beda displayed no more emotion than she would if Fargo were holding a bouquet of flowers.

"It's against the law to carry a concealed weapon in New York," Ronnie said, his Adam's apple bobbing. "I could report you and have you arrested."

"For defending myself?" Fargo stepped to the left so he could shoot without fear of hurting Beda. "Drop the knife or die."

Ronnie Kemp's face was a mask of fury. He elevated his arm, and for several seconds it appeared he was going to disregard the command and attack.

"For God's sake, son," Dalbert interceded. "Do as he wants or he'll gun you down where you stand."

Straightening, Ronnie defiantly stared at the Colt's

muzzle, then flipped the knife onto the table and folded his arms across his chest. "Very well. But this isn't the end of it, not by any means."

"No, it isn't," Fargo agreed, certain the two of them would have a final showdown before the whole affair was over with. Sliding the revolver up under his shirt, he headed for the hallway. "I'm turning in. I'll be on my way at first light." A heated, bitter exchange ensued, but he couldn't care less what they were arguing about. He was out of earshot within moments.

For all of Lucius's wealth, the Kemp clan was as miserable a pack of malcontents as Fargo had ever run into. They couldn't get along if their lives depended on it. Ronnie and Beda were spoiled to the core. Laurel lacked gumption. Dalbert was a wealth-crazed no-account. And Berton was a two-legged mouse. That left Lucius, a pale shadow of the powerful individual he once was.

Footsteps suddenly pattered to Fargo's rear. He spun, but it was only the maid, Marta, carrying an armful of folded towels and washclothes. "I want to be alone," he said. Alone to think, and to congratulate himself on the fine mess he had stumbled into.

"My apologies, sir, but Mr. Kemp instructed me to refill your wash basin and provide you with these." Marta gazed at his waist, at the slight bulge his Colt made. "Please don't take offense. I'm not Ronald. I actually like you."

"Don't let the others hear you say that." Fargo noticed how the swell of her bosom hinted at charms not readily apparent, and roved his gaze to the hem of her uniform, which only fell to the middle of her milky thighs. With a toss of his head he walked on. He really did need to get an early start. Indulging his fondness for the opposite gender would keep him up late and leave him tired and listless.

"Might I say, sir," Marta chirped, her short legs pumping to keep up, "how much I admire what you did? No one has ever stood up to Ronald like that before. It was long overdue."

"You don't sound very fond of him."

"Quite perceptive sir. He's obnoxious. He treats the staff as if he's somehow superior to us, when not all that long ago he wasn't making much more money than we do. He struts around like a peacock, barking orders as if it's his God-given right."

"Is he staying the night?' Fargo asked.

"Not to my knowledge, sir, no. None of them are. Berton has a home in New Jersey and will be leaving shortly. Dalbert lives in Manhattan. Beda has her own place just a couple of miles from here."

"And Ronnie?"

"He rents a loft down by the Hudson River. He's always had a special fondness for water. For over a year he worked as a longshoreman, back before his uncle gave all of them their fortunes. Ronnie has squandered most of his on jewelry, clothes, and loose living." Marta glanced behind them, then said quietly, "To be honest, I despise him. He always associates with the most unsavory characters. And no matter how much Lucius gives him, it's never enough. He always wants more."

"What's your opinion of Camilla?" Fargo was putting his life at risk for the heiress. He might as well learn all he could about her.

"Oh she's the salt of the earth," Marta said sweetly. "A nicer person you'll never meet. All those mean things Ronald said weren't the whole truth. Yes, she's very devoted to her work. But she's not out to make a name for herself. She feels sorry for the Indians, for how they've been treated. By learning all she can about the tribes who were wiped out, she can preserve their memory for future generations."

"She told you that?"

"Those were her exact words, yes" Marta confirmed. "So you see, Camilla is much more decent than Ronnie let on."

Fargo came to the stairs and started up. "What can you tell me about Beda and Pandora?"

"Not much, I'm afraid. They tend to keep to themselves. They don't go flying off the handle all the time, like Ronnie does, although I did see Pandora blow up once at something Ronnie said. She slapped him silly, she did, and he didn't try to defend himself. He's a coward, that one. Rumor has it he was challenged to a duel once but he refused to meet his challenger on the field of honor."

"I thought dueling was illegal."

"Oh, it is. But rich men do it all the time. Last year two senators were set to fight over remarks one made about the other. They had picked their seconds and bought new dueling pistols and everything, but the governor got wind of it and stopped it at the last minute. He said it would set a bad example."

Fargo reached the landing. "Do you think Lucius did the right thing choosing Camilla as his heir?"

"Out of all of them she's the nicest," Marta said. "I heard him say his fortune should be used to benefit mankind, and she's the only one who tends to think of other people before she thinks of herself."

"What about her brother, Laurel?"

"He's a hard one to figure. He never shows much interest in anything, even in his uncle's millions. When Lucius announced he had chosen Camilla, Laurel was the only one who didn't raise a fuss."

Fargo had learned more in two minutes of talking to her than he had in the entire two hours spent with the family. "Too bad I have to get such an early start. I wouldn't mind taking you out on the town tonight."

"Me, sir?" Marta said, tickled. "I'm just a maid."

"You're also a woman," Fargo remarked, "and a pretty one, at that. You must have a husband or boyfriend stashed away somewhere."

"Not on your life." Marta laughed. "I'm young yet. I won't be ready to settle down for quite a spell."

"A girl after my own heart," Fargo said, and winked. He was rewarded with a crimson tinge that crept up her neck to her rosy lips.

"You flatter me, sir. A handsome devil like yourself must have his own share of women pining after him."

They were almost to Fargo's room. He fished the key from his pocket. "I'd invite you in, but I wouldn't want to get you into trouble."

"I have to go in anyway," Marta said. "To hang up the towels," she added hastily.

Fargo went to insert the key into the hole when he heard a sound from within, the muffled hint of movement and a faint clink. Motioning to the maid to stay where she was, he reached under his shirt, lightly grasped the latch, wrenched and pushed. The door flew wide, slamming against the wall hard enough to shake a painting on the wall.

Jeffrey was over by the dresser. He nearly jumped out of his skin, and almost dropped the bottle he had been about to place on top. "It's only me, sir! I've brought the whiskey you requested."

"About damn time." Fargo entered. The closet door was slightly ajar, yet he distinctly recollected shutting it after placing his saddlebags and bedroll in the closet right before supper. He looked at Jeffrey. "Has anyone else been in here?"

"Not to my knowledge, no, sir." The younger man angled toward the corridor.

Fargo thought it strange Jeffrey didn't want to know why he had asked. "Hold it," he said, and opened the closet. The bedroll lay on the floor beside his saddlebags, not on top as he had left it. "I don't like it when people go through my things."

Jeffrey tried to act indignant. "I have no idea what you're talking about, sir. All I did was bring your whiskey and a new set of glasses. I would never stoop to snooping into a guest's personal effects."

"Is that a fact?" Fargo did as he had done to Ronnie; he clamped his left hand onto Jeffrey's throat and dug his fingers in deep. Looming over the smaller man, Fargo shook him like a wolf shaking a fawn. "What were you looking for?"

Jeffrey didn't resist, didn't struggle. His mouth moved but no words came out. Only tiny whimpers, his eyes pleading to be let go.

"I can't hear you," Fargo said, and shoved the servant against the dresser.

"It wasn't me!" Jeffrey whined, and recoiled when Fargo strode toward him. "I mean, it wasn't my idea! Mr. Kemp asked me to go through your effects and report back to him on what I found!"

"Which Mr. Kemp?" Fargo already knew, or thought he did.

"Laurel!" Jeffrey revealed. "It was Laurel!"

Bewildered, Fargo didn't try to stop Jeffrey from slinking past and darting out the door. *Why in the world had Laurel put the simpleton up to it?* he wondered. Camilla's brother and father were the two he thought he could count on the most, the two who cared for her the most and would suffer the most if she were never found.

Marta was shaking her head. "What's happening to this family? I just don't understand any of this."

"That makes two of us," Fargo said. Hunkering, he sorted through his belongings to ensure everything was still there, and checked the Henry to be sure it hadn't been tampered with.

Deeply troubled, Fargo rose and closed the closet. It was one thing to have made an enemy of Ronnie Kemp. But now he had to watch his back around Camilla's own brother. He contemplated marching downstairs and demanding to know what Laurel was up to, but he doubted Laurel would come right out and tell him.

Resentment boiled up within him and Fargo fought down an impulse to smash a fist against the wall. Here he was, trying to help them, and what did they do?

Ronnie wanted him dead. Laurel was snooping around. Lucius had kept crucial information from him. Dalbert treated him with contempt. Beda disliked Camilla enough to hope he failed to find her, and Pandora might have tried to murder him. It was ridiculous. Every hand was against him. He couldn't rely on anyone.

"Sir?"

Fargo had forgotten about the maid. "You can leave the towels and go." He moved to the dresser, opened the bottle, and sat down, his mind in a whirl. He was close, so very close, to telling the whole family to go to hell, and leaving.

Marta closed the door. "Sir, I almost forgot. Webster instructed me to tell you there is a portrait of Camilla in the music room, so you'll know what she looks like." Marta came to the bed. "The music room is right next to the study."

"Thanks. I'll stop there tomorrow on my way out." Taking a long swig, Fargo smacked his lips, then wriggled the bottle at Marta. "Care for some?"

"Don't mind if I do." She dropped the towels and wash cloths on the quilt, tilted the whiskey to her mouth, and drank with enthusiasm. "Not bad," she said, smacking her lips louder than he had.

Her hips were inches from Fargo's face, her thighs temptingly near. "Your employer won't mind you drinking on the job?"

"I won't tell if you don't," Marta said, placing a hand on his shoulder. "I'm supposed to do all in my power to make you feel at home." The pink tip of her tongue rimmed her lips invitingly. "You wouldn't happen to have a few suggestions as to how I can best go about doing that, would you?"

Fargo chuckled. "As a matter of fact, I might."

9

Women never ceased to make Skye Fargo grin. They liked to brand men as philandering brutes who only had one thing on their minds; men were animals, men were lustful, men were always looking to get up under a woman's skirts. Yet in the same breath, women were fond of portraying themselves as saintly creatures who never indulged their physical urges. They were too refined, too dignified to even think about sex.

The truth, though, as Fargo had discovered, lay somewhere between the two extremes. Not all men were obsessed with lovemaking, just as not all women were the paragons of righteous virtue they made themselves out to be. He had met plenty of women who liked a frolic under the sheets as much as any man.

Marta the maid was one of them. As Fargo placed his hands on her rounded bottom, she grinned seductively and moved up against him, coquettishly pressing her nether mound against his mouth. "I am at your complete beck and call, sir," she said, her eyes aglitter with mischievous deviltry. "Do with me as you will."

Fargo inhaled the dusky scent of her firm body and felt himself stir lower down. For one so small, she was superbly proportioned. Her bosom, her hips, her legs, were as fine as a man could want. Her close-cropped hair, the shortest he had ever seen on a woman, was alluring in itself. A ripe mouth and full cheeks completed the portrait of sensual desire she presented.

"No one will come looking for you, will they?" he asked. It wouldn't do to be interrupted.

Marta removed his hat and tossed it on the bed. "I've been assigned to you, and only you. I have no other duties to attend to." She ran her fingers through his hair. "No one will miss me for hours, handsome."

"All the better," Fargo said, and rubbed his chin lower, over her nether mound to the junction of her thighs. Her uniform was smooth as silk. When he thrust his chin between her legs, he felt the heat her womanhood was giving off. He also caused her to squirm and giggle throatily.

"Something tells me this will be a night to remember." Marta bent and kissed his forehead, her lips incredibly soft and moist.

"I'll do my best," Fargo said. Running his hands to the bottom of her uniform, he slipped his fingers under the hem and caressed her smooth inner thighs. She sighed softly and arched her back.

"Before you go any further, you must promise me that what we do here tonight stays in this room. You must never tell another soul. I don't want to lose my job over a dalliance. Agreed?"

"It is hard being a woman in this day and age," Marta complained. "Men tend to put us on pedestals. And if we don't live up to their ideals, they accuse us of being sluts. Take Mr. Kemp, for example."

"Lucius?" Fargo was more interested in exploring her body than in jawing, but he recalled Kemp's comment about Camilla and wanted to learn more.

"The very same. He is quite the prude, that one. To him, sex is sinful unless it is between a man and his wife. Gossip has it that when he was choosing his heir, he picked Camilla because she is the only one of all his nieces and nephews who has never gone to bed with anyone. Supposedly, she's a virgin. To Mr. Kemp, that makes her more virtuous than the rest."

"Supposedly?" Fargo said.

"There is talk that maybe she isn't as virginal as her uncle would like to believe," Marta responded. "Even so, compared to the others, she's practically holy. Pandora's escapades are legendary. She is insatiable. She's had more lovers than anyone can count, and she doesn't care who knows it."

"What about Beda?"

Marta traced the outline of Fargo's right ear with a fingertip. "She is quiet, that one. Always keeping to herself. But under the surface she's a hellcat. Those who have worked here the longest say she is almost as wild as Pandora." Marta traced the other ear. "Ronnie, it goes without saying, revels in debauchery. He frequents the most expensive bawdy houses and is on a first-name basis with the most notorious prostitutes in the city."

"And Laurel?" Fargo inquired.

"I can't say with any certainty. He's more discreet than even Beda. Rumors are mentioned from time to time, dark rumors having to do with the summer he spent at a lake with some friends. His uncle, you might have noticed, hardly ever speaks to him. They are estranged, those two, and no one will tell me why."

Since she was being so free with information, Fargo delved further. "Why didn't Lucius leave more of his fortune to his brothers?"

"You've met Dalbert. Do you need to ask? Where do you think Ronnie gets his taste for night life? Dalbert would gamble most of it away in no time." Marta's hand strayed to his chin. "As for Berton, he's a dullard. They say he has the business sense of a snail. Not only that, he is much too trusting of others. Much too gullible. He wouldn't hold onto the fortune for long, not with all the sharks we have in New York City. And I don't mean the kind with gills." Her features saddened. "All Lucius has done, all his years of hard work and perseverance, would end in ruin."

Fargo was about done with his questions. "You sound as if you admire him?"

"He's a demanding employer. He always expects the best out of those who work for him. But he is also fair to a fault. And he is without a doubt one of the most generous people I have ever known. Last year alone he gave hundreds of thousands of dollars to charity." Marta bent her lips toward his. "Now then. Which would you rather do? Talk ourselves to death or put our mouths to better use?"

"Do you need to ask?" Fargo mimicked her. Pulling her close, he rolled her onto the bed on her side and laid flush against her. His body dwarfed hers.

"I should warn you," Marta said. "I'm a screamer. I might bite you to keep from crying out so we won't be overheard."

"Now who's doing too much talking?" Fargo asked, and silenced her by covering her lips with his. Their tongues met and swirled like two lovers in an erotic dance, sending pleasant tingles down his spine. He pried at the buttons at the front of her uniform and when they were undone, he slid a hand inside.

"Mmmmm," Marta mewed. "You have warm fingers. I like that in a man."

Fargo was warm all over and growing warmer. He made short shrift of her undergarments, exposing a pair of perfectly round, swollen breasts, like two halves of a grapefruit. Her small nipples were erect as tacks, and when Fargo pinched one she arched her back and sighed.

"You've done this before," Marta said playfully.

"Once or twice." Fargo devoted the next five minutes to stimulating her breasts. He kissed them, licked them, squeezed them. Enticed lower by her dusky scent, he nuzzled a moist path to her navel, inserted his tongue, and felt her shiver. Her thighs widened, and her legs rose to wrap around him.

125

Abruptly, without forewarning, the door shook to several loud knocks. "Mr. Fargo? Are you in there?" Beda Kemp called out. "We need to talk."

Fargo looked up. He had a bulge in his pants the size of an axe handle and wasn't about to stop. Placing a finger to his lips, he motioned for Marta to lie still, but she stiffened and eased out from under him.

"Please," Beda Kemp insisted. "I know you wanted to turn in early. I won't take up much of your time."

Marta was frantically gathering up her discarded undergarments. She shook her head when Fargo gripped her wrist and tried to pull her back onto the bed. "I know her," Marta whispered. "She won't go away until you answer."

As if to prove the point, Beda yelled, "Mr. Fargo? I hear you moving around in there. Have the decency to let me in, will you? It's my brother who made you mad, not me."

Although he was loathe to do so, Fargo rose, pulled his shirt down over his manhood, and reclaimed his hat. "What about us?" he whispered. "I'd like to take up where we left off later on."

"I'll return if I can after everyone else has turned in." Marta, almost dressed, jerked a thumb at the door. "If she catches me in here there will be hell to pay. To spite me she'll tell her uncle."

"Then we won't let her catch you," Fargo whispered. Pecking Marta's cheek, he whisked her into the closet. "Don't make a peep."

Beda pounded louder. "Quit playing games! I won't take no for an answer!"

Checking himself in the full-length mirror, Fargo called out, "Hold your horses. I'm not dressed." He waited another ten seconds, then opened the door and stood in the doorway so she couldn't get past. "What the hell is so important it couldn't wait until morning?"

Beda had brought a glass of rum and she sipped

some before replying, "Aren't you going to invite me in?"

"No." Stepping out, Fargo shut the door behind him. "Now that you've got me up, I might as well go for a stroll. I can use the exercise." To forestall an argument he headed for the stairs, leaving her with no choice but to follow if she really wanted to talk to him. She swiftly caught up.

"I must say. You're one of the rudest men I've ever met. It wouldn't have hurt for you and I to sit down in the privacy of your bedroom."

"What would your uncle say?" Fargo said. It could have been his imagination, but he had detected a suggestive hint to her comment.

"Who cares?" Beda said. "Uncle Lucius doesn't run my life. Not after he showed me exactly where I stand by choosing Camilla over the rest of us." Bitterness oozed from her every pore. "And to think, once I admired him. Once I tried my best to please him, to live the kind of life he expected of me. Not anymore."

Fargo descended two steps at a stride. Midway down, by a sheer fluke, his still-rigid manhood became snagged in his pants. He reached down to free himself, then saw Berton and Laurel climbing toward him.

"I thought you were turning in," the son said with a barbed look at Beda. "Where is she taking you?"

"Not that it's any of your business, cousin," Beda shot back, "but he's the one taking me. I was going to strip him naked and make passionate love in his bedroom."

Berton clucked like a flustered hen. "Now, now. Enough of that kind of talk. We're family, and we should try to get along. Son, I want you to apologize to Beda."

"Why should I?" Laurel sulked. "You know how conniving she can be. She'll try to wrap Mr. Fargo around her little finger just as she's tried to do with the rest of us."

"If I were a man," Beda said haughtily, "I'd slap your face and formally challenge you to a duel. Say what you will about me, but we both know you're not much better. You have a dark side to your personality. Or have you forgotten—"

"Don't you dare!" Laurel barked. "All you have is hearsay, not proof. Until you do, I'll thank you to keep your mouth shut." Shouldering on by, he stomped up the stairs, saying as he passed, "I warn you, sir. She's a viper. Trust her at your own peril. I know things she doesn't know I know."

"What does that mean?" Beda asked, but received no reply.

Berton bowed his head and walked on. "I'm sorry," he said to Fargo. "They haven't always spatted like this. When they were little, all five of them were as close as peas in a pod. It's Lucius. His darned last will and testament. It's turned them against one another."

"Money will do that," Fargo remarked. Of the whole bunch, Bert was the only one he felt sorry for. Unlike the others, Bert wasn't money-hungry. All that mattered to him was finding his daughter and preserving the Kemp family. A hopeless task given the circumstances.

Berton looked back. "The Good Book says the love of money is the root of all evil. Truer words were never written."

"I beg to differ," Beda said with surprising venom. "Being rich beats being poor any day of the year. Show me a rational person who would rather live as a beggar than in the lap of luxury."

"Money can't love," Bert said.

"But it can put food in your belly and clothes on your back and a roof over your head," Beda argued. "Can love do all that?"

"Love feeds the soul, not the body," was Berton's parting salvo, and he hurried after his son.

Beda rolled her eyes toward the ceiling. "Amazing.

Simply amazing. How can he have lived so long and learned so little? When he's broke and fending for himself he'll see the light. But by then it will be too late."

"I doubt Lucius will let his brother starve," Fargo said.

"The future isn't written in stone," Beda said enigmatically, and clasped his elbow. "Can I convince you to change your mind about going for a stroll? It's chilly out. We'd be much more comfortable in the dining room. Everyone else has left and we'll have it all to ourselves."

Fargo saw no reason to object. He'd bought Marta plenty of time to slip out of his room and make herself scarce. "So long as I get a cup or two of coffee, it's fine by me."

A maid was cleaning off a few odds and ends from the grand table. She scuttled off at Beda's bidding and was back in two shakes of a lamb's tail with a pot and china cups and saucers.

Fargo sat at the head of the table so he could see if anyone entered. Filling his cup, he added sugar and cream and said, "So let's hear what's so important it couldn't wait until morning."

Beda was stirring her coffee, her head bent, her eyes hidden by her hair. "I want you to be honest with me. Realistically, what are your chances of finding Camilla?"

"Two in ten."

"That's all?" Beda said.

Fargo couldn't say whether she was upset or glad. "Too much time has gone by. Odds are it's rained a few times. There's been a lot of dew, a lot of frost on cold mornings. I'll be lucky to find a single track."

"All things considered, then, Uncle Lucius is sending you on a wild goose chase."

"I don't want to dash anyone's hopes, but yes, that's the size of it," Fargo said. "It would be different if they'd had horses. Under the right conditions hoof-prints can last for weeks."

"It will be a rough time," Beda said.

"Hunting for them will be hard work," Fargo agreed. "I'll have to cover as much territory as I can before the first snow hits, and hope I get lucky."

"I was referring to how my uncle will react if you can't find his precious Camilla," Beda set him straight. "He'll have to select a new heir. Ronnie is out of the question. Laurel has a blemish he can never erase. Pandora is as wild and reckless as Ronnie. That leaves only one of us in the running."

"You?"

Beda smiled confidently. "Me. So you'll excuse me if I hope your search is an utter failure." She thought-fully fingered her cup. "To be honest, Camilla brought this on herself. She had no business going off into the deep woods with those misfits."

"Misfits?" The more Fargo learned about Beda Kemp, the less he liked her. She had a habit of putting her own interests before everyone else's. In that respect she was as selfish as her brother.

"What else would you call idiots who go around unearthing old bones?" Beda said. "Is that any way for a grown person to spend their life?" Beda shook her head. "Camilla could have done any number of sensible things. She could have gone into business for herself. She could have opened a clothing store. Or an art gallery. But no. She got it into that silly head of hers she could make a difference in the world by digging up the past."

Fargo was tired of Beda's company. Polishing off the rest of his cup, he set it down and rose.

"Leaving so soon?"

"I can't think of a reason to stay."

"How about fifty thousand reasons?"

About to turn, Fargo slowly sank back down. He had an inkling what she was leading up to, and he wanted to hear her say the words, wanted to find out how far she was willing to go. "I'm listening."

Beda glanced toward the kitchen, then toward the hallway. They were completely alone. "Two-in-ten odds aren't good enough. There's still an outside chance Camilla will turn up alive. So I'm here to convince you to boost those odds. Say, to zero in ten."

"I'm still listening."

"Our uncle is offering you ten thousand dollars to track her down. By pooling our resources, some of us can offer you fifty thousand dollars *not* to find her. All you have to do is ride around in the woods for a couple of weeks, then tell Uncle Lucius you didn't come across any trace of the expedition." Beda placed her hand on his. "What do you say? Fifty thousand dollars to do absolutely nothing?"

"Ever seen a black widow spider?" Fargo asked.

Blinking in confusion, Beda shook her head. "Can't say that I have, no. What do spiders have to do with anything?"

"Some people think black widows are the prettiest spiders around. They're a shiny black color, except underneath where they have with a bright-red hourglass mark."

"Fascinating," Beda said, mildly irritated. "What's your point?"

"I'm getting there. Black widows aren't just pretty. They're dangerous. Their bites are venomous. You'd never know it to look at them that they can be deadly." Fargo stared at her for several seconds. "Get my point yet?"

Beda wasn't the least bit amused. "Damn you. Who are you to sit in judgment on me? You don't stand to lose a fortune if Camilla is found. And for your information, offering you fifty thousand was my sister's idea, not mine. If it were up to me, I wouldn't offer you a cent. But Pandora likes to cover every contingency."

"When do I get to meet this wonderful sister of yours?" Fargo asked. He was under the impression she wasn't at the estate.

"Maybe never," Beda said evasively. "She's been busy."

"Did she enjoy her stay at the Imperial Inn?"

Beda started to answer, then caught herself and grinned. "You think you're clever, don't you? But all you've been so far is lucky. And no one's luck lasts forever. You don't realize it, but you're caught up in a war. A war that can only have one outcome."

Fargo remembered the longshoreman, Stevens, using the exact same words. Coincidence? Not by a long shot. He decided to quit sparring and go for the throat. "Whose idea was it to have me killed on the way here? Yours? Your brother's? Or was it another of Pandora's contingencies?"

"I don't have the foggiest notion what you're talking about." Beda's expression grew wary.

"War, remember? The war for the Kemp fortune." Fargo reached across and grasped her wrist so tightly, she winced. "There's one thing you've overlooked. Once you start spilling blood, there's no telling where it will stop. Before this is over some of your own might be shed."

"Was that a threat?"

"No, a fact of life." Fargo pushed his chair back and rose. "Did you honestly think you could try to kill me and I wouldn't do anything about it?"

Smirking, Beda pushed her own chair back. "What can you do? Where's your proof?"

Fargo thought of the compact. It alone wasn't enough. And it was all he had. The letter he had taken from the Imperial Inn and the identification card belonging to Martin Stevens had been ruined. Cheryl Taylor hadn't realized they were in his pants pocket when she washed his buckskins and they had ended up in soggy bits and pieces.

"The police would laugh in your face," Beda gloated. "And any judge in the state would dismiss the case out of hand."

Leaning on the table, Fargo gave it to her plain. "Who said anything about having you charged. This is personal. The wise thing to do is turn yourselves in while you still can."

"Is that so?' Beda laughed. "We're not stupid, you know."

Sighing, Fargo straightened. "I'm serving notice. Tell your brother. Tell your sister. The next attempt on my life will be the last."

"Or what?" Beda taunted. "You'll shoot Pandora and me in cold blood? The great Trailsman? The knight errant in buckskin who regularly rescues damsels in distress?" She shook her head. "Highly improbable. You see, I know more about you than you suspect. When Uncle Lucius told us he was hiring you, I did some research at the library and read some interesting accounts. Like the time you saved the members of a wagon train stranded in a blizzard. Or that time you saved some people from the Apaches."

"So?"

"So all the stories had one thing in common. They went on and on about how you're a man of honor. How your word is your bond. They mentioned your reputation as a womanizer and a gambler. But for all your flaws, they made it plain you're not a killer. You don't go around gunning down defenseless people. So your threats are worthless."

Fargo turned to leave. She thought she had him all figured out but she was wrong.

"Last chance, big man," Beda said. "Fifty thousand dollars is nothing to sneeze at. It's more money than you'll see in your lifetime. Think of all the things you could do, the sights you could see."

It would be a waste of Fargo's time to try and explain. She would never understand. "You've been warned," he said. He was almost to the doorway when she made a puzzling statement.

"Things aren't as they seem. People aren't as they pretend to be. Your scruples are no substitute for common sense. Quit before it's too late."

"I can't," Fargo said. No matter what they had in store for him, he would see it through to the end. He ambled out, and nearly collided with Webster.

"Here you are, sir," the butler said. "I've been searching all over. My employer would like a word with you in the study before you retire."

Lucius Kemp was in his wheelchair by the small table, several sheets of paper, a pen, and a bottle of India ink in front of him. "Thank you for coming," he said cordially. "I won't keep you. But it's important we clear the air."

"Over what?" At the rate Fargo was going, he would be lucky if he got to bed before midnight.

"My nephew Ronald, for starters. His antics at supper were despicable. He has no say in Camilla's rescue. Absolutely none. I've given you free reign to do as you please, without hindrance." He handed a couple of sheets to Webster, who relayed them.

"To Whom It May Concern," Fargo read the first aloud. *"The bearer of this document has full and legal right to act in my stead in every and all matters as he may choose, without restriction. His will is my will. Failure to cooperate with his requests will reap the most dire legal consequences."* Under it was Kemp's scrawled signature. The second sheet was a letter of introduction to the head of the search operation, a woodsman named Owen Hamilton. "Are these necessary?" Fargo asked.

"I think they are." Lucius began to turn his wheelchair. Webster immediately leaped to do it for him but Lucius waved him off. Rolling the chair over to Fargo, he squeezed Fargo's forearm with unexpected vigor. "Mark my words. You are to find my niece. I don't care what it takes or how much it costs. Don't let anyone or anything stand in your way."

"What if someone in your own family tries to stop me?" Fargo bluntly asked.

Lucius Kemp didn't bat an eye. "When I said anyone, I mean *anyone*. If you have to, dispose of them as you deem fit." He paused, his features hardening. "Just in case that's not plain enough, let me spell it out for you. If someone tries to stop you, kill them. Kill them dead."

10

Half an hour of tossing and turning convinced Skye Fargo he wasn't going to get to sleep any time soon. His mind was racing like an arrow in flight. He couldn't stop thinking about the missing heiress and those conspiring to keep her missing. The same person, or persons, were to blame for the attempts on his life, and he would very much like to find out who it was before he set off for the wilds of northern New York. Unfortunately, since Martin Stevens's identification card and the letter to the Imperial Inn had been destroyed, he didn't have any idea how to go about it, short of pistol-whipping each of the Kemps until the guilty party confessed.

Fargo closed his eyes and tried yet again to doze off. Suddenly he remembered the slip of paper he had found on the second longshoreman, the one with "Joe's Shanty" written on it, and an address. Tossing the blankets off, he hurriedly dressed. By the clock on the dresser it was a little past eleven. Plenty of time for him to pay the place a visit and get back in time for a few hours' sleep.

Quietly opening the door, Fargo confirmed the hallway was empty, then tread lightly to the stairs. He preferred to slip out unnoticed, and at the bottom he stopped to listen. The great house was quiet, Slinking down a hall that brought him to a rear door, he was reaching for the latch when a cough behind him brought him around in a crouch.

Webster stood calmly a few feet away, smiling and acting as if it were perfectly ordinary to find a guest skulking about the mansion in the dead of night. "Might I be of assistance, sir?"

"Don't you ever sleep?" Fargo gruffly rejoined, annoyed the manservant had come up on him unnoticed.

"I usually retire at midnight, sir," Webster said, "long after everyone else. It's my responsibility to ensure the staff has performed all their daily duties as required, and that everything is in order for tomorrow."

"So you go around checking up on them?" Fargo said.

"If I don't, sir, no one else will. And they have a tendency to slack off unless I 'crack the whip,' as a military man might say." Webster nodded at the door. "Forgive my curiosity, sir, but where might you be bound at this time of night?"

Fargo gripped the latch. "I need to go into the City." He could have said he was going for a late stroll, but the butler was bound to keep an eye on him and might report his departure to Lucius Kemp. "And I'd take it as a personal favor if no one else knows."

"As I mentioned before, sir, I can be the model of discretion when I need to be," Webster assured him. "But, again, if you'll pardon my presumption, how do you plan to get there?"

"How else," Fargo said. "On my horse."

The butler looked as if someone had shoved a broomstick up his backside. "I wish you wouldn't, sir. Certain quarters in the City aren't safe at night. Footpads are as thick as fireflies. And denizens of the criminal element lurk in many an alley and dark corner."

Civilization and the wilderness were alike in that regard, Fargo reflected. Once the sun went down, the predators came out. "I have to go," he insisted, opening the door.

Webster made bold to place a hand on his arm. "Hear me out, sir. I didn't mean you shouldn't. I merely meant you shouldn't go by horseback. No one rides a horse through the City this late."

"It will take too long if I walk." Fargo was six paces from the door before the butler caught up.

"Please, sir! I would never forgive myself were you to come to harm." Webster sounded sincere. "Might I suggest an alternative? I'll have the stableman ready a carriage and select one of our drivers to take you wherever you desire to go. It's eminently safer."

Fargo mulled the proposition over. On the one hand, he didn't care to have anyone know where he went. On the other, a driver could get him about the city much faster than he could manage on his own. "I like the idea. On one condition."

"What might that be, sir?"

"You can convince the driver to keep it to himself."

"Whoever I ask to help, sir, will be as discreet as I am. But I'm afraid I must impose a condition of my own." Webster paused. "It would be wrong of me not to inform my employer. I am pledged in his service, and it is a matter of personal pride that I perform my duties diligently." He glanced back at the mansion. "I care not one whit about the rest of the Kemps. Dalbert is a degenerate, and his children have been spoiled to the point of ruin. Berton is sloth personified. Laurel is so self-absorbed he would make an excellent sponge." Catching himself, Webster stated contritely, "I shouldn't have said that. It's not my proper place to comment on the character of my employer's relatives. Suffice it to say, my only loyalty is to Lucius Kemp, and to Lucius Kemp alone. Accordingly, with your consent, tomorrow morning I will mention that you took a late trip into the City but plead ignorant of all other particulars. Agreed?"

Fargo saw no harm in Lucius knowing. "Agreed," he said.

"Then let me escort you to the stables."

The night air was brisk. A northwesterly breeze rustled nearby stately maples and stirred the drooping leaves of several weeping willows. Fargo expected the butler to lead him to the main stable but Webster proceeded around it and across the yard to a quaint cottage. The windows were dark but after a few light raps the glow of a lamp lit the interior and an elderly man in a nightcap and nightgown opened the door. His spindly features rippled in surprise.

"Mr. Webster? What's brought you here at this ungodly hour?"

"My apologies, Porter. One of our guests must go into the City. How long will it take you to rouse one of the drivers and have a carriage rigged?"

Porter raised the lamp higher so he could see Fargo's face. "That depends on where this gentleman wants to go."

Fargo had the address memorized. "Joe's Shanty on Logan Street."

The butler and the stableman both blinked, and Webster said, "My word, sir. That's down on the docks, not far from the fish market. A most unsavory area, inhabited by a most unsavory element."

Porter expressed it more plainly. "It's one of the most dangerous parts of the City, sir. A night hardly goes by that someone isn't beaten and robbed, and at least once a month some poor soul is foully murdered."

"I urge you to reconsider," Webster said.

"If you don't want to help out, I can always take my horse," Fargo responded.

The butler shook his head. "Please, no. It would put you at too great a risk. We must take every precaution we can. You are too valuable to Mr. Kemp. He feels you are his last hope at finding Camilla." Webster turned to Porter. "Have a coach ready to leave in fifteen minutes."

"Might I suggest the coupe instead of a coach or phaeton?" Porter recommended. "It's a lot smaller and better suited to the narrow streets in the harbor district."

"Whatever you deem best," Webster said.

The butler now led Fargo around to the other side of the stable. Adjacent to it was a long, low building, open at the front, and lined up inside were over a dozen vehicles; a full-sized coach, a country brougham, a luxurious landau, and more. Shortly thereafter they were joined by Porter, now fully dressed, and a much younger man in a neat uniform and high hat. The pair bustled to a small vehicle at the far end. Grabbing the tongue, they pulled it into the open and presently had a fine roan in harness.

Porter came toward them. The young man climbed into the seat and followed.

"Is that Williams?" Webster asked, nodding at the driver. "I would have thought one of the older men would be more appropriate."

"Begging your pardon, but Williams knows the docks better than any of the others," Porter said. "He was raised there, you know."

"No, I didn't." Webster gave the young man a critical appraisal. "I can't stress how important it is that you return Mr. Fargo to us safe and sound."

"Have no fear, sir," Williams answered, eager to prove his reliability. "I'll watch over the gentleman as if he were my mother."

"You are not to let him out of your sight," Webster directed. "Where he goes, you go. Whatever he does, you do."

Fargo reached for the door but Williams was off the high seat and opening it for him before his fingers could touch it.

"Permit me, sir."

The interior was plushly furnished. Fargo settled into a soft seat covered with rich leather, and waited while Williams lit a brass lantern mounted between the body of the coupe and the high seat. Rosy light spilled through the front window, filling the compartment.

Webster stepped closer. "Please be extremely careful, sir. Mr. Kemp would be devastated if you came to harm."

"He's not the only one," Fargo said. At a crack of the whip, the horse clattered down the gravel drive to the front gate. The guards opened it for them and they rattled out into the street. A knock on the front of the coupe drew Fargo's attention to a tiny sliding door above the glass. He pulled on the small knob.

Williams had shifted partway in his seat. "Forgive my disturbing you, sir," he said, speaking loudly to be heard above the noise of the wheels and the thud of hooves. "Mr. Porter told me you want to go down to the docks but he didn't say where, exactly."

"Have you ever heard of a place called Joe's Shanty?"

The young man whistled. "Indeed I have. It's one of the worst bars in the City. Owned by an old longshoreman named Iron Joe who caters to the seafaring crowd."

"You've been there?" Fargo inquired. Williams didn't strike him as the type to frequent a waterfront dive.

"I've driven Mr. Kemp there on occasion, yes."

"Which Kemp?" Fargo asked. As if he couldn't guess.

"Ronald, mostly. Although once or twice I've taken Dalbert there, too," Williams said. "You wouldn't catch me within ten blocks of the place on my own. Dalbert insisted I go in with him once, and I don't mind admitting I was scared half to death. The looks those roughnecks give you. Most every man I saw had a knife or a dagger on his belt."

"Thanks for the warning," Fargo said.

"There's more," Williams volunteered. "About a

141

year ago there were reports in the newspaper of people disappearing from the harbor area. The police suspected they were shanghaied, and Joe's Shanty was listed as one of the establishments under suspicion. So keep your wits about you in that devil's den."

Fargo intended to.

New York City late at night was vastly different from New York City by day. Gone were the teeming throngs of pedestrians, the unending stream of traffic. The sidewalks were nearly deserted. Most streets were empty. Darkened buildings loomed over inky thoroughfares, the darkness broken here and there by a lit window or a street lamp. Menacing figures lurked in gloomy doorways. Others furtively prowled the shadows.

At one point Williams brought the coupe to a stop at an intersection and glanced both ways, apparently unsure which way to go. Instantly, a middle-aged woman appeared at the right-hand door, her bloated face filling the window. She had on twice as much makeup as she should, to conceal the ravages of time and a life spent in wanton neglect. Pursing her thick red lips, she smiled as seductively as she knew how and winked at Fargo.

"Good evening, handsome. Would you care for some companionship this fine frosty night?"

Fargo shook his head.

"Don't be so hasty," the woman said, bending so her more-than-ample bosom swelled like overripe melons. "I can give you a time you'll never forget. You name it, I'll do it. Just so it doesn't involve bottles. I got one stuck once . . ."

Williams bent over the side. "Here, now! Enough of that! I won't have the likes of you accosting my passenger. Be off with you!"

"The likes of me?" the woman bristled, and crooked a painted fingernail. "Watch your manners, sonny. A lady has to make a living too, doesn't she?"

"You're not a lady. You're a whore."

The woman's fleshy face contorted and she made as if to haul the young driver from his perch. "Step down here and call me that and I'll scratch out your eyes, you miserable lout. What do you know, anyhow? You're nothing but a wet-nosed kid."

The coupe rattled on. Fargo looked back and saw the prostitute standing forlornly in a circle of lamplight, stooped in sorrow. He pulled the curtain and didn't open it again until he smelled the unmistakable scent of salt water. They were nearing the docks. Somewhere a tug horn blew and was echoed by another far off.

The waterfront district pulsed with life and vitality. Busy taverns, bars, and houses of ill repute lined street after street, bursting with light and color. Rowdy merrymakers were making the rounds of their favorite watering holes. Ladies of the night were also abundant, with two or three on every corner. Like fishermen trolling for fish, they displayed their physical wares for the swarms of brawny dock workers, carefree sailors, and dandified city dwellers who flocked there each night.

Police were present, as well, but they kept a low profile. Many, Fargo had been told, were paid to look the other way when minor crimes were committed. Perhaps it was true. He saw plenty of drunks ignored by the officers they passed. And a couple of fistfights were taking place right out in the open, but the police didn't bother to put a stop to them.

Two sets of rules seemed to apply, one set for New York City by day, another set for New York City by night. In the light of day the police were diligent in holding crime to a minimum. But at night, when the city's wilder denizens were abroad, the best the police could hope to do was keep the widespread violence and rampant lust from spilling over from the waterfront into the peaceful, law-abiding neighborhoods that bordered it. The waterfront was a powder keg, and the police had the unenviable task of preventing the fuse from being lit.

Fargo noticed that the nearer the coupe drew to the docks, the rowdier the night life became. Raucous laughter, lusty curses, and the babble of loud voices filled the muggy night air. Now and again he glimpsed ships at anchor down by the wharves, their masts stripped of sails. Smaller pleasure crafts lined a dock to the south.

Williams turned the coupe off a major thoroughfare onto a narrow side street. He had to haul on the reins to avoid running down a pair of grizzled men who were staggering along arm-in-arm and singing off-key. "Move aside!" he bellowed. "Let us by!"

One of the old salts made an obscene gesture, at which both laughed hysterically as they tottered to the curb.

Williams turned again, onto an even narrower and considerably darker street. His nervousness was apparent in the looks he cast to either side and by the way he held the whip ready to hit someone if he had to. "We're almost there, sir," he announced.

Joe's Shanty was only a block from the wharves. It sat well back, an ugly, squat building hiding in the shadows like a bloated toad waiting for prey. Its windows were shuttered, and were it not for loud, tinny music, and the din of voices, Fargo would never have suspected the establishment was open for business.

The coupe came to a stop across the street. Williams swung down, his whip still in hand, and yanked on the door. "It's not too late to change your mind, sir. This is no fit place for a gentleman."

"Dalbert and Ronald wouldn't agree," Fargo said, sliding out.

"True, sir, but they're not gentlemen, not in the strictest sense of the word." Williams nearly jumped when a man in a blue coat and woolen cap strode out of the night and marched on by.

Fargo started to cross but stopped when the younger man glued himself to his elbow. "Where do you think you're going?"

"You heard Webster, sir. I'm not to let you out of my sight. Where you go, I go. Whatever you do, I'm to do."

"Like hell." Fargo would have a hard enough time alone. He couldn't watch his own back and the driver's, too.

"But what will I tell Mr. Kemp if something happens to you?" Williams protested. "It's my duty."

Pivoting, Fargo jabbed him in the chest. "Tell him I slugged you. Tell him I tied you up. Tell him any damn thing you want. But you're to sit up on your seat until I get back." Without awaiting a response, he wheeled and crossed to a short walk that brought him to the entrance.

Fargo opened the door. A blistering wave of sounds, sights and odors overwhelmed him. Joe's Shanty was filled to capacity; every stool, every chair, every table was occupied, every foot of floor space crammed. Cigar and cigarette smoke hung as thick as fog. In a far corner a piano player in a vest and derby pounded the keys of an old piano.

Most of the patrons had salt water in their veins. There were seamen galore, and almost as many longshoremen. Mingled among them were rakes and rogues in suits and silk hats. Women hung on many an arm, and through the crowd threaded barmaids balancing trays laden with drinks.

Fargo closed the door and stepped into the light. Almost immediately a subtle change occurred. The babble of voices dropped a level. Curious stares were bestowed, and whispering broke out. His clothes were to blame. He was the only man in the whole place dressed in buckskins. They branded him as someone who was as out of place there as a sailor would be in a saloon in the middle of the prairie. He regretted not having the foresight to find clothes that fit in better.

The harm had been done. There was nothing he could do but shoulder through the crowd to the bar. It was jammed, and Fargo thought he would have to shout to get the attention of the bartender, but the longshoremen and seamen at his end moved to either side as if they wanted nothing to do with him.

A portly barman shuffled his way. Fargo requested a whiskey, and the man produced a dirty glass from under the counter, and filled it from a bottle that wasn't much cleaner.

"Anything else, mister? We have eats if you're hungry."

"I could use some information," Fargo said.

The bartender's grin faded and a hostile glint crept into his dark eyes. "What kind of information?"

"I'm looking for a man by the name of Martin Stevens. I know he likes to come here from time to time. Have you seen him lately? Or know anyone who might know where I can find him?"

"Is he a friend of yours?" the barman suspiciously asked.

"I've played cards with him a few times. Lost my shirt. He said if I ever stopped by here, he'd give me a chance to win some of my money back." Fargo had worked out the lie in advance. It was plausible enough to be believed.

The bartender's pudgy mouth tweaked upward. "That Stevens sure does like to gamble, I'll grant you that." He scanned the crowd. "To tell the truth, though, I haven't seen him for a couple of weeks. Him and his friend Jim Chandler used to be in here almost every night. Those two don't go anywhere without each other."

Chandler. Fargo now had the name of the second

longshoreman who had tried to kill him. "Is his friend here now?" he played innocent.

"I don't see him, no."

"Too bad," Fargo said. "I won't be in town long and I was hoping to get together." He tipped his glass. The rotgut seared a fiery path down his gullet to the pit of his gut where it exploded like a cartridge flung into a fire. "Good whiskey," he said.

The man was flattered. "I don't water down my drinks like some places do. When you buy my booze, it's the real thing." He swished his hand at a coiling wreath of cigar smoke, then peered toward a table over by the left wall. "Wait a minute. See that stocky guy with the red beard?"

Fargo couldn't miss him. The man in question was another longshoreman with a ruddy face and a flaming beard that spilled over the front of his dark-blue coat clear down to his waist. He was involved in a card game with four others of his breed.

"That there is Ned Grant. He's another of Marty's close friends. Go on over and introduce yourself. Maybe he can help you out."

Fargo dipped into a pocket and placed ten dollars on the counter. "I'd be grateful if you did the honors. Longshoremen aren't the friendliest bunch I've ever met."

Chortling, the barman scooped up the money. "Ain't that the truth. They tend to keep their own company. Safer that way, I suppose." He came around the end of the bar. "Give me a second. If I wave, it means he's agreed to talk to you."

Fargo's luck was holding. His sole purpose in coming was to learn if anyone there had ever seen Martin Stevens in the company of Dalbert or Ronald Kemp. But he had to exercise caution. He couldn't come right out and ask. Men like these didn't like snoops. Grant would tell him to go jump off a pier. He had to be clever and wait for the right moment.

The bartender had bent over the table. Grant and two of the other players were studying him. At a nod from Grant, the barkeep beckoned.

Fargo knew better than to act too eager. He let Ned Grant speak first.

"So you know Marty, eh?"

"Not well, no. But he did win over a hundred dollars of my money," Fargo said.

Grant's beard creased in a smile. "He's won a lot of mine, too, from time to time." Grant nodded at the longshoreman to his right, who got up and walked off. Ten seconds later the man was back with an empty chair, which he placed next to Grant's.

"Have a seat, friend. We're having us a friendly game and you're welcome to sit in."

Hesitating for effect, Fargo asked, "Will Martin join us later?"

"I honestly can't say," Grant said. "None of us have seen him in a while. But if he's going to show up anywhere, it'll be here. So why not have some fun while you're waiting?"

"And give you a chance to take my money?" Fargo retorted.

Ned Grant's whole body shook with mirth. "You've seen right through us. The boys and me were figuring on fleecing you of a few bills. Hope you don't mind?"

"I admire an honest man," Fargo said, and slid down. He only had forty dollars left. The rest was at the mansion. Laying the bills in front of him, he commented, "I hope this is enough."

"Hell, that's more than most of us have," Grant responded. It was his turn to deal. Cutting the cards, he announced, "Jacks or better to open. Nothing wild. Anyone caught dealing from the bottom of the deck will have an anchor tied to their legs and get dumped into the harbor." He grinned, displaying tobacco-stained teeth. "Any questions?"

Fargo shook his head. Over the next forty-five minutes

he won a few pots and lost a few, and was seven dollars to the better when it came his turn to deal. He dealt each card slowly and methodically so no one could accuse him of cheating. His hand consisted of two queens, two nines and a three. Grant opened. When it came his turn, he took one card. It was a long shot but he wound up with another nine. Soon the others folded and it was down to the red-bearded longshoreman and him.

"You know," Grant idly remarked while upping the ante two dollars. "I've been thinking about Marty. I haven't seen him since that rich brat came to see him a while back."

Fargo perked up his ears. The description fit Ronnie Kemp to a *T*. "Rich brat?"

"Some kid from upriver. Supposed to have money to spare." Grant showed his hand. He had three kings. "He was in here a while ago, in fact. Heard him say he was going down the street to the Yardarm Tavern."

"I'd like to talk to him," Fargo said, displaying his full house. "Maybe he knows where Marty got to." Raking the pot, he sorted his winnings.

"That's a damn good idea," Grant declared. "And there's no time like the present." Pushing back his chair, he rose. "Excuse us, boys. I'm going to take our friend to the Yardarm and point out the brat to him."

Fargo could recognize Ronnie on sight, but he had to play along. "I could use some fresh air," he commented, stuffing the money into a pocket.

Ned Grant smiled and plowed a path to the back of the room and a rear door. "This way is shorter," he said. He went out first, into an alley mired in gloom.

Wary of a ruse, Fargo waited until the longshoreman had gone a few yards, then stepped outside. The instant he did, he registered movement to his right and started to swivel, but it was already too late. Something smashed against the side of his head and the near-total darkness became complete. He never even felt his body hit the ground.

149

11

A slight rocking sensation filtered through the haze of pain in which Skye Fargo was mired. With a jolt, he regained consciousness. A pungent odor assailed him, and suppressing a cough, he opened his eyes and took stock.

He was shackled to a wall. Or so he assumed until he identified the rocking sensation for what it was, and the smell of sea water eclipsed that of the musty ship's hold in which he was being held. His wrists were manacled to a bulkhead but his legs were free. To his right were crates stacked chest-high, and on one lay his hat and Colt. Someone had frisked him while he was unconscious, but they hadn't done a very thorough job. He could feel the sheath of his Arkansas toothpick still strapped to his right ankle, and by twisting his leg so the hilt rubbed against it, he verified the knife was still there, too.

A lantern sat on another crate, the flame set low. Dim light also came through a doorway off to the left. Overhead, the hatchway was closed.

Fargo reckoned that Grant and company had brought him to one of the vessels at anchor in the harbor. Which one hardly mattered. Getting the hell out of there did. The shackles were old and dotted with rust, but he strained against the chains to no avail. As for the manacles themselves and the rings partly imbedded in the bulkhead, they were thick enough to withstand a buffalo.

Again Fargo surged outward, bracing his feet against the wall and throwing all the strength in his whipcord physique into the effort. It did no good. The manacles bit into his wrists, drawing blood, and the chains held fast.

Temporarily defeated, Fargo slumped and mulled over his predicament. There had to be a better way. He could shoot the manacles off if he could get his hands on the Colt, but it was well beyond his reach. Or he might be able to work his wrists loose given enough time, and if he didn't mind rubbing them down to the bone.

Frowning, Fargo propped his feet against the bulkhead. He had to get out of there now, before his captors returned. Once more he flung himself outward. Once more the chains brought him up short. He continued to apply all his might, continued until his shoulders throbbed and his wrists were fountains of torment. Leaning back, Fargo cast about for another means of freeing himself, but there simply was none.

Footsteps clomped hollowly in the hallway. Muted voices drew near, and a shadow filled the opening. A moment later into the hold strolled Ned Grant and two of the longshoremen who had taken part in the poker game at Joe's Shanty.

"You've come around already?" Grant said in mild surprise. "It's only been half an hour. Usually, a blackjack is enough to keep most men out for eight to ten."

"The people you've shanghaied, you mean?" Fargo guessed.

"Not me, friend," Grant said, and motioned at the deck above their heads. "All I do is supply the raw material. Captain Sanders of the *Rose Marie* does the actual shanghaiing." He leaned on a stack of crates. "Now then, suppose we get down to business. Where are Martin Stevens and Jim Chandler?"

"How would I know?" Fargo said.

Grant nodded at the taller of his companions, a man

with a beaked nose and a scar on his chin. "Teach him some manners, Finch."

Fargo braced himself, but the punch to his stomach doubled him over. Gasping for breath, he fought fleeting nausea and swallowed bitter bile that rose in his throat.

Finch drew back a fist to do it again.

"Belay that," Grant said, and came over. "Listen, friend. We can pound on you all night if that's what you want. We'll knock your teeth out. We'll bust your bones. Hell, we'll cut off an ear or two and maybe gouge out an eye. But why put us to all that bother and you through all that misery if you don't have to? All we want is to find out what happened to our friends."

"What makes you so sure I know?" Fargo responded.

"It's like this," Grant said, folding his arms across his chest. "Marty and Jim are good friends of mine. I was with them about two weeks ago, playing cards at the very table we were seated at tonight, when a blue blood asked to join our game. I'd seen him before. One of those snooty rich types. The kind who look down their noses at everybody but like to hobnob with riffraff for the thrill of it."

"This blue blood have a name?"

Grant smirked. "That would be telling. The point here is that he had a business proposition for Marty and Jim. It's well known those two will do anything for a dollar. And I mean anything." He paused. "Care to guess what the business proposition was?"

"Beats me." Fargo glanced at the third longshoreman, wishing he, too, would venture closer.

"The blue blood wanted someone killed," Grant disclosed. "A frontiersman who always wears buckskins. A tall guy partial to a white hat and a red bandanna. With blue eyes and a brown beard. Sound like anyone you know?"

"Go to hell."

Grant laughed. "The Trailsman. Isn't that what they call you? Scout. Tracker. Man-killer." He looked Fargo up and down. "You don't look so tough to me."

Now the other two cackled, and Finch declared, "Let's have us some fun with this ape, Ned. How about if I whittle on his ears for starters?"

"Last chance, Trailsman," Grant said. "I'd take it, were I you. Finch loves to carve. He's a real master. Whatever's left will be dropped in the drink for the sharks, courtesy of Captain Sanders. He owes us a favor or three."

Finch reached into a coat pocket and produced a long folding knife with stag handles. "Say the word, Ned."

Fargo backed against the bulkhead as if the sight of the knife had unnerved him. 'Stevens and Chandler are here in New York City," he lied. "Not ten minutes from the harbor."

Grant arched an eyebrow. "What do you take me for? If Marty and Jim were back, they'd have contacted me by now. No, my hunch is they tried to kill you down in Pennsylvania, where that blue blood sent them, and you killed them instead. Otherwise, you wouldn't still be breathing."

"They did try to kill me," Fargo admitted, "but I slipped through their fingers and they trailed me to New York. Last night they tried again and were arrested. The last I saw of them, they were being dragged off to jail." He hoped he sounded convincing.

"Jail?" Grant said. "Which precinct was this?"

"I never asked," Fargo said. "All I can tell you is that one of the officers was named O'Malley."

Finch flicked the knife open and raised the tip to Fargo's neck. "This bastard is lying through his teeth. Let me start in."

"Maybe he isn't," Grant said. "I had a run-in with a cop named O'Malley once. He hauled me in for drunk and disorderly. But I'll be damned if I can remember which precinct he was with." He pushed the knife away from Fargo's throat. "Hold off until Brink and me get back. We shouldn't be gone long."

"Where are you going?" Finch inquired.

Grant made a beeline for the doorway. "Where do you think, you numbskull? To check on the Trailsman's story. If Captain Sanders comes down and wants to know why our guest isn't dead yet, tell Sanders he will be before the *Rose Marie* sails at dawn. Sanders has my word."

Fargo's gambit had worked. He had gained a reprieve, however brief. Now he had to somehow gain the upper hand before Grant and Brink came back.

Finch backed up and roosted on a crate next to the lantern. He was sulking over being denied his sadistic pleasure. Absently stroking the blade as if it were a lover's leg, he remarked, "I hope they don't take too long. I want to do you good."

"Any chance of my getting some water to drink?" Fargo requested.

"When whales can whistle," Finch snapped.

Fargo sagged as if in despair and bowed his chin to his chest. He had thought of a ploy that might work, but for it to succeed he had to find out where the keys were. "I guess there's no chance you'll loosen these manacles, either?"

"For a million dollars," Finch said, and grinned.

"You probably don't even have the keys," Fargo said glumly. Amazingly, the longshoreman took the bait.

"They belong to the captain of this vessel, not to us." Finch bobbed his head to the left.

Fargo shifted and spotted a single large key suspended from a hook. He hadn't noticed it earlier because it was partly in shadow. Like his Colt, it was well out of reach.

Finch went on, saying, "Captain Sanders is as black-

154

hearted a scoundrel as ever lived. You name it, he does it. Smuggling. Shanghais. Slave running. Hell, he even runs a disposal service, as he calls it, and dumps corpses in the ocean for certain powerful people in New York City and Boston." Finch sighed in envy. "I'd give anything to be in his shoes."

"Buy a ship of your own," Fargo said.

"With what? Money doesn't grow on trees."

"Would five thousand dollars be enough?"

Finch sneered. "You expect me to believe that some yokel who runs around in deerskin has that much money to his name?"

"I do now," Fargo said. "It's how much Stevens and Chandler were paid to kill me. I have the money hid at my hotel."

"Five thousand?" Finch said, his greed transparent. "With that much I *could* get my own vessel. Maybe not as big as this one, but big enough to make my start."

"Free me and it's yours."

Finch thoughtfully hefted the knife. "Damn me if I'm not tempted, mister. But I'm not stupid enough to go against Ned Grant or risk the wrath of Captain Sanders. The captain would have me keelhauled, just for the hell of it. So I'll make you a better offer." Suddenly advancing, he held the knife low down. "You tell me where the money is or I'll cut off the last thing any man ever wants to lose."

"Grant told you not to touch me, remember?" Fargo reminded him.

"But Ned isn't here, is he?" Finch countered. "I'll claim you were acting up. That I tried to quiet you down and you kept on yelling so I had to poke you to shut you up." His smirk was positively vicious. "Now where's the damn money?"

Fargo glanced at the blade and licked his lips to give the impression the threat had scared him. "Room 24 at the Imperial Hotel." He mentioned the hotel in

Pennsylvania because it was the first one that popped into his head.

"The Imperial?" Finch said. "Never heard of it, but I can find it quick enough."

Lowering the knife, he carelessly started to turn. "If all frontiersmen are as yellow as you, it's a wonder there's any of you left."

Fargo tensed, and when the cocky longshoreman took another step, he pumped his legs high and scissored them together, locking his ankles tight around Finch's neck. Finch instinctively grabbed at his boots to force them apart, but whipping to the left Fargo slammed the longshoreman against the bulkhead. Finch cried out and lost his grip on the knife. It clattered to the planks underfoot as Fargo squeezed, and wrenched. Frantic, Finch clawed at Fargo's boots but couldn't separate them. Within moments Finch was the color of a beet and sputtering for breath.

"Now you listen to me, you son of a bitch," Fargo snarled as he continued to apply pressure. "Get the key and undo these manacles or I'll snap your scrawny neck." To stress his demand, he slammed Finch against the bulkhead, not once but three times.

"Stop! Stop!" Finch croaked, blood seeping from a gash on his forehead. "I'll do it! Just give me a minute to catch my breath."

"No." Fargo levered his legs in a powerful surge that smashed the smaller man into the hard wood with the force of a battering ram.

Squawking and gasping, Finch punched at Fargo's shins and knees. Yet another swing against the bulkhead left him stunned, and bleeding even worse from a new wound.

"I won't say it again," Fargo warned. His stomach muscles were corded into knots, his limbs as taut as wires. He couldn't keep them tense like that indefinitely, though. He had to force Finch to comply quickly.

The skinny longshoreman numbly glanced at the hook, then tottered toward it. After a single step Fargo's ankles brought him up short. Half-heartedly, he extended an arm and announced, "I can't reach."

"Try harder!" Fargo ordered, clamping his legs with all the force he could muster.

Finch reached out but his wriggling fingers were an inch or so shy.

"Again!"

Leaning as far to the left as he could, Finch touched the hook. "I tell you I can't!"

Fargo slammed him into the wall yet again crunching the longshoreman's teeth together. Whining, Finch rose onto the tips of his toes and at last his forefinger curled around the key itself.

"Don't drop it," Fargo commanded.

A fraction at a time, Finch slid the key off the hook. It almost slipped from his fingers but he held on, clasping it to his chest as if it were worth its weight in gold.

"Undo the manacles," Fargo commanded. Yanking the longshoreman toward him, he wrapped both hands around the other's throat, then lowered his legs.

They were virtually nose-to-nose. Anger replaced Finch's fear, but he obediently inserted the key into a manacle, and twisted. At a distinct click the manacle rasped open.

"Now the other one," Fargo said. He would only let go when he was completely free. He didn't like it when Finch stalled by fumbling at the lock and inserting the key backward, and he gouged his thumbs deep into the longshoreman's flesh. "I'll count to three." Without pausing, he cracked out, "One. Two. Thr—"

The other manacle parted and fell, its chain jangling.

"There!" Finch barked. "I hope you're happy, you bastard."

Pivoting, Fargo slammed him against the bulkhead

and reached for the left-hand shackle. "Let's see how you like it."

"Like hell," the longshoreman said, and exploded into violence.

Fargo was caught flat-footed. Finch had done everything he had demanded so far, and he wasn't expecting Finch to fight back. But that's exactly what the man did. Muttering under his breath Finch lunged at Fargo, trying to gouge out his eyes with the key. Automatically, Fargo ducked. He grabbed Finch's wrist but the weasel jerked loose and stabbed the key at his throat. Only a lightning side-step saved him. But it also gave Finch room to move, and the longshoreman dove for the knife.

Fargo sprang to intercept him. His right arm forked the other's waist and together they rolled half a dozen feet and thudded against some crates. Simultaneously, both heaved onto their knees. Fargo threw an uppercut that Finch avoided, and Finch retaliated by stabbing the key at his right eye. Dodging, Fargo seized the other's forearm and wrenched sharply, and was rewarded with a yelp of agony. The key went skittering into the shadows.

Cornered beasts were always doubly dangerous. Finch hissed like a viper and rammed his shoulder into Fargo's sternum, knocking Fargo backward. Instantly, Finch leaped for the knife again and palmed the stag handles.

Fargo lunged, seeking to seize the longshoreman's wrist, but Finch whirled with startling swiftness and lashed the cold steel at his face. Jerking aside, Fargo shoved upright. Finch did the same. For a few frozen moments they confronted each another, each waiting for the other to make the first move. Finch accommodated Fargo by thrusting at his groin. Skipping to the side, Fargo swivelled and delivered a left-cross to Finch's jaw that failed to land squarely but clipped Finch hard enough to drive him back half a step.

"I'll gut you like a fish!" the longshoreman vowed, and the knife descended in a glittering arc.

Fargo danced to the right, just out of reach. His gaze alighted on the crates, on the one on which his hat and Colt rested. In three bounds he could reach it, but he had to get past Finch's flashing blade.

Or he could try another tactic.

Fargo feinted as if about to spring, and Finch immediately sheared the knife at his jugular. Throwing himself to the rear, Fargo fell onto his back with his knees tucked to his chest. Sensing victory, Finch started to close in and skirted to the right to avoid being kicked. But Fargo had no intention of kicking him. Instead, he had slipped his right hand up under his boot, molding his fingers to the Arkansas toothpick. Now, as Finch speared the folding knife at his chest, Fargo flipped onto his shoulder and drove the toothpick into the base of Finch's throat, clear to the hilt.

The longshoreman stiffened and pulled back, unleashing a scarlet geyser. Clutching at his ravaged jugular, he staggered against the crates. His eyes widened and he bleated in terror. He tried to speak but all that gushed from his mouth was blood. Sobbing, he sank to his knees, the knife clattering useless at his feet.

Fargo rose and claimed the Colt. Ensuring it was still loaded, he looked up. Finch had melted onto the floor and was convulsing spasmodically. Eventually he uttered a low groan, then was still.

Donning his hat, Fargo walked over and cautiously crouched. He felt for a pulse but there was none. A few swipes of the toothpick on Finch's pants cleaned the blade of blood, and he slid it into its sheath. About to straighten, he heard voices and the tread of approaching footsteps.

Fargo darted into an opening between two crates. Barely had he done so than Ned Grant filled the doorway.

"Finch? You were right. The Trailsman was lying—"

Grant turned to stone. He saw the empty manacles and then his friend lying in a spreading crimson pool. "Fargo's escaped!" he bellowed. It didn't seem to occur to him that Fargo might still be in the hold. Spinning, he dashed into the hallway, nearly tripping over the raised lip at the bottom of the door. "Alert Captain Sanders! Have him call out the crew! We've got to stop the Trailsman from reaching shore!"

Boots drummed into the distance. Rising, Fargo headed for the doorway but stopped beside the lantern. He thought of what Finch had told him about the owner of the vessel. He thought of the countless slaves borne against their will from the land where they were born. He thought of the scores of innocents the captain had shanghaied. And picking the lantern up, he adjusted the wick so the flame was as high as it could be, raised the lantern aloft, and flung it toward the opposite end of the hold.

The glass globe shattered into fragments. Kerosene spewed and instantly combusted. Flames engulfed the top of a crate, spreading rapidly, and in a span of moments ignited a second.

It wouldn't be long before the entire hold went up.

Fargo didn't linger. He vaulted through the doorway and raced down the hall in the opposite direction the longshoremen had taken. A companionway loomed out of the murk and he ascended the wooden steps three at a stride. At the lower deck, he flattened against the wall and peeked around the corner before showing himself. It was well he did.

An alarm bell sounded, pealing loudly in the vessel's cramped confines. Out of a doorway further down spilled crewmen in various stages of undress. Some were shrugging into shirts. Others were pulling on pants. Barreling to the left, they disappeared up another companionway.

Fargo glided after them. With any luck they would

lead him to the upper deck, and from there he could find the gangway and make good his escape.

With no forewarning whatsoever, another crewman stepped from the crew's quarters. He was fully dressed, and wedged under his wide leather belt was a dirk. On spying Fargo he let out a yell and snatched at his weapon.

Fargo was faster. The Colt streaked up and out and the barrel slammed the seaman across the temple, sending the man reeling back through the doorway. Pivoting, Fargo ran to the companionway and started up, but he had only gone a third of the way when half a dozen crewmen materialized above. Baying like a rabid pack of wolves, they swooped toward him, knives and daggers glimmering in the glow of a lantern held by one of their number.

Pivoting, Fargo leaped to the bottom. A couple of long strides carried him past the junction and into the crew's quarters. The man he had slugged was out cold between bunks. Pressing his back to the bulkhead, Fargo cocked his Colt.

Into the hallway charged the crew. Whooping and hollering, they raised enough racket to be heard in New Jersey. Then, inexplicably, the uproar died. Fargo suspected they had figured out where he was and were preparing to rush him. A cry of horror proved differently.

"God Almighty! Do you see what I see?"

"Smoke!" bawled a shipmate. "Smoke coming from hold number two!"

"The ship's on fire!" declared a third.

Pandemonium erupted. Some of the crew rushed toward the hold; others pounded back up the companionway to spread the alarm.

Fargo was only a few yards behind. In all the confusion, they didn't think to look behind them, and he reached the upper deck without further mishap.

The *Rose Marie* was a clipper, her long, graceful hull low to the water. The sails on her three high masts were furled, and she rode at anchor a stone's throw from a dimly lit dock, to starboard. Much of the deck space was filled by cargo waiting to be lowered into the holds.

Sprinting to a huge net suspended from a hoist, Fargo hunkered as more crewmen appeared, all of them yelling and gesturing at once. From the forecastle hastened more, several in smart uniforms. And up on the quarter deck, a broad-chested man wearing a frock coat and a tricorne hat appeared at the forward rail and began bellowing commands.

Captain Sanders, Fargo guessed.

Most of the crew poured below decks to combat the fire. Others scrambled to a mound of water casks that hadn't yet been placed in storage, while still others flew to the sides to lower large buckets.

The deck in Fargo's vicinity was deserted. Hunching low, he moved toward the bow. He passed barrels piled shoulder-high and lumber that would be used to effect repairs while at sea, if need be. He passed kegs of rum and containers of foodstuffs. Then, ahead, he spied the gangway.

Suddenly, beside it, Ned Grant and another longshoreman reared. Both were armed with pocket pistols and both took hasty aim and fired.

Leaden hornets sizzled the night as Fargo threw himself behind a large pile of thick rope. Another pistol cracked, from the quarter deck, and a slug dug a furrow in a plank an inch from his hip. Whirling, Fargo saw Captain Sanders silhouetted against a tapestry of stars. He fired once. The captain flung out his arms, arched his spine as if impaled by a Sioux lance, and toppled over the rail.

Boots hammered the deck, converging rapidly.

Surging erect, Fargo sent two slugs into Ned Grant's chest, rotated, and sent two more into Grant's companion. Like ungainly fowl skewered in midflight, they pitched headlong to the deck.

Fargo raced along the side rail to the gangway and sped down it onto the dock. A mountain of cargo hid him until he was shrouded by the Stygian ebony of a narrow alley. Not that he need have worried. The crew wasn't after him anymore. Their main concern, their *only* concern, was the welfare of their ship and their ill-gotten livelihoods.

Fargo glanced back. Roaring flames twenty feet high and monstrous coils of thick smoke streamed skyward from amidships. The hold was an inferno. Nothing the crew or anyone else could do could stop the conflagration. Within the hour, perhaps less, the vessel would be a charred husk, and come morning crowds of curious gawkers would arrive to gaze on her blistered remains.

The *Rose Marie* would die as her evil master had; her days of slave running and smuggling forever ended.

Wearing a grim smile, Fargo ran to find Williams and the coupe.

12

Northern New York was ablaze with brilliant autumn hues. Splashes of red, orange, and yellow painted the verdant forest canopy for as far as the eye could see. From a clearing on a sawtooth ridge, Skye Fargo gazed out over the limitless expanse of forest stretching to the horizon and asked, "How much longer?"

"We'll be there in an hour," Fred Johnson answered. "An hour and a half at the most."

Fargo spurred the Ovaro on. Johnson was one of the many woodsmen hired by Lucius Kemp. He had found the pair waiting for him at the stable the morning he set out.

Webster had been there, too, hovering over Kemp like a mother hen over a stricken chick, insisting Kemp stay bundled in a heavy coat to ward off the morning chill.

"You requested a guide," Lucius had announced, "and Mr. Johnson knows upstate New York like he does the back of his hand. I've had him waiting here since I sent for you, for just this purpose."

"You took a lot for granted," Fargo said.

Lucius winked. "Not at all. I did my homework, as they say. I knew you weren't the type of man to refuse a plea for help."

Johnson wasn't much of a talker. On the long ride north he kept pretty much to himself although at one point he admitted that while he had done a lot of hunting in the upper regions of New York, he wasn't as familiar with the territory as Lucius Kemp had Fargo believe. "I doubt anyone is, mister. The only folks who ever get up this way are hunters like me, and then only a couple of times a year."

"What about Indians?" Fargo asked.

"What about them? The Iroquois and their kin were driven off long ago. The last wild bucks were killed off during my great-great-grandpa's time. No one has seen an Indian hereabout since. That is, until all this trouble started."

"Have you seen him? The one they call Redface?"

"No, and I pray to God I never do. The last man who did took an arrow in the shoulder. They say he's trying to drive the search parties off. Why would he do that, do you think, unless he had a hand in whatever happened to Miss Kemp?"

Yet another riddle to add to the long string Fargo had to occupy himself with during the many hours they spent on the trail.

Upstate New York proved to be more wild and rugged than Fargo had imagined, a spectacular region of purple peaks, rushing streams, high waterfalls, and sparkling lakes. Steep rocky gorges slashed the mountains. Birch, maple, spruce, and white pine thrived. Deer and bear sign were everywhere.

In the past two days the only evidence of human habitation they had come upon was a dilapidated cabin. Fargo had knocked, and when no one answered, he'd opened the door. Inside was an old chair and a rickety bench.

"Some hunter's place, I reckon," Johnson said.

Now they were nearing the destination and Fargo couldn't wait to get there. He wasn't the only one.

"I'm so sore from all this riding I won't be able to sit for a month of Sundays." Johnson tugged on the rope to their pack horse. "We sure got here fast. Must have set some kind of record."

"Lives are at stake," Fargo reminded him.

"I ain't complaining, mind you," Johnson said. "No one wants that poor gal to be found more than me. I never met her, but from what I hear she was a real peach. A lot like my own daughter."

As always, the forest hemmed them in close, cloaking them in shadow. A carpet of leaves lay underfoot, dulling the hoof falls of their mounts. Fargo rode with his right hand resting on the butt of his Colt, alert for movement and sound. He heard the gurgling of a stream well before he spotted it. White froth rimmed the jagged tops of rocks out in the middle. To the west a gravel bar jutted midway across, and Fargo elected to cross there. As he reined the Ovaro around, he caught sight of a prone figure on the other side, half-sprawled across a log.

Johnson had seen the figure, too. "Land sakes! Do you see what I see?"

A tap of Fargo's spurs galvanized the stallion into a trot. He slowed near the end of the gravel bar to ensure the water was shallow enough, then plunged in and forged to the opposite bank. The grass was slick and the pinto slipped twice before gaining purchase.

The figure on the log groaned as Fargo came to a stop and vaulted from the saddle. As carefully as he could, he turned the man over and lowered him onto his back. On the left temple was a wicked wound caked with dry blood.

The man stirred. He was big-boned and hefty, and wore a flannel shirt, overalls, and boots, all the worse for wear. Brown eyes fluttered open, and suddenly, in a panic, the man grabbed for an empty knife sheath at his hip.

"Calm down," Fargo said, gripping the fellow's shoulders. "We're not out to hurt you. Who are you? What happened?"

"You're white!" the man declared. He tried to sit up but couldn't. Another groan escaped him. Gingerly probing the wound, he swore a few times, then said, "That rotten heathen about did me in!"

"An Indian did this?" Fargo asked, scanning the area. Johnson had crossed and was sliding from his sorrel.

"It was Redface himself. He's a fiend, just like everybody claims." The man managed a wan smile. "Sorry. Where are my manners? I'm George Weaver. I'm up here from Syracuse looking for those university people."

"You're one of Owen Hamilton's men?" Johnson asked. "I don't recognize you."

"No, no, I'm here on my own," Weaver said. "Word has it that whoever finds the heiress will be set for life."

"Another one of those," Johnson said in mild reproach, and glanced at Fargo. "The woods are crawling with men like him. Someone started a rumor Mr. Kemp is willing to fork over a million dollars for Camilla's safe return. He never made any such offer, but they keep coming anyway."

"So I've heard." Fargo was more interested in something else. "Tell me about Redface," he directed as he bent to examine the man's wound.

"There's not a whole hell of a lot to tell," Weaver said. "I was watering my horse when I sensed someone was behind me. There he was, as bold as you please; his face all red and fierce-like. He asked me what I was doing here—"

"He speaks English?" Fargo said.

"As good as I do," Weaver confirmed. "He ordered me to leave. I'm not about to let an uppity redskin boss me around, so I reached for my pistol. He was quicker, though, and walloped me on the head with a tomahawk. Tried to split my head open, the bastard."

Fargo noted the angle at which the weapon had struck. "He hit you with the flat of the tomahawk, not the edge."

"I know what I saw, mister," Weaver said tersely. "That savage was armed to the teeth and out for white blood. I've learned my lesson. As soon as I'm fit, I'm heading back to Syracuse. I don't make much money as a butcher, but I'll live a heap longer."

Rising, Fargo gauged the position of the sun, which was low in the western sky. "Fred, I want you to boil a pot of water and bandage Mr. Weaver. Stick with him until morning. I'll send some men to keep you company."

"You're pushing on alone? Are you sure you can find the base camp without my help?"

Fargo forked leather. "If I can't, I'd better take up a new line of work." Come hell or high water, he was bound and determined to reach it before another day was out.

Weaver raised his head, his teeth clenched from the pain. "Hold on there, mister. What if that savage returns?"

"Tell him the same thing you told me," Fargo advised. "That you're heading home as soon as you're fit. It should pacify him." If Redface was as bloodthirsty as everyone made him out to be, Weaver wouldn't be alive.

"Should?" Johnson asked. "I'd feel a heap safer if you'd stick around."

"You'll only be by yourselves a couple of hours," Fargo promised, and spurred into the pines. They should be safe for that long. He put them from his mind and concentrated on weaving among the densely spaced boles. Soon he ascended a gradual incline to a rise sprinkled with boulders, and from there trotted down into a tract of poplars. Sparrows flitted among the branches, and somewhere to the right a catbird screeched. In another half an hour the trees thinned and a glade broadened before him. In his haste to reach the base camp he moved into the open without looking both ways and regretted his lapse when a stern command rang out.

"Stop where you are, white man!"

A lone warrior had risen from concealment. He wasn't much more than twenty years old, clad in deer-hide leggings and moccasins. His hair, reminiscent of the Pawnees, was worn in a spiked crest down the center of his head. The sides were clean-shaven. He was armed to the teeth, with a knife and a tomahawk at his waist, a lance and quiver slanted across his back, and a bow in his hands. A barbed shaft was nocked to the sinew string.

As was customary among many tribes, the young warrior had painted his chest and face. But where the Sioux or the Cheyenne were content with a few streaks on their forehead and cheeks, the young warrior had painted his entire face with red ocher. From chin to hairline, he was vivid scarlet.

Reigning up, Fargo held his hands out from his sides to demonstrate his friendly intentions. "You must be Redface."

"It is good you have heard of me," the young warrior said in flawless English. "Since you know who I am, you must also know what I want you to do."

"Leave the territory?" Fargo said. "I've heard of your campaign to drive off all the whites. But it's a lost cause. You can't fight greed."

"I do what I do to try and save lives." The young warrior cautiously sidled nearer. "Are you here to join the search for the missing whites?"

"Lucius Kemp hired me to find his daughter and the people who were with her, yes," Fargo confessed.

"You have come a long way for nothing, then. Turn around and go. Do not sneak back or the next time I see you, I will hurt you."

"Like you did the man down by the stream?" Fargo said.

"He would not listen to reason," the young warrior responded. "I tried to explain but he reached for his pistol. He is like the rest of your kind. All he saw was the color of my skin. His ears were closed to my words."

"My ears are open. I'd like to learn more. Mind if I light a spell?" Without waiting for permission, Fargo swung down.

Instantly, the young warrior tensed and drew the string back another quarter of an inch. "I warn you, white man. Take another step and it will be your last. Get back on your horse and ride off."

"I can't," Fargo said. "I have a job to do."

Anger made the young warrior careless. "Why is it your kind are so stubborn?" Advancing so the barbed point of his arrow was a mere six inches from Fargo's sternum, he snapped, "I will not tell you again. Too much is at stake. Go! Now!"

Fargo raised both hands, palms out, and started to turn toward the stallion. "All right. Just don't release that string—" And as he uttered the last word he was already whirling and shifting. His right forearm struck the bow at the exact split-second the warrior let the arrow fly. The shaft streaked past, missing him by a cat's whisker. Grabbing the bow, Fargo wrenched it from the other's grasp. He thought Redface would try to hold on, but instead the young warrior resorted to the tomahawk and bone-handled knife. The two weapons flashed in the sunlight as they streaked up and out.

Retreating, Fargo blocked a rash thrust of the knife with the bow, deflecting the blade into the string and severing it clean through.

The young warrior was incensed. Whipping the tomahawk overhead, he whooped shrilly and attacked.

By keeping the bow between them, Fargo evaded a rain of blows. He countered, jabbed, blocked. Then, gripping one end of the bow in both hands, he swung it like a club. The warrior ducked, pivoted, and was on him before he could swing again. A smashing blow of the tomahawk jarred the bow from his fingers. Smooth steel sought his throat, but he skipped aside. For a moment he was in the clear and could draw his revolver without hindrance, but he left it in the holster. He wanted the younger man alive.

The warrior, though, had no such compunctions. Like a wolverine gone berserk, he pinwheeled his arms without letup, seeking to prevail by force rather than finesse. The razor edges of his weapons flashed like lightning.

Again and again Fargo saved himself with a heartbeat to spare. Relying solely on pure reflex, he sprang to either side, to the rear, whatever was called for. He was always in motion, always striving his utmost to make it difficult for his adversary to connect. Inadvertently, he backed against a maple, and the young warrior thought he saw his chance. Yipping like a coyote, the warrior swung the tomahawk in an arc.

Fargo ducked barely in time and wood slivers showered onto his hat. Levering his right shoulder, he planted a fist in the young warrior's gut, low down, and the warrior doubled over, wheezing noisily. Capitalizing, Fargo landed a left to the jaw, then a right across to the temple that jolted the young warrior onto his heels. An uppercut ended their fight and left the warrior sprawled on his back in the dirt, dazed but not quite unconscious.

Drawing the Colt, Fargo kicked the knife out of the other's reach. The warrior stubbornly held onto the tomahawk, though, relinquishing it only when Fargo gouged the Colt's muzzle against his left cheek. Moving back a safe distance, Fargo flung the tomahawk a dozen feet from them, and sat on a nearby log. "Suppose we try this again."

"You are not going to kill me?" the young warrior asked in obvious puzzlement. "Most of your kind would."

"There you go again," Fargo chided. "Marking all whites with the same brand." He leaned on his free hand. "What are you up to? Why don't you want the search parties to find Camilla Kemp?"

"I do want her and the others found," the young warrior declared. Grunting, he rose onto his elbows. "It is for their sake I do what I do."

"Convince me."

"May I sit up?" the warrior requested, and when Fargo nodded, he slowly did so. Rubbing his jaw, he commented, "You are a strange one, white man. What is your interest in this?"

"I've already told you," Fargo said. "Camilla Kemp's father hired me to find them."

"Yet another one," the warrior said in disgust. "Hundreds precede you. They blunder through the woods like so much cattle, obliterating tracks, erasing sign."

"Is that why you're chasing everyone off? You want to find the expedition yourself?"

"I would like nothing more." The stripling squared his shoulders. "I am of the Lenape," he stated, as if that clarified things.

"A Delaware?" Fargo thought a moment. "Are you any relation to the guide Camilla Kemp hired?"

"Tonekotay, as the whites call him, is my father," the young warrior proudly declared. "You can call me Nayokona, although that is not my true name. My people do not reveal their true selves to outsiders."

Some Apache bands, Fargo was aware, did the same. They considered it bad medicine. "Nayokona it is. But what you've been doing makes no damn sense. Some of the whites you're trying to scare off are experienced woodsmen. They can be of help in finding your father. So can I."

"You do not understand. Those who took my father captive are too smart for the white searchers. They

172

have been lying low, as you whites would say, and will stay in hiding until the search parties leave."

Excited, Fargo rose. "You know for certain they were taken hostage? You found sign? Who is to blame?"

"I found some sign, yes, but not much. I suspect—" Nayokona stopped and shook his head. "No, I should not say until I have more proof."

"Will you show me where you found it?" Fargo asked, glad he had heeded his instincts and not gunned the younger man down.

"Yes. On one condition."

"Name it." Fargo would agree to anything that hastened his rescue of the expedition members—or conclusively proved they were dead.

"The other whites must leave," Nayokona said. "Only when the woods are quiet again will those we seek come out of hiding."

Fargo stroked his chin. The young warrior's argument had merit. "You must suspect the kidnappers are still in this general area."

"I know they are. They, or their scouts. Clever warriors, skilled at concealing their spoor."

Fargo had been toying with the notion that maybe the kidnappers were white, that maybe it was part of a plot by one of Camilla's cousins to do away with her and thus force Lucius to choose another heir. "You're sure the kidnappers are Indians?"

"As sure as I am that I am Lenape," Nayokona said. He hesitated, clearly inclined to say more, but reluctant to do so. "Their moccasins give them away. The soles are shaped like this." With the tip of a rigid finger he drew a crescent in the dirt. "Moon moccasins, my people call them. Worn by the Old Ones, by those we call the Shadow People."

Every frontiersman worthy of the name knew that no two tribes fashioned their footwear exactly alike.

One of Fargo's first lessons in tracking was to learn the difference between tracks made by his friends the Sioux, and their various enemies. Cheyenne soles were straight. Crow soles were slightly curved. Pawnee soles were unusually wide across the balls of the feet. The Kiowa wore moccasins that were tapered at the front, like the business end of their lances. Arapaho soles were pear-shaped. "Shadow People?" he said. "I've never heard of a tribe by that name."

"I do not know the white name for them," Nayokona said. "Many winters ago they were a powerful nation. Now they live in the shadows. They move like ghosts, and strike without warning. The elders of my tribe say that to see them is to die."

Once again Fargo was reminded of the Apaches. Neighboring tribes like the Pimos and Maricopas lived in mortal terror of the fierce raiders, so much so that spotting one was considered the worst of omens. Whites tended to dismiss the notion as superstitious nonsense, but try telling that to the scores of Pimos and Maricopas the Apaches had slain.

Holstering his Colt, Fargo picked up the tomahawk, reversed his grip, and offered it to the Delaware, handle-first. "I believe this is yours."

Nayokona stared, then accepted the weapon. "You surprise me more and more. What now? Will you come with me to where I saw the tracks?"

"Tomorrow would be better," Fargo suggested. It was almost dusk, and there wasn't much they could do in the dark. "I need to talk to the other whites. In the morning they will all leave, and I'll meet you wherever you want."

"When the sun has risen that high—" Nayokona pointed at a spot in the sky that corresponded to about ten in the morning. "I will meet you on the west slope of the bald mountain to the northwest." Swiveling, he pointed at a barren crest in the distance. "You will find me near a ravine at the bottom."

"I'll be there," Fargo promised.

The Delaware gathered up his knife and bow. As he entered the pines he said over a shoulder, "Take care, white man. Some of the others searchers are like children. They shoot at anything that moves, or open fire at the slightest sound."

Fargo watched until the young Delaware was lost amid the gathering gloom of approaching sunset. Remounting, he flicked his reins and galloped westward. Their talk had given him a lot to ponder, and he was still mulling his options when several pinpoints of light blossomed into a trio of campfires. He was hundreds of yards out, but noisy chatter and the nickering of horses was borne to him by the stiff breeze.

They weren't taking many precautions. Frowning, Fargo rode nearer. He was within a stone's throw of the meadow in which the camp was situated when a shrill challenge was issued.

"Halt! Identify yourself!"

A rifle cracked and a slug whistled past Fargo's head. "Hold your fire, damn you!" he bellowed as a lanky figure separated from a cluster of oaks and came toward him.

A skinny youth of fifteen or sixteen lowered a Kentucky rifle. "You're a white feller! I was afeared you might be Redface."

A dozen or more men hastened from the encampment, several bearing blazing brands hastily snatched from the campfires. "What's the shooting about?" a towering colossus in a deerskin hat and coat demanded. "Lyle, is that you?"

"Yes, sir, Mr. Hamilton, sir," the youth acknowledged. "This jasper sort of snuck up on me."

"On a *horse*?" Owen Hamilton had a great booming voice to match his stature. "Hell, boy. Who are you trying to kid? You were dozing and didn't realize he was there until he was right on top of you. Then you fired without thinking. Isn't that how it went?"

Lyle sheepishly bowed his head.

Hamilton rotated, his broad face creasing in an apologetic smile. "You'll have to forgive the boy, stranger. He's a tad green behind the ears." He extended a torch so the rosy glow bathed the stallion. "Let me guess. You've heard there's a whopper of a reward for whoever finds the Kemp expedition, and you've come to join the madness?"

Fargo flourished the papers provided by Lucius Kemp. "No, I've come to take over," he said. "These will explain everything."

"You don't say?" Hamilton gave his Sharps rifle to a companion, unfolded the letter of introduction, and held it near the torch. His mouth moved as he read the contents. "I'll be tarred and feathered," he exclaimed. "It's true, boys. I've been replaced. Mr. Kemp has put this gent in charge of the whole operation."

Not many liked the idea. Ignoring glares of open hostility, Fargo rode past them into the meadow. Sixty or seventy men were present, the majority ringed around the three roaring fires. Their mounts were tethered willy-nilly. Saddles, blankets and packs were strewn at random, leaving little space to move about.

Hamilton and the others had trailed after the pinto, and by the time Fargo swung from the saddle, whispers were spreading like wildfire. Undoing the flap to one of his saddlebags, Fargo retrieved his battered tin cup and filled it from a pot resting on a flat rock. He sipped leisurely, letting the news sink in, and when those surrounding him fell silent, he gazed across the fire at Owen Hamilton. "First things first. About two hours south of here is a stream—"

"I know of it," the woodsman said.

"Fred Johnson is there, tending a man named Weaver. I need you to send six volunteers to stay with them until Weaver is fit enough to head home. It shouldn't take more than a day or so."

"You sure don't waste time giving orders," Hamilton said.

Fargo surveyed the cordon of unfriendly searchers. "I've got more. Have the horses tied in a string. They'll be easier to protect. And tell the men to spread their bedrolls in sections, like the army does, so it's not so cluttered."

"Anything else?" Hamilton asked a trifle testily.

"Just one more thing." Fargo had given his conversation with Nayokona long, hard thought and reached an inescapable conclusion. "In the morning I want you to disband the searchers."

An audible intake of breath came from those around him.

"You want me to do what?" Hamilton asked, incredulous.

"Call off the search. Thank everyone for their help and tell them they can head back to civilization. Their services are no longer required."

The hulking backwoodsman strode around the fire and planted himself in front of Fargo. Placing ham-sized hands on his wide hips, he said with a low snarl, "The hell you say. The only way that will happen is over my dead body."

13

Skye Fargo believed Nayokona's account of the Shadow People. Particularly the Delaware's claim that they were lying low because of all the whites in the area. He had seen the same thing himself countless times out West. When army troops or other large groups of whites ventured into Indian territory, the Indians invariably melted into the wilderness. Oh, there were exceptions, friendly tribes like the Shoshones and the Flatheads who always welcomed whites with open arms, but by and large most Indians distrusted whites and shunned contact.

Fargo was convinced the Shadow People would only come out of hiding if the searchers were sent home. He'd expected resistance to the idea. Most of the searchers, after all, were motivated by money, and as he had witnessed in the gold fields of Colorado and California, where the prospect of becoming rich was concerned, people could be downright fanatical.

So now, as Owen Hamilton towered over him like a riled grizzly, Fargo calmly sipped more coffee then said, "You saw the papers from Lucius Kemp. Buck me and it's the same as bucking him."

"Does Mr. Kemp want us to disband?" the backwoodsman defiantly demanded. "Is it his idea or yours?"

"Mine," Fargo admitted.

"That's what I figured," Hamilton said. "But unless you can give me a damn good reason, I'm not about to tell these boys to call it quits. Not when there are lives at stake."

Fargo glanced up. Judging by the woodsman's expression, Hamilton was sincere. He cared about the missing people.

"Kemp's niece isn't the only one who has disappeared," Hamilton continued. "And two of the others are women, students of Professor Petticord's. So long as there's a chance they might be alive, it'll be a cold day in hell before I give up."

Grumbles of agreement rose from some of the men and several appeared ready to pounce if Fargo protested. Sipping more coffee, he stalled, buying time to think. Kemp had told him that Owen Hamilton was one of the first to offer help finding the missing expedition. A native New Yorker, Hamilton lived near Albany and made his living by hiring himself out as a guide to hunting parties from the big cities. Most of his clients were well-to-do, and they thought highly of his skill. His fame had spread throughout the tristate region. It was why Lucius Kemp chose him to lead the search effort.

But all that aside, Fargo couldn't let the big woodsman intimidate him. He had made up his mind and he intended to stick by his decision. Slowly straightening, he replied, "It isn't open to debate. Whether you like it or not, tomorrow morning all of you are heading back."

"Who the hell do you think you are, riding in here out of the blue and bossing us around?" Hamilton angrily demanded. "For two bits I'd toss you back on your horse and send you packing."

"Don't even try," Fargo warned. He knew it was the wrong thing to say the moment he said it, but the harm had been done.

Owen Hamilton had fingers as thick as railroad spikes and knuckles as large as walnuts. His right hand clamped like a vise onto the front of Fargo's shirt and he lifted Fargo half off the ground. "No one tells me what to do," he said flatly.

Fargo bristled at being manhandled. Struggling to control his temper, he responded, "I'll say this only once. Let go of me."

"And what if I don't?"

A flick of Fargo's wrist sent the hot coffee into Hamilton's eyes. The woodsman reached up to wipe at them with his sleeve, and in that moment Fargo rammed his left knee into Hamilton's groin. Most men would have doubled over in agony. Hamilton merely grunted, shook his head like a great, shaggy lion, and clamped his other hand onto Fargo's shirt.

"You shouldn't ought to have done that."

The ground and the sky switched positions as Fargo was swept above the woodsman's head, shaken like a hare in the grip of a terrier, and then heaved half a dozen feet. Onlookers scrambled to get out of the way, but some weren't quite fast enough and inadvertently cushioned Fargo's fall. The tin cup skidded from his fingers as he crashed onto his right shoulder. Rolling into the open, he heaved upright.

A living wall of sinew and bone slammed into Fargo with the impact of a runaway train. Fargo's lungs deflated like punctured balloons. Arms of banded steel circled his chest and squeezed, and it was all he could do to keep from blacking out. Sucking in air, he found himself nose-to-nose with the backwoodsman.

"No one has ever broken my bear hug," Hamilton boasted.

Fargo believed him. It felt as if every rib in his body was on the verge of caving in. His arms were pressed to his sides and virtually useless. His legs, though, were free. Swinging them as far back as they would go, he pounded his boots against the bigger man's shins. It had no effect.

Hamilton grinned. "You'll have to do a lot better than that."

"Fair enough," Fargo said, and smashed his forehead into Hamilton's broad face.

The woodsman staggered a step or two, steadied himself, and applied even more pressure, the veins in his temples bulging as if fit to burst. Blood trickled from his nose. "You made me bleed! No one has ever done that before."

"I'm just starting," Fargo said. What worked once would work twice. Again he drove his forehead into Hamilton's face. Again Hamilton tottered, and the bigger man's grip momentarily weakened. Exerting all the power in his whipcord body, Fargo broke free. He had hardly set himself, though, when a looping right clipped his chin and reeled him rearward, into the ring of onlookers. Several seized him and shoved him back toward Hamilton.

"Beat the hell out of him, Owen!" someone hollered.

"Stomp him to a pulp!" another cried.

Fargo raised his fists in time to deflect a right cross to the jaw that would have dropped him like a poled ox if it connected. His forearms stinging something awful, he circled, alert for an opening. The woodsman had adopted a boxing stance, but his arms were too far apart to afford much protection for his stomach. Instantly, Fargo delivered a series of punches to the gut. It was like hitting a washboard. Hamilton's abdomen was banded thick with hard muscle. All the big man did was snort.

"That sort of tickled."

Fargo ducked a left to the cheek, dodged a right to the chest. Hamilton had swung too hard and his momentum carried him another step forward. Taking advantage of the mistake, Fargo landed a solid blow to the left kidney, a blow that jolted the woodsman onto his heels and elicited a sharp oath.

"Come on, Owen!" a fellow searcher bawled. "Quit playing with him and get it over with!"

"Bust his skull wide open!" enthused another partisan.

Hamilton tried. He closed in fast, swinging without letup, a battering barrage that would have crumpled a lesser man where he stood. But Fargo was no Milquetoast. He blocked almost every punch. Those he couldn't block, he avoided. It angered Hamilton, who husked like an enraged bull and redoubled his attack.

Fargo was always in motion, always circling or skipping aside. He lost track of where he was in relation to the campfire until he took a step to the right and his leg was seared with heat and pain. Laughter greeted his mistake. He looked down and saw his foot in the fire. Jerking back, he spared himself serious injury, but the lapse of attention proved costly. A knuckle-crowned fist crashed into his ribs, and the next thing he knew he was on his back in the dirt, dazed and aching, and the backwoodsman was lumbering forward to finish him off.

"You've got him now, Owen!" a man shouted.

So it seemed. Fargo twisted to his left and attempted to stand, but his legs were as wobbly as wet reeds. Mentally resisting the sense of weakness, he pushed onto his knees.

"I'm fixing to kick you from here to New Jersey," Hamilton declared, and lashed out with a heavy boot.

Fargo dodged it, but just barely. Shifting, he felt the boot scrape his temple. He lunged up, wrapped both arms around the woodsman's stout leg, and heaved. Hamilton was upended into a group of smirking searchers who couldn't scatter in time, and four of them went down along with their champion, limbs and bodies entangled.

Owen Hamilton was furious. Bellowing loud enough to be heard in Brooklyn, he hurled men from his right and left, bowling over others who didn't get out of his way fast enough. Curses were heaped on him as he started to rise, but he ignored them.

Like a bee stinging a bear, Fargo flew in close and

let fly with a flurry to the head and neck. He opened a cut on the woodsman's brow and another on the chin, but he couldn't keep Hamilton from regaining his feet. Once more the bigger man towered over him. Once more he was put on the defensive.

Then Fargo's luck changed. He saw that the campfire was now behind Hamilton, and lowering his head and shoulders, he charged. A fist caught him in the shoulder but didn't stop him from slamming into Hamilton's legs.

The woodsman was knocked into the flames. For a second he stood riveted in shock. But only for a second. To escape the searing heat he hurtled into the clear, smashing others aside. His left pant leg had caught on fire and he frantically slapped at it to smother the flames before they spread higher.

Fargo didn't relent. Slipping in closer, he braced himself, tensed his entire body, and let fly with a searing uppercut that caught the woodsman full on the jaw. Not once, not twice, but three times Fargo connected, and at the third blow Owen Hamilton went as stiff as a fence post, teetered like a tree in a gale, and toppled.

A silence gripped the onlookers, who were packed four and five deep. They stared anxiously at Hamilton, waiting for him to get back up and resume the fight. But their leader was out to the world, his eyes closed, his mouth slack. It took ten full seconds for the reality to sink in. Muttered exclamations of disbelief changed to keen resentment as, one by one, they turned their attention from their fallen leader to the one who had brought him low.

"You were lucky, mister," one of their number growled.

"That's all it was. Dumb luck," agreed someone else. "Ain't one man in a thousand who can lick Owen."

A scruffy specimen in clothes that hadn't been

washed in a month of Sundays pushed to the front and shook a hairy fist. "I say we do as Owen wanted and send this bastard on his way! Who's with me?"

A chorus of belligerent whoops and yells greeted the suggestion. Several men started menacingly toward Fargo, a few reaching for revolvers. Others started to level their rifles.

Fargo's hand leaped to his Colt. Forged steel sparkled in the firelight, and the angry men stopped cold. Pivoting a full three-hundred-and-sixty degrees, Fargo said loud enough to be heard by those in the back ranks, "I'll say this one last time. Lucius Kemp hired me. Lucius Kemp put me in charge. If you don't like it, take it up with him. Until then, you'll all do as I tell you."

"But why in hell do you want us to leave?" a scarecrow asked. "Some of us have been at this for weeks with nothing to show for it but blisters and sore feet."

"I was countin' on going home rich," groused a porkish character.

No one seemed inclined to taste lead, but Fargo didn't lower his Colt just yet. "A lot of you were only thinking of lining your pockets," he said. "A lot of you thought finding Camilla Kemp would set you up for life." The vultures betrayed the truth of his statement by the greed that spread from face to face like a windblown forest fire. "But you're stumbling all over yourselves, no closer to finding her than the day you started."

"And you expect to do better?" a fellow in store-bought clothes challenged.

"Maybe not," Fargo conceded. "But my only interest is in bringing the expedition back alive. How many of you can say the same?" That shut them up. Guilt suppressed the greed, and some turned away in budding shame. "I wouldn't ask you to go if it wasn't for the best. Go home. Get on with your lives. From here on out I'm doing this my way."

Muttering and mumbling, the majority moved toward the other campfires.

Satisfied the situation had been defused, Fargo shoved the Colt into its holster. He scoured the grass for his tin cup, refilled it, and squatted. He suddenly felt tired, very tired, but it would be hours yet before he dared lie down to sleep. He wouldn't put it past some of the greedier searchers to try and stick a knife between his shoulder blades so they could go on searching unhindered.

Only a few men had remained to help revive Owen Hamilton and assist him in rising. Rubbing his square jaw, the backwoodsman wasted no time. He balled his massive fists and strode forward.

Sighing, Fargo stood, his hand on the Colt. He had hoped to avoid further violence. "That's far enough," he said.

Hamilton halted and slowly unclenched his thick fingers. "You throw one hell of a punch, mister. No one has ever licked me in a fistfight, and I've been in more than my share." His mouth curved in a lopsided grin. "I was beginning to think no one could."

Fargo shrugged. "There's a first time for everything."

"It was my fault. I admit it," the backwoodsman said. "To mend fences I'd like to apologize."

"Apology accepted," Fargo said.

Hamilton stayed where he was. "This still isn't settled, though. I meant what I said a while ago. Unless you can give me a good reason why the hunt should be called off, I'm going to march over to the other fires and ask those coons to help run you off." Hamilton paused. "We'll do it, too. You might drop a few of us, but we'll settle your hash, permanent-like."

It was no idle threat. The majority of searchers would be all too glad to dispose of anyone who stood between them and their fondly imagined riches. "Tell me something," Fargo said. "Why are you so dead set on giving me hell?"

"Is that what you think? You've got me pegged wrong. Lucius Kemp is free to pick whoever he wants to lead the search so long as the welfare of his daughter and the others are put above all else."

"My sentiments, exactly," Fargo assured him.

"Then why in God's name are you calling off the search?" Hamilton asked. "You don't think you can find them by your lonesome, do you?"

Fargo motioned, and the two of them hunkered an arm's length from one another. After refilling his battered cup and pouring another for the colossus, Fargo related the gist of his talk with Nayokona. The big woodsman listened in amazement, withholding his comments until Fargo concluded. "So now you know. If I'm loco, say so."

"I'll be damned," Owen Hamilton gazed into his cup and swirled the contents. "For weeks Redface has been terrorizing the dickens out of my men. For weeks we've tried to catch him so we could find out what he's up to, but he's always outwitted us. And now you come along and do in one day what we couldn't do in over twenty."

"It was luck more than anything else," Fargo said, and recalled Beda's remark that his luck wouldn't hold forever.

Hamilton lifted his gaze to the murky forest. "The thing of it is, that Delaware could be right."

"You've found sign?"

"I wish to hell we had. All this time there's been nothing. No tracks. No partial prints. Not so much as a smudge. It's as if the expedition never existed." Hamilton dropped his voice to a near-whisper. "This is just between us. But every so often, I've had the feeling me and the boys were being watched. That we were being spied on. But I could never catch whoever was doing it, and it spooked me some. I'm no babe

186

in the woods. Whoever is out there, they're like a bunch of ghosts."

"It sounds as if the Shadow People deserve their name," Fargo said.

"I've heard a few tales over the years," Hamilton said, and leaned back. "I was born and raised on a farm, but farm life was too dull for me. I always liked to hunt, so I earned money supplying meat for our neighbors. I always dropped the biggest deer, the fattest bears. After a while word got around, and I was contacted from all over by rich men like Lucius Kemp. Citified dandies who couldn't track a bull moose in a foot of snow. They pay me to do the tracking and they do the shooting. Lazy as sin, but they pay real well."

"Those tales you heard?" Fargo prompted.

"Oh. From time to time I share drinks with other hunters and woodsmen. You know how it is. I've learned that in the past ten years, at least six men have disappeared up in this neck of the woods. There might be more. No one has kept a tally."

"No trace of them was ever found?"

"None whatsoever. A lot of the old-timers won't come anywhere near here. There was one I met who told me a crazy yarn about a run-in with green Indians in this very area."

"The Indians wore green buckskins?"

"No, not their clothes. He swore their *skin* was green. That they were green men." Hamilton looked around as a man came over to fill a coffee cup, and resumed when the man had walked off. "The old-timer was up here after black bear, and one evening he saw a husky bruin pawing at a log on a slope above him. So he snuck higher to get within rifle range. But when he raised his head again for a look-see, the bear was dead, its hide riddled with arrows, and a pack of green-skinned warriors were standing around it, about to carve it up."

Green-skinned Indians? The notion seemed preposterous. Fargo was inclined to dismiss it as yet another tall tale. Hunters, like fishermen, were forever embellishing their stories. Bear, elk, and deer, like fish, became considerably larger in the telling. But suppose the old hunter wasn't lying? Were the green-skinned warriors the Shadow People of Delaware legend? And what relation, if any, was there between the green-skinned warriors, the Shadow People, and the lost tribe Camilla Kemp had been seeking, the fierce Killamak? Were they three different tribes or one and the same?

Owen Hamilton was having similar thoughts. "Maybe the old hunter wasn't touched in the head, like I'd figured. Maybe those green warriors are the same ones the Delaware told you about. If they are, finding them will take some doing. Which brings me back to my original question. Even if the Delaware and you find these Shadow People, what then? Are the two of you planning to take them on by yourselves?"

Fargo hadn't thought that far ahead.

"You'll need help, so why don't we compromise?" Hamilton proposed. "Why don't I send most of the men back but keep, say, a dozen or so to help you and the Delaware out?"

"If the Shadow People are out there watching, they'll know," Fargo mentioned.

"Not if we outsmart the bastards," the woodsman said. "I'll lead the whole kit and kaboodle south so the Indians will think we've given up. But I'll sneak on back with ten or twelve men I can trust, men who care more about finding the expedition than about lining their pockets, and we'll hide out until we hear from you. How does that sound?"

Fargo liked the idea, but it entailed a certain risk. If the woodsman and his men were spotted, the Shadow People would stay hidden. The mystery would never be solved. Yet he couldn't deny Hamilton's help might be needed should bloodshed result. He had to weigh the potential harm against the potential benefit and hope to heaven he made the right choice. "Where will I find you if I need you?"

Hamilton smiled. "How about by that stream where you left Johnson and that other fellow? What was his handle? Weaver?"

"That will do just fine," Fargo said. "But no fires. No noise. Keep your horses muzzled and hobbled. And don't let anyone stray off on their own."

"I'll make that clear to the men I choose," Hamilton said.

"No hunting, either," Fargo directed. "A gunshot can carry for miles."

"We'll set snares and deadfalls to catch game. With only a dozen mouths to feed, a few rabbits or squirrels will tide us through each day." Hamilton offered a hand. "Are we agreed, then? You'll accept my help?"

Fargo shook. He deemed it wise not to say anything to Nayokona unless he absolutely had to. The young Delaware might regard their plan as a betrayal of his trust.

"For the first time in weeks I have high hopes Miss Kemp and her friends will be found," Hamilton commented. "When I arrived and took over, I thought it would only be a matter of days. but the days dragged into weeks, and now it's almost been a month. If any of them are still alive, it'll be a miracle."

The two of them stayed up late talking. The more Fargo learned about the woodsman, the more he admired him. Hamilton wasn't typical of his breed. He had completed six whole years of schooling and could read and write. They had a lot in common in that they both loved the wilderness and shared a deep wanderlust, an irresistible urge to always see what lay over the next horizon. Hamilton had married young,

189

though, and now had three sprouts to support, so he limited his wandering to New York and parts of surrounding states.

Fargo mentioned some of the sights he had seen in his travels; mountains that reared miles high, unending vistas of grassy prairie, herds of milling buffalo over a million strong, canyons so deep the sun never touched their bottoms, rivers so wide they couldn't be crossed on horseback.

"I've always wanted to take a gallivant west of the Mississippi," Hamilton said with undisguised envy. "To take a gander at the Rockies, and those geysers folks say gush right out of the ground."

"Maybe some day you will."

"Not if my wife has anything to say about it," the woodsman responded. "Patty's content right where we are. Her parents live just up the road from us, and she has a lot of kin in and around Albany."

Yet another example, Fargo reflected, of why he was in no hurry to rope a woman and settle down.

As if Hamilton could read minds, he said, "I don't blame her. A family needs roots. A home for the kids, and kinfolk to lend a hand when times are tough." The big woodsman smiled. "My Patty has a heart of gold. She's let me go off on hunts for weeks at a stretch and never complains. When Lucius Kemp's messenger showed up on our doorstep, she said it was my duty to go help out. She even helped me pack. As much as I want to see the West, I'd never leave her for the world."

Most of the searchers had turned in when Fargo finally spread out his bedroll and slid under his blankets. His saddle served as his pillow, and he slept on his back with his right hand resting on the Colt.

By daybreak the camp was abuzz with activity. Owen Hamilton stepped onto a stump and gave a short speech. He thanked the men for their help, informed them the search was over, and instructed them to gather up their effects and be ready to ride out by eight. The news didn't go over well. A lot of dire glances were cast at Fargo. But they did as Hamilton had commanded.

Fargo saddled the Ovaro and indulged in a last cup of coffee before leaving. When he saw the big woodsman coming toward him, wearing a frown, he rose. "Is something wrong?"

"A hitch in our plans. I almost forgot. One of the search parties is still out and isn't due back until tomorrow or the next day." Hamilton was embarrassed by his lapse. "I've been sending them in relays to cover more ground. Ten men to a group. They go out for a week at a time, then report back."

"Someone will have to stay here and wait for them." Fargo saw no way around it.

"They're my responsibility," Hamilton said. "I'll stick around, along with the twelve men I've selected. As soon as the last search party shows up, we'll head for the stream and wait to hear from you."

"Fair enough." Fargo put his cup in his saddlebags and forked leather. "With any luck, a week from now this will all be over." They shook, and he spurred the stallion northward. At long last his hunt for Camilla Kemp could begin in earnest.

Skye Fargo was over halfway to the bald mountain when he realized he was being shadowed. Once the feeling that he was being watched came over him, he couldn't shake it. He tried telling himself it was his imagination, but it grew stronger as the minutes went by. He scoured the woods from under his hat brim, but saw no one. Nor the slightest hint of movement.

Fargo suspected the Shadow People. He was moving through a thick belt of saplings, and to prevent an ambush he angled toward more open ground. Shucking the Henry from its scabbard, he levered a round into the chamber and rode with the rifle across his thighs. He had gone another fifty yards when his shadower made a mistake. A patch of high weeds swayed as if bent by the wind. Only there was no wind. It had fallen deadly still, so still that he heard the beating of a crow's wings as it flew overhead.

Pretending he hadn't noticed, Fargo threaded through a last stand of slender trees. He continued to watch the weeds from his hat. Suddenly the snout of a rifle poked into view, aimed in his direction.

Fargo reined to the right to put an oak between himself and the bushwhacker. Not a second too soon. The rifle boomed, and a slug gouged a furrow in the trunk as he went by. Snapping the Henry to his shoulder, he reined toward the weeds and banged off several rapid shots. The other rifle was yanked out of sight, and a figure rose and raced westward.

Jabbing his spurs, Fargo galloped in pursuit. He couldn't see the figure clearly yet but he could tell the bushwhacker wore buckskins. An Indian, he assumed, until the man glanced back and he beheld a craggy, bearded countenance.

The Ovaro reached the weeds. Twisting in midstride, the bushwhacker tried to bring his rifle into play. Fargo never hesitated. He stroked the trigger, pumped the lever, and stroked the trigger again.

The fleeing figure was cored through the torso. Stumbling wildly, the man grabbed at his chest and keeled headfirst to the earth. The rifle slid from his grasp. Clawing at the ground, he sought to rise but couldn't.

Fargo reined up ten feet out and warily slid down, his sights squarely centered on the bushwhacker's head.

"Don't shoot, mister!" the man bleated, pink froth flecking his lips. "I'm done for! You've bucked me out in gore."

Fargo kicked the killer's rifle farther away. "Who the hell are you?" he demanded. "Why did you try to do me in?"

"M—m—money," the man sputtered. The froth bubbled over his grizzled chin. "I did it for the money!"

"Someone paid you? Who?" Fargo bent lower, his finger curled around the Henry's trigger. "Talk, or you'll die that much sooner."

"They did," the man said. He was weakening fast, and his eyelids fluttered like the wings of a frantic butterfly. "Hired a bunch of us—"

"Who?" Fargo's gut involuntarily tightened. He was sick and tired of being a target. A reckoning was long overdue.

"The young ones," the bushwhacker gasped. "They paid good money. They don't want you to—" Whatever else he was going to say was cut short by violent convulsions. Hissing and spitting, he rolled from side to side, his arms and legs undulating like snakes. His contortions ended with a loud whine, and his chest seemed to fold in on itself.

"Damn." Lowering the Henry, Fargo squatted and went through the man's pockets. He found a wad of bills amounting to four hundred and eighty-four dollars, which he stuffed into his pants. Collecting the man's rifle and revolver, Fargo placed them in his bedroll, tied the roll down, and remounted.

It stood to reason the bushwhacker had a horse hidden somewhere nearby. Fargo roved back and forth over ten minutes but couldn't find it. Since time was pressing, he wheeled the pinto and moved on. The bushwhacker's mention of "young ones" puzzled him. Did it refer to some of the Kemps? Or someone else? Had they also hired the longshoremen? More importantly, how many more attempts on his life would there be before it was over?

By maintaining a gallop, Fargo arrived at the bald mountain at the appointed time. Paralleling the bottom, he soon came to the mouth of a wide ravine that slashed the west slope as if cut by a sword. Nayokona wasn't there.

Rising in the stirrups, Fargo placed a hand across his eyes to shield them from the sun's harsh glare and swept the mountain from bottom to top. A few blackbirds and a whitetail doe were all he saw. Kneeing the stallion into the ravine, he examined the ground. No fresh tracks were visible, but several old, faintly discernible smudge marks made by flat soles, presumably moccasins, made him wonder if they were the prints Nayokona had spoken of. The sign of the Shadow People.

One way to find out, Fargo thought, and started up the ravine. The Ovaro's shod hooves rang on the stones underfoot.

"Wait!"

Out of the brush jogged the young Delaware, dressed in a breechclout. His whole body was now daubed in red ocher, and he was heavily armed, as before. He had been running hard and was winded.

"I was beginning to think you wouldn't make it," Fargo said, drawing rein.

"There is much going on," Nayokona said. "A new group of whites has arrived and pitched camp east of here. I saw them from higher up."

Fargo remembered the ten-man party Hamilton was waiting for. "How many were there?"

"Fifteen or sixteen," Nayokona said. "They were on horseback. I thought they were more searchers. But when they came close to the meadow where the rest of the searchers are camped, they changed direction and hurried to the north to avoid them. It was most strange."

"Maybe they didn't want to be seen," Fargo said, thinking of the bushwhacker. "Were all of them men?"

"I could not tell. But why would white women come here? It is too dangerous."

"We'll check on them later," Fargo said. "Right now all I care about are these tracks." He pointed at the smudges. "Where do they lead?"

Nayokona smiled. "Not many would recognize them for what they are. You have the eyes of a hawk." His smile widened. "Or of a Delaware." He headed up the ravine. "They were fresher when I found them. It was after a rain."

Fargo trailed close behind. The fact that the legendary Shadow People made mistakes was encouraging. They weren't invincible. They possessed extraordinary abilities, but they were human.

Twenty yards in, Nayokona stopped and crouched. "This was the first complete footprint I discovered."

Faint but unmistakable was the crescent shape the young warrior had alluded to previously. Dismounting,

Fargo examined it closely. The maker of the track had been moving at a swift pace and the foot had slapped the ground with the full weight of the man evenly distributed. The stitching along the heel and toes was imprinted in the soil, a crisscross pattern similar to that used by some of the Plains tribes. Fargo placed his own foot next to it. His was two inches longer but not nearly as wide.

"Come. There are more." Nayokona climbed higher.

Fargo led the pinto by the reins. The ravine's steep sides were higher than the Ovaro, limiting his view of the surrounding woodland, which he didn't much like. Anyone could sneak up on them without them knowing it. But he didn't intend to be there that long.

"When I am discouraged in my search, when I worry that I will never set eyes on my father again, I come back here to touch the tracks and prove to myself they are real," Nayokona said.

"Have you found tracks anywhere else?"

Nayokona frowned. "Only here, and above. You will see shortly." Some loose stones slid from under his foot and he almost slipped. "The Shadow People hardly ever leave sign of their passing. My grandfather used to say it is because they have mastered the art of walking on air. But my grandfather believed many odd things. He swore that in the dawn of time hairy giants roamed this land. And that in certain lakes, to this day, dwell creatures that will overturn canoes and eat those in them."

Fargo spied more smudges and another partial print. "Did your grandfather speak English as well as you do?"

"Not a word. It was my father and mother who encouraged me to learn. To survive in the white world, they said, I must know the white tongue. So I took lessons from a missionary."

"You must have been his prize pupil," Fargo said. Many Indians found the white tongue difficult to master, just as many whites found Indian tongues incomprehensible. He'd always had a knack for new languages, which had served him in good stead in his wide-flung travels.

"My people have a saying. When someone goes to the trouble to learn something, they should learn it the best they can."

"Wise words," Fargo remarked. The ravine had narrowed to the point where they had to hike in single file. Around the next bend a section of the left-hand slope had been eaten away by the heavy rains and oozed to the bottom like a miniature mudslide. Outlined in the now-dry mud were two complete crescent-shaped tracks made by two different individuals.

"I think there were four of them," Nayokona said, indicating partial prints to the right of the slide.

"Five," Fargo said, and pointed at barely perceptible marks near the right rim. "One of them was up there, serving as a lookout."

The young warrior scrambled up for a better look. Stones and dirt cascaded from under him, and he had to drop onto his hands and knees to gain purchase. "I had not noticed these. Truly, you are one of the best trackers, red or white, I have ever met."

"We'll find more before we're done," Fargo predicted. Legends to the contrary, the Shadow People were no more stealthy or crafty than the Apaches or any one of a dozen other Western tribes.

Nayokona jumped to the bottom and resumed climbing. "Perhaps we will succeed where no other Delaware ever has. But I will be honest with you. I do not think my father or any of the others are still alive. Not after all this time."

"You never know," Fargo said. Maybe the Killamak weren't as bloodthirsty as they were made out to be. Maybe they adopted or enslaved some of their captives.

"I know the stories the elders tell," Nayokona said. "The Shadow People have no hearts. They show no mercy. They were a small tribe, yet the Hurons and the Iroquois feared them. Disease brought them low, not their many enemies. Disease they caught from white men." Nayokona paused. "They must hate your kind more than they hate anyone."

Fargo hadn't thought of that. It added new urgency to their quest.

The ravine narrowed even more. Twenty feet above them the end was in sight. Fargo had to tug on the reins to induce the stallion to negotiate a final steep incline that brought them out on a grassy shelf. From the north end they were afforded a splendid view of the terrain to the north. Mile after mile of unbroken forest canopy. Mile after mile of unexplored woodland.

"They are out there somewhere," Nayokona said, and gestured at the grass. "Here is where I lost their trail."

Fargo scoured the shelf rim. Grass seldom retained prints for long. Horse tracks, yes, but then horses were a lot heavier. At the northwest corner he stopped. Below it the grass was sparse. Descending, he inspected the soil intently. It was harder packed than the ravine, and rocky. But fortune smiled on him. Fourteen feet down, in a patch of barren earth no wider than his palm, he discovered a crescent-shaped heel imprint. "They went this way," he said.

Nayokona bounded down to see for himself. "For the first time since I started looking for my father, I think I might find out what happened to him."

Forty feet lower, in heavy woodland, Fargo found another partial. After that, though, they covered hundreds of yards without finding so much as a scuff mark. Acting on the assumption the Shadow People had held to a northwesterly bearing, Fargo pushed on for over three-quarters of a mile over exceedingly rough terrain. Finally he halted, willing to concede temporary defeat.

"We have lost them," Nayokona said. "Just when I got my hopes up."

"Maybe we should separate," Fargo suggested. "We can cover twice as much ground in half as much time."

"I will go north. You go west," the Delaware said. "We will meet here when the sun is there." He pointed at where the sun would be about three in the afternoon. "Is that acceptable?"

Nodding, Fargo swung onto the pinto. For the next two and a half hours he conducted a broad sweep. Repeatedly crisscrossing back and forth, he concentrated on tracts where the vegetation was thinnest. But he might as well have been tracking will-o-the-wisps. As the sun approached midafternoon, he reined the stallion eastward and was the first to arrive at the spot where he was to meet the Delaware. Nayokona wasn't there. A handy oak offered a suitable backrest, and he sat down to await his new friend.

Ten minutes elapsed. Twenty minutes. Half an hour.

Fargo wasn't worried. As he had learned firsthand, the young warrior could take care of himself. He grew drowsy, and although he had no intention of dozing off, he did and slept soundly until a nicker awakened him. Blinking, he sat up and was mad at himself when he saw the sun low in the western sky. He had slept most of the afternoon away!

Nayokona still hadn't returned.

Something was wrong. Fargo rose and stepped into the stirrups.

In the young Delaware's eargerness to find his father, Nayokona hadn't tried to hide his trail. So following it was easy. His tracks led into the densest stretch of forest Fargo had ever seen, a primordial realm of oppressive shadow and unnatural quiet, of moss-shrouded trees, thorn-laced thickets, and immense boulders. The stallion's hooves fell dull and alien on spongy soil carpeted by dead leaves. The awful silence began to fray at his nerves. He had never been in woods so silent. So devoid of life. He didn't spot a single bird, a solitary squirrel.

Fargo suspected he was nearing the Canadian border. It might be five miles off, possibly ten. There was no established boundary to go by. He did note a change in the vegetation, with more pines and firs and spruce than before.

The Ovaro began to act skittish. Ears pricked, nostrils flared, it seemed to sense impending danger.

Suddenly the Delaware's tracks stopped cold. Nayokona had turned from side to side, as if scanning the undergrowth, then raced to the northwest.

Mystified, Fargo leaned low, half-hanging from the saddle horn. He saw no other tracks, yet he was certain the young warrior was being chased. Broken stems and crushed twigs testified to the speed at which Nayokona had been moving. An enormous log had blocked his path and the Delaware had vaulted it with deceptive ease. Fargo had to go around. On the other side Nayokona had paused and wheeled, like an animal at bay, but only for a few moments. Then he had run on.

Gazing back, Fargo saw something he had overlooked; an arrow sticking from a spruce tree. He slid down and clambered over the log. The shaft was one of Nayokona's. It was imbedded several inches and resisted his attempts to pull it out. Whoever he had fired it at must have dodged it.

Fargo sprinted to the pinto. Climbing on, he rode as rapidly as he could given the thickness of the undergrowth. Nayokona had barreled on through a thicket, but Fargo skirted it to spare the pinto. In doing so he stumbled on tracks paralleling the young warrior's. Crescent-shaped tracks. Eight pairs, as best Fargo could judge. A band of Shadow People, or Killamak, as he now preferred to refer to them, hot after their quarry like a pack of ravenous wolves after a fleeing deer.

The length of Nayokona's stride showed he had been running flat out yet the Killamak had slowly gained. Fargo passed another arrow, this time stuck in a lightning-charred stump. He didn't stop to try and remove it.

The sun was dipping below the horizon. Second by second the sky drew darker. It wouldn't be long before night fell, dashing any hope Fargo had of overtaking Nayokona anytime soon.

The trail became a lot harder to read, forcing Fargo to go slower. He lost precious minutes but there was nothing else he could do. Frustration welled within him, and he stubbornly plugged on until near-complete darkness gripped the land. Then, and only then, did he bring the stallion to a stop.

The night was moonless and much of the starlight was obscured by clouds. Fargo couldn't see his hand at arm's length. The only way he could continue to track was by torchlight, a potentially perilous undertaking since the torch could be seen for miles. The smart thing to do was wait until daylight.

Swearing under his breath, Fargo slid down and looped the reins around a limb on a small pine. He removed his saddle and saddle blanket, spread them near the tree, and eased onto his back.

Suddenly a guttural screech slashed the night. It came from the north, from deeper in the wilderness, and while it resembled the high-pitched scream of a mountain lion, it was different enough to give Fargo cause to suspect something else was to blame. He listened for a while, but it wasn't repeated.

The Henry across his legs, Fargo lowered his chin to his chest and tried to sleep without much success. His mind was in a whirl of agitation. He felt he had let the Delaware down, even though he had done his best.

Soon other cries spiked the night. The bleat of a frightened doe, the hooting of an owl. Fargo also heard the melancholy howl of a wolf, still more proof he must be close to Canada, or have crossed over without being aware.

Fargo closed his eyes. No sooner had he done so than another unearthly screech silenced everything else. It was answered to the west, and soon they spread to all quarters of the landscape. Strident, piercing cries, unlike those of any animal Fargo ever heard. High-pitched and eerie, they possessed a bestial quality that hinted at something other than human.

It was close to midnight when Fargo succumbed to a dreamworld consisting of darkling spectral images and eerie sounds. A harsh shriek near at hand jarred him awake, and as he sat straighter, it was mimicked by an identical cry to the south. Whatever was making them was a lot closer.

The Ovaro stamped the ground, a sure sign it was disturbed.

Off among the pines a twig crunched with startling clarity. Fargo's scalp prickled as a coal-black shape loped out of the depths of the woods. It was thirty feet out and seemed unaware of his presence. He saw the stallion's head bob, and thinking the pinto was about to whinny, he sprang to its side and placed his left hand on its muzzle.

The black shape stopped. From its throat issued a feral shriek like those Fargo had already heard. Up close the effect was doubly unnerving. Fargo tried to distinguish the thing's features but it was like trying to see water at the bottom of a well. Another shriek, to the southwest, lured the creature off, and once it was gone Fargo let out the breath he hadn't realized he was holding.

Fargo didn't sit back down for over an hour. The constant shrieking had him on perpetual edge. Twice he heard the vegetation crackle at the passage of something big; whether animal or human he did not know. He wondered why the shriekers were running all over the place in the middle of the night and making enough racket to raise the dead. What did they hope to accomplish? He heard yet another cry, heard it answered, and was stunned to realize the shrieks were signals.

It was the Killamak, and they were hunting someone. Either Nayokona. Or him.

The rest of the night was a nightmare of furtive sounds and beastly screams. Toward daylight the shrieks ended and Fargo enjoyed an uninterrupted hour of solid slumber. It wasn't enough. As a pink tinge splashed the eastern sky, he stiffly rose and stretched to relieve a kink in his back. Food could wait. He threw on his saddle and was under way before sunrise.

The tracks were still plain as could be. In a quarter of a mile Fargo emerged from the trees into a field. A ring of flattened, torn grass marked the spot where the Killamak had overtaken the Delaware. Nayokona had struggled mightily but been overcome by weight of numbers.

Was the Delaware dead? Fargo found smears of blood, but not as much as there would be if Nayokona had been gravely wounded. From there the trail angled to the northwest. At the tree line Fargo found more proof the young warrior was alive. The Killamak had briefly halted, and mixed in among their crescent prints were those of the Delaware. Nayokona had been limping but he was moving under his own power.

Heartened, Fargo trotted in pursuit. Once again the woods lay in the grip of an unnatural quiet. Fargo figured he must be near a Killamak village. It would explain why large game was missing, but not the absence of smaller animals and birds.

Dawn arrived, chill and windy, and from out of the north rolled more clouds. Not long after, a sinuous bank of fog seemed to seep up out of the very earth, shrouding the forest in a vaporous preternatural twilight.

Wispy, serpentine tendrils coiled around Fargo and the Ovaro. He slowed to a walk, riding uneasily. Every couple of minutes he stopped to listen. If there was a village nearby, he'd hear barking dogs and the laughter of children long before he saw it.

The fog was so thick that Fargo could no longer see the sign. Sliding off, he swished at it with a hand, causing a small ripple. He spied a track and moved on, reduced to a snail's pace and chafing at the delay.

It couldn't possibly get any worse, he reflected.

Then feet pattered on the leaves. Fargo pivoted to the left but all he saw was fog. The same when, moments later, something pattered to the right. He palmed the Colt, his skin crawling with the conviction he had found the Killamak—or they had found him. Movement suggested they were encircling him.

Fargo vaulted into the saddle. He started to rein around, but a glance revealed several dark figures barring his escape. There were already Killamak to the right and Killamak to the left so he spurred the stallion forward. Since the war party was on foot, he should be able to outdistance them within moments.

Suddenly the fog parted enough for Fargo to glimpse four or five crouching forms waiting in ambush. On an impulse he reined to the right, and there was another one. Fargo didn't stop, didn't slow down. He jabbed his spurs hard and the Ovaro slammed into the crouched Killamak, bowling him over.

Fargo had a fleeting image of a snarling face, hate-filled eyes, and skin that appeared to be green. He was denied the opportunity to ponder how that was possible. For out of the fog leaped a burly human toad. Their shoulders impacted, and Fargo was knocked sideways. His left boot slipped out of its stirrup and he began to fall. Quickly, he gripped the saddle horn, and had nearly straightened when another darkish shape hurled itself at him from up high.

They were jumping out of the trees! Fargo ducked, but not low enough. The Killamak crashed into him full force and they fell, locked together. As they hit the ground the Killamak shrieked a ghastly cry just like those Fargo had heard during the night, and within seconds the fog disgorged more green-skinned, brutish forms. Five, six, seven of them flung themselves on top of him and struggled to pin his arms and legs.

Fargo resisted. He punched one man, kneed another, slugged a third with the Colt. He almost broke loose but there were too many. As he surged upright and took a step, an iron hand clamped onto his ankle. He toppled, and his legs and arms were seized. The Colt was ripped from his grasp.

The unthinkable had happened.

He was a captive of the Shadow People.

15

Skye Fargo's shoulders and hips ached and his arms and legs were sore and stiff. He had the Killamak to thank. After capturing him, several had gone off into the fog and returned carrying a long, trimmed branch, to which he had been lashed by his wrists and ankles. The pole had been hoisted onto the shoulders of a couple of brawny warriors, and the whole band had trekked to the northwest in single file.

That had been an hour ago and they were still on the go. The Killamak moved like ghosts, making no more noise than the breeze, never once speaking aloud. To communicate they used hand signals. Not the traditional sign language of tribes west of the Mississippi, in which Fargo was fluent, but a system uniquely their own.

Their green skin, Fargo observed, was the result of the dye applied to every square inch of exposed skin. From head to toe, they were the same shade as the vegetation around them. Wavy black lines had been added to their chests and faces. It was perfect camouflage. In the thick green woodland, with its many shadows, they were virtually invisible.

Their weapons consisted of bows and arrows, bone-handled knives, and war clubs, with the clubs being favored. Only one warrior carried a lance, and it was shorter by half than those of the Sioux or the Cheyenne. Small deerskin breechclouts were their only clothing besides their moccasins. A few wore green wristbands. One sported a green headband, and it was he who appeared to be in charge.

Their moccasins, Fargo saw, were crescent shaped for a reason. Their feet were unnaturally curved, almost deformed, in that their toes and heels curved inward. But it didn't hamper them. They moved with the fluid agility of cougars.

There was something about the Killamak that Fargo found distinctly unnerving. They had an air of brutishness about them, of untamed savagery enhanced by their stooped posture, their thick, beetling brows, and their dark, beady eyes. They were short in stature, more beastlike than human, squat and heavy and corded with muscle. Manes of black hair tumbled over their knobby shoulders. When one grinned wickedly as they were binding him, Fargo saw that they filed their teeth to tapered tips. The warrior had pointed at Fargo's head, smacked his thick lips, then rubbed his stomach. Some of the others chuckled.

Fargo was mystified. He'd taken it for granted the Killamak would somewhat resemble other Eastern tribes. The Iroquois and Hurons were tall and well-proportioned, like the Delawares. But the Killamak were exactly the opposite.

The Old Ones, the Lenape called them, and maybe there was some truth to it. Maybe the Killamak were holdovers from an earlier age, from the time when hairy giants did roam the land and monsters filled the lakes. He began to understand why the other tribes had shunned and feared them.

For two more hours the Killamak bore him through fog-draped woodland. Tireless, imbued with inhuman stamina, the pair carrying him showed no more strain than if he were a leaf. They were always alert, always on their guard. Frequently they paused to sniff the air.

Their sense of smell was acute. Shortly after the band started out, they abruptly halted, all of them with their heads thrown back and their nostrils quivering.

At a gesture from the warrior wearing the headband they crouched low, their dark eyes fixed to the north. Soon a black bear appeared. Grunting and huffing, it passed within thirty feet of them without suspecting the warriors were there.

The terrain became more rugged, a formidable tangle of trees, deadfalls, and boulders, impassable to anyone on horseback. Fargo was glad the Ovaro had trotted off when he was caught. There was no telling what the Killamak might have done to it; some tribes were quite fond of horsemeat.

At last the woods ended. Before Fargo's wondering gaze unfolded a spectacle the likes of which few white men had set eyes on in centuries. A crude palisade of rough-hewn logs, sharpened at the top to thwart invaders, enclosed a two-acre tract. At a cry from the leader a gate was opened from within, creaking on leather hinges.

Fargo craned his neck as they entered. Most of the enclosed space was devoted to a large longhouse. As near as he could tell, the frame had been fashioned from elm-wood poles over which strips of elm bark had been placed. Approximately seventy-five feet long and twenty-five feet wide, it had a square opening at the top for ventilation. There were no windows, only doorways at both ends.

Killamak were busy at a variety of tasks. Two old women were curing a hide on a wooden rack. A hunter was skinning a freshly killed buck. Another was plucking feathers from a plump duck. Younger women were minding a few small children. The females had the same beetling brows and flat faces of the males. They wore deerskin aprons but no tops. The upper halves of their bodies were covered with flowery patterns and symbolic designs. One woman had two yellow stars radiating outward from her nipples. Another had a blue triangle bordering her navel. The children were completely naked.

Fargo's captors halted, and the leader gave a fierce yell. The villagers stopped what they were doing to greet the war party, and more filed from the longhouse. Before long Fargo was ringed by over two dozen of the brutes. Only seven were children under twelve or so, a disproportionately small number, Fargo thought. Intensely curious, they examined him closely. A few poked his chest and sides. Others pulled at the whangs on his buckskins. An older woman was fascinated by his beard and kept pulling on the hairs. They didn't act hostile, but they weren't friendly, either.

Suddenly a commotion broke out. The women gathered up their children and moved back. The warriors stiffened and bowed their heads.

Out of the longhouse strode another Killamak. Slightly taller than the rest, he was broad of shoulder and wide of girth. A bearskin robe and an eagle-feather headdress marked him as someone of importance. His chest had been dyed green, like the rest of the men, but his face, arms and legs were a bright yellow. He held a long, smooth hardwood staff, with which he motioned at the warrior in the headband, who stepped aside so he could approach.

It had to be their chief. "Do you speak English?" Fargo asked, not really counting on an answer and not getting one.

The chief's cold, sinister eyes dissected him as if he were a calf being sized up for slaughter. Blunt fingers pried at his shirt, at his belt, his boots. The leader made a slow circuit, then bent and looked Fargo in the eyes. Any hope Fargo entertained of convincing them he was friendly evaporated. Raw, unyielding hatred was mirrored in that dark, beady gaze, a hatred that eclipsed all reason or understanding.

"Your people still blame my kind for the epidemic, don't you," Fargo said, more a statement than a question.

Barking a few words in the Killamak tongue, the chief rose to his full height and struck without warning, cuffing Fargo across the cheek.

Fargo was rocked sideways, his face spiked by torment. He tasted the salty tang of blood and spat it out. "Try that when I'm not trussed up, you bastard," he growled.

The chief uttered a brittle, mirthless, sadistic laugh, and wagged his staff at the warrior in the headband. The warrior, in turn, addressed the two Killamak who had been carrying Fargo, and they stooped and lifted the pole. The rest followed as the chief led the way around the near corner of the longhouse.

Fargo braced for the worst. Ronnie had told him the Killamak tortured their enemies, and he wouldn't put it past them to start right in. His dread mounted when he saw what was on the other side of the dwelling.

A wooden platform approximately twelve-foot square had been erected, complete with a short flight of steps. Climbing them, the chief smirked and pointed at an object in the center. He said something, and laughed.

It was a solid block of wood six feet long and three feet wide. Reddish stains discolored the top and dried gore encrusted its sides. Leather straps were attached, their purpose self-evident. Beside it rested a long ironwood club with a large ball-like head. The use it was put to was also apparent. Lined up in obscenely grinning rows around the base of the altar were scores of human skulls that all had one thing in common; they had all been crushed from behind, most likely by the very same club that now waited menacingly for its next victim.

The chief was showing Fargo the fate the tribe had in store for him. Fargo pretended to be indifferent and looked away, at which the chief laughed louder, then gave a short speech.

In due course Fargo was carried into the longhouse. The doorway was scarcely big enough to admit an average Killamak. There was no door, as such, but just inside, propped against the left wall, was a sturdy solid wooden barrier that could be placed over the opening and braced by a thick log.

A wide central open aisle was the hub of Killamak life. Cooking pots were situated at regular intervals, directly under the holes in the ceiling. On either side were living quarters, narrow compartments on raised fur-covered platforms where families slept and stored their personal belongings. Above each compartment, running the length of the building, was a wide shelf for added storage space. Curtains fashioned from cured hides afforded some small measure of privacy.

Fargo was conveyed midway into the longhouse and deposited none-too-gently on the dirt floor. A pair of warriors untied the cords that bound him. At a word from the chief, they hauled him to his feet and shoved him toward a deer-hide curtain. Another Killamak pushed it aside. Fargo tried to move fast enough to suit them, but the circulation in his legs had been cut off for too long and he wobbled as if drunk. He stayed upright only by a supreme force of will. Again the chief barked, and Fargo was given a hard push. He lifted his leg to clear the platform, but stumbled and tripped and sprawled on his face. As he rolled onto his side, the curtain was flung shut. Sitting up, he peeked out.

The Killamak were dispersing. Four hefty guards had been left to guarantee he didn't go anywhere.

Fargo began rubbing his tingling legs to get the blood flowing again. He wasn't about to sit around waiting for the end to come. He'd rather die fighting and take as many of them with him as he could.

The platform was covered with furs. From the rear, where the furs were piled highest, came a low groan. Shifting, Fargo crawled nearer. A man lay on his stomach in the shadows, arm flung outward, as if tossed there by the Killamak and too weak to move. Gingerly, Fargo gripped a shoulder and rolled the other captive over. "Nayokona!"

The young Delaware was in pitiable shape. He had been severely beaten. His mouth and nose were caked with dry blood, his left eye was practically swollen shut, and his lower lip was puffy and split. His right eye slowly opened and he blinked in confusion. He had to swallow a few times before he croaked, "They caught you, too, my friend?"

"Afraid so." Fargo slipped an arm under Nayokona's and gently raised him high enough to prop him on a bundled elk hide. "There. You should be a little more comfortable."

"How long have I been here?"

"Since sometime early last night would be my guess," Fargo said.

"That is all? It seems much longer." Nayokona coughed, and a new drop of blood seeped from a corner of his mouth. "They knocked me down and kicked me again and again. The men and the women. I do not remember anything after that."

"What did you do to get them so mad?" Fargo was lucky he hadn't shared the Delaware's punishment.

"Nothing that I know of. I resisted when they tried to take me hostage but they did not seem angry then. Only later, when we arrived at their village."

"Did you kill any?"

"No." Nayokona licked the drop from his lips. "They tied me, and brought me here on a pole. Their leader came out, and the moment he saw me, he yelled and raged and started to kick me and the others joined in. I have no idea why."

The curtain parted. Framed in the opening was a shapely woman in her twenties. Her oval features were haggard and drawn, her face streaked with grime. Formerly lustrous blonde hair hung limp and disheveled. The tatters of a once-plain dress clung to her bosom and thighs, revealing more than it hid. "I think I know the answer," she said. Stepping onto the platform, she closed the curtain behind her.

"Camilla Kemp!" Fargo said, rising. Elated, he gripped her shoulders and smiled broadly. If she was alive, the others might be, too. "Your uncle hired me." He gave his name. "I traveled all the way from Missouri to help track you down."

Instead of greeting the news with joy, Camilla frowned and sadly declared, "I wish you hadn't come. You've brought another death down on my head. As if there weren't enough already."

"How do you mean?"

"They're all dead, Mr. Fargo. Professor Petticord. Harold Baxter. Heather and Estelle and Thomas. They're all dead." Tears dampened Camilla's green eyes, and her rosy lips quivered. "It's my fault. They joined the expedition at my request. And they suffered the most horrible deaths imaginable."

Fargo steered her over near Nayokona and she listlessly sank down. "The Killamak killed them all?" The legends, then, were true in at least one respect. The Shadow People were as bloodthirsty as they were made out to be.

"Thomas died when we were attacked," Camilla said. "He took a spear through the heart. The rest of us were captured alive and brought here. Professor Petticord had been wounded in the shoulder and was as weak as a kitten. But that didn't stop them from dragging him out the first night and tying him to their horrible altar." Tears streamed, and she choked down a sob.

"There's no need to talk about it," Fargo said.

"No. It's all right." Camilla took a deep breath. "They made us watch, you see. They hauled us outside and held our heads so we couldn't turn away. Professor Petticord was tied down. He looked at me and told me to never give up hope, and then their leader swung that terrible club and smashed the professor's head as if it were a rotten squash. I can still hear the sound."

"I'm sorry," Fargo said, but she didn't hear him. Absorbed in her recital, she shuddered at the memory.

"That wasn't the worst part, though. They pried apart his skull and scooped out his brains with a wooden spoon and placed them on a plate. And then—" Camilla clasped her arms to her chest—"and then they passed around the plate and every Killamak ate a mouthful."

Fargo envisioned the nightmarish scene in his mind. "Is that what they did to the rest?"

"Harry Baxter was the next to go, about a week after we got here. They dragged him out kicking and screaming. He begged for his life. He pleaded and cried. But it did no good." More tears gushed, and she doubled over. "He screamed for me to help him but there wasn't anything I could do."

"You can't blame yourself." Fargo sought to comfort her by holding her close. She appeared not to mind.

"Harry loved me, Mr. Fargo," Camilla said softly. "He had no real interest in anthropology. He majored in it because I liked it. And now he's gone. Him and Estelle."

"Estelle?"

"One of the professor's students. She came along for extra credit. She was a cute young thing, so carefree and full of life. The Killamak put her with Harry the night before he was to die, and she had to give herself to him."

"Give herself?" Fargo recollected a Shoshone custom of allowing strangers who spent the night to share their blankets with a willing woman.

"Part of their ritual," Camilla detailed. "Sort of like the last meal for a condemned criminal. Only in their case it's a woman. A captive woman." She wrung her hands in the furs. "They didn't give one of us to the professor because he was so weak. But Harry and To-nekotay—"

"My father!" Nayokona sat up. "Is he dead too? Have the Shadow People slain him?"

"You're his son?" Camilla covered her face with her hands. "Dear God. Is there no end to the lives I've ruined? No end to the horror?"

"Please. I must hear more." Grimacing, Nayokona placed his hand on her arm. "Tell me everything. It is important."

Camilla took a deep breath. "He was a brave man, your father. The bravest of us all. The day we were attacked, he killed three Killamak. That's probably why they beat him so often. They gave Heather to him the night before he was to die, but your father refused to touch her. So they tortured him." She looked at the young Delaware. "They did things I don't dare repeat or I'll go mad. Sickening, disgusting atrocities. Yet he never cried out. He never begged for mercy, as Harry had done. He died nobly."

Nayokona averted his face and it was a while before he spoke again. "My heart is happy to hear your words."

"They killed Heather anyway," Camilla said. "A sweet girl who never harmed a living soul, and she was tied to their altar and had her brains dashed out." Anger crept into her voice. "The mighty Killamak! The lost tribe! Once the most feared of all! A tribe that rivaled the Iroquois and the Huron! I devoted my career to them, to proving they were everything legend claimed. I saw them as a great, mythic people. But I couldn't have been more wrong."

In the violence of her emotion, she began to tremble. Fargo gave her a light squeeze, saying, "We all make mistakes."

"Most mistakes don't cause the deaths of our friends and colleagues," Camilla snapped, and shook a fist at the hide curtain. "The Killamak! Savage animals is what they are! Primitives who take perverse delight in torturing others! To think, I once admired them! I once thought of them as mysterious and noble!"

Fargo tried again. "How were you to know? A legend is just another name for a tall tale and tall tales always stretch the truth."

Camilla Kemp put her fists to her temples and hissed through slitted lips, "I've never been a vengeful person. But if I could, I would wipe them off the face of the earth. I would kill every last man, woman, and child, and I would be doing the world a service."

Fargo glanced at Nayokona. The young Delaware had lain back down and placed a forearm across his face, over his eyes. He was taking the death of his father hard. Fargo wished there was something he could say or do to lessen the warrior's sorrow but there wasn't. Camilla was proof of that.

"But then, why bother?" she said, and a budding maniacal gleam lit her eyes. "They're killing themselves off. Given time, Nature will succeed where everyone else has failed. The Killamak will cease to exist."

"They will?" Fargo was worried about her state of mind. She was dangerously close to breaking.

"Haven't you noticed?" Camilla said. "According to the legends, the Killamak were a robust, handsome people. But look at them. They're stunted and deformed. Largely infertile, too, I suspect, or there would be a lot more children." The scientist in her asserted itself and she rambled on. "The smallpox epidemic that wiped most of them out is to blame. Centuries of inbreeding have taken a fearsome toll. There can't be more than three or four dozen left. Another generation or two and they won't be able to have any children at all. The Killamak will fade into oblivion as they so rightfully deserve." She had settled down at last. Dabbing at her eyes, she said, "Please forgive my outburst. It's the strain. I've been alone for weeks now, with no one to talk to except the Killamak."

"You speak their tongue?"

"A little, yes. I picked up a smattering from a journal kept by a French trapper who spent some time among them before the epidemic turned them against whites. I've learned more since they captured me."

"We need to find out what they've done with my revolver," Fargo said. "I intend to get you out. You and Nayokona, both."

Camilla smoothed her tattered dress. "I appreciate the sentiment, Mr. Fargo, but you're deluding yourself. We're watched twenty-four hours a day. At night they bar the entrances and post sentries on the palisade." She bit her lower lip. "There's no escape, I'm afraid. We're all going to die, and no one will ever know what became of us."

Not if Fargo could help it. "Did the chief send you to talk to us? Or do they let you have the run of the place?"

"Except for an old woman who follows me everywhere I go, I'm pretty much left on my own," Camilla said. "They know I'm not going anywhere. Even if I made it to the woods, they'd hunt me down in no time. They can track by scent, just like dogs."

"What do you think they did with my Colt?" Fargo asked. He still had his gunbelt and plenty of cartridges. He also had the Arkansas toothpick. The Killamak hadn't thought to look inside his boot.

"My guess is their leader has it," Camilla said. "They've seen white men use guns and know guns are deadly. Tenecicomesh collects them but hasn't quite figure out how to make them work."

"Is that the chief's name?"

Camilla nodded. "As best as I can pronounce it. He's a mean one. He enjoys cracking skulls, enjoys inflicting pain. He laughed when Harold begged to be spared, laughed when Heather cried and whimpered.

So did most of the others. They have no compassion, no mercy."

Nayokona lowed his arm. "There is one thing I would very much like to know. Why do the Killamak eat brains?"

"They believe all people have a soul or spirit essence, and that it's housed in the human brain. When they eat the brains of their captives, they think that they are eating some of the spirit essence. They think its energy, its strength, will flow into them and make them stronger." Camilla swiped at a stray bang. "I've read about tribes in South America who believe something similar, only they eat the heart."

"They ate my father's brain?"

"No, as a matter of fact," Camilla said, and the young warrior radiated relief. "It's sort of complicated, but they won't eat the brain of anyone who has slain a Killamak. Something to do with it tainting the essence and bringing bad luck to whoever eats it."

"Again you have made my heart glad," Nayokona said. "I, too, will do what I can to help you escape these devils."

The curtain abruptly parted and Tenecicomesh stepped onto the platform. Behind him were six burly warriors, well-armed. The chief gazed contemptuously down at Fargo and the Delaware, then growled at Camilla, who translated.

"The great chief, as he styles himself, says the two of you are to be sacrificed. One of you will have your brains eaten tomorrow night. The other later on."

Fargo slowly rose. It took every ounce of self-control he possessed not to take a swing and wipe the vicious sneer off Tenecicomesh's face. "Tell this bastard that if he harms us, other white men will come. More white men than there are blades of grass. They will bring many guns and they will destroy his people."

Camilla did as she was bid but Tenecicomesh was

218

no fool. He laughed, and turning to her, he went on at some length.

"He says you lie. He says his scouts have told him that most of the whites have gone." Camilla blanched. "For lying to him, he has decided you will be the first to die. Tomorrow night when the moon is overhead, his people will feed on your essence."

Tenecicomesh said something more, something that brought a crimson tinge to Camilla's cheeks.

"What is it?" Fargo asked.

"He reminded me of their custom. When they sacrifice an enemy, they always kill a female captive to act as his guide in the next world since he can no longer think for himself. An act of kindness, the chief calls it." Camilla paused. "The night before the sacrifice, the man and the woman are put together so they can get to know one another and will be compatible in the spirit world."

Fargo glanced at Tenecicomesh, then at her. It couldn't be.

"I'm to be your guide," Camilla disclosed. "I'm to die when you do. But tonight you and I must make love."

16

It was after sunset when the Killamak leader returned. By then Skye Fargo had learned more of what was expected of him. Camilla explained that if either of them refused to go along with the ritual, they would be sadistically tortured like Nayokona's father.

"He was a long time dying," she stressed.

To Fargo the idea was preposterous. He liked to make love as much as any man—hell, more than most, if his unending string of dalliances were any indication—but being forced to do it whether he wanted to or not went against his grain. He resented being told what to do by anyone, especially a smug son of a bitch like Tenecicomesh. "We don't have to go through with it," he said for Camilla's sake. "We can fight our way out when they come for us, gun or no gun."

"And be slain before we reach the entrance?" Camilla shook her head. "I won't have another death on my conscience. Not yours, not Tonekotay's son. Not if I can help it. I thought I made that clear?"

Nayokona studied her with renewed interest. "You would give yourself to him to gain an extra day of life?"

At that, Camilla blushed and glanced away.

Fargo studied her, too, debating what to do. Under ordinary circumstances he wouldn't hesitate to go to bed with her. She was immensely attractive. Her blonde hair, her green eyes, the ample swell of her cleavage, and the creamy contours of her thighs were enough to excite any man. But these weren't ordinary circumstances. She was being denied the right to say no if she wanted. The Killamak were forcing him on her, and Fargo had never forced a woman to go to bed with him his whole life long. "I understand how you feel," he said, "but we won't do it if you don't want to."

"You don't know what you're saying," Camilla replied. "You didn't see what they did to Tonekotay."

Fargo grasped her hand and she entwined her fingers with his. Her palm was warm to the touch. "Some things are worth fighting for." He'd always known he might buck out in gore some day. Few frontiersmen lived to a ripe old age. Life on the frontier was too violent and unpredictable.

Camilla faced him. "I can't let you suffer on my account. No woman could. For my own peace of mind we have to do as they want."

Fargo thought back to his talk with her uncle. She was so attractive and alluring, she must attract men like honey drew bears. It said a lot about her willpower that she was still a virgin. He figured she must be saving herself for the right man, so he gave her one more chance to back out. "What they want doesn't matter. Follow my lead when they return. We'll either get away or die trying."

"It would be suicide," Camilla insisted.

Fargo had a brainstorm. "What if we only pretend to make love? That would let you off the hook."

"They would know."

"How?" Fargo wouldn't put it past the Killamak to have the entire tribe stand around and watch.

"I'll be examined afterward by one of the women," Camilla revealed, and shuddered. "A very thorough examination. If we don't go through with it, she'll know." She touched his cheek. "It's sweet of you to try and spare me, but I've made up my mind."

That had been hours ago. Now, as the hide curtain

was jerked aside by Tenecicomesh, Fargo rose from the furs and helped Camilla to stand. The chief snarled at her, and motioned. Behind him were half a dozen warriors.

"He says we are to go with them to a special place," Camilla translated. "He warns us not to try any tricks or he'll have you gutted and strangled with your own intestines."

Most of the warriors held war clubs. Half were on the right, half on the left, blocking the center aisle. Camilla stepped down first. Fargo glanced over a shoulder at Nayokona, who was propped against the wall. "Get as much rest as you can while we're gone. You'll need your strength when the time comes."

Tenecicomesh assumed the lead and headed toward the opposite end of the long house. The chief strode with his head high, his staff striking the earthen floor with each stride.

Women were busy preparing stew in the giant pots. Every compartment was occupied. In some, mothers and daughters were sewing hides, or brushing their long black hair with combs made from porcupine quills, or painting their torsos. The men, for the most part, were sitting around talking. As the procession filed by, everyone shot to their feet. The warriors bowed their chins. The women dropped to their knees.

"They think they're doing us a great honor," Camilla said.

Fargo saw a giant wooden chair or throne that stood in the center of the open space up ahead. Bearskin pelts similar to the one Tenecicomesh wore were draped over the back and sides. On a bench beside it, on the right, were undamaged human skulls. On a bench on the left were weapons confiscated from white captives; guns, knives, and swords lying in a jumbled pile. His pulse quickened when he glimpsed his Colt.

Two of the hefty guards either noticed or were

smarter than they seemed. They closed in, their shoulders brushing his, and hefted their war clubs, intimating the outcome if he attempted anything rash.

Tenecicomesh climbed a pair of short steps to his throne. Facing his followers, he intoned a few words, took his seat, and signaled. Two warriors promptly gripped Camilla by the wrists, ushered her to the steps, and compelled her to kneel.

Fargo didn't think she was in any danger so he didn't interfere. The chief gave a short speech, made a few passes in the air with the hardwood staff, and touched it to Camilla's shoulders. Then it was Fargo's turn. He allowed them to push him to the steps, and knelt. The bench with the guns was only a few feet away, a temptation almost too great to resist. But he'd never reach it with the warriors so close.

Tenecicomesh went through the same motions as he had with Camilla. When he was done, he rose and elevated his arms overhead. Wolfish whoops erupted from every throat, male and female, young and old, raising the rafters with their din. At a nod from Tenecicomesh, warriors seized Fargo and Camilla and forcibly guided them to an empty room a dozen feet past the throne. Without ceremony they were flung inside and the curtain was snapped shut.

"Oh my," Camilla said.

The chamber, by Killamak standards, was lavishly furnished. Soft hides covered the platform and the wall. Others separated it from adjacent compartments. A small wooden tray had been set at one end. On it were a pitcher of water and a heaping plate of venison jerky.

Fargo was ravenous. Hunkering, he grabbed a handful and sat back. The venison was freshly made and delicious. He offered a piece to Camilla, but she declined.

"I couldn't eat at a time like this."

The bars that supported the curtains didn't quite

reach to the overhead shelf, and rosy light from the cook fires streamed in the gap. It was bright enough for Fargo to see how embarrassed she was, and to want to kick himself for not being more considerate. "Well, you know how men are. Always thinking of their bellies."

A halfhearted grin was his reward. "My grandmother used to say that the way to a man's heart was through his stomach. It must be true. Every woman I've ever met has agreed with her."

"It's still not too late to back out," Fargo made one final effort. "I won't hold it against you."

"You wouldn't, but I would," Camilla looked down at herself. "I'm such a mess. I wish they'd let me bathe. I'd rather we did it on a nice bed with pillows and a quilt and everything, but this will have to do."

Fargo had no need to ask what "it" was. She was nervous, talking to hear herself talk. He slid closer to suggest it might be best if she changed her mind, but she suddenly reached out and placed her hands on both sides of his head.

"Promise me you'll be gentle. Promise me you'll treat me like a lady." Camilla's grip tightened. "And promise me that if by some miracle we make it out alive, you'll never tell another soul."

"I promise," Fargo said, and held up the piece of jerky. "Care for a bite?"

"All I want is to get this over with," Camilla said, and glued her mouth to his.

Fargo was momentarily taken aback by the passionate urgency in her kiss, and even more so by the knowing manner in which she glided her satiny tongue into his mouth and swirled it around his own. Even more unexpected was the hand she lowered to his lap and the sensual way in which she rubbed his inner thighs. Most virgins would be much too shy to do such a thing. It had an undeniable effect, and dropping the jerky, he wrapped his arms around her and pulled her body close. His chest cushioned by her bosom, her legs pressed against his, slowly he lowered her onto her side.

After a while Camilla broke the kiss. She was breathing heavily and her voice was husky. "You do that really well."

"I try," Fargo said, wondering how a virgin would know. He nuzzled her ear and teased the lobe with the tip of his tongue, then sucked it as he would a nipple. She responded by gasping and arching her back.

"You're making me break out in goosebumps!"

Fargo was going to do a lot more than that before he was through. He switched to her neck, licking and sucking it until she squirmed and cooed in rising need. Her fingers stroked the back of his neck and kneaded his broad shoulders. Slowly lathering a path down across her collar bone to the valley beneath her mounds, Fargo immersed himself in the exquisite softness of her cleavage. It was like lying between two pillows. Her breasts were marvelously soft and pliant. When he lightly kissed one, she shivered all over.

Plucking at the dress, Fargo slid it partway off her left shoulder. Her left globe slid loose and her nipple jutted toward him in silent invitation. He rimmed it with his lips and gently pulled, eliciting a low groan. Her fingernails scraped his biceps. He tweaked her nipple, then sucked on it a bit.

Camilla sighed and wriggled her hips back and forth, her eyes hooded. Her cherry lips creased in a languid smile. "You do have a knack, don't you?"

Although Fargo was still willing to give her the benefit of the doubt, he had to admit that if someone were to offer him odds, he'd take ten-to-one odds against her being as pure as driven snow. Or week-old snow, for that matter. He would find out soon enough. She clearly wanted him, and he could no more say no to a beautiful woman than he could give up breathing.

The circumstances were unusual, to say the least. Fargo listened but heard nothing to indicate the Killamak were outside the compartment, eavesdropping. Nor, when he scanned the curtains, did he see any shadows. Evidently Camilla and him were to be left alone. Another part of the ritual, no doubt.

Struck by an idea, Fargo stopped sucking on her nipple and whispered, "How long?"

"How long what?" Camilla dreamily replied, her right hand rising to trace the outline of his jaw.

"How much time do we have before the Killamak come for us?"

Camilla giggled. "Oh, don't worry. They won't barge in on us in the middle of things. We have all night together."

Did they, indeed? Fargo mused. An avenue of escape had opened. But before he could put his plan into effect, he had to convince the Killamak he had entered into the spirit of things and that attempting to escape was the farthest thing from his mind.

Fargo eased Camilla onto her back. In the pale half-light her skin acquired a lustrous sheen that accented the upthrust curve of her rounded globes and the smooth contours of her thighs. He slid a hand between her willowy legs and they parted to admit him. Caressing them from hip to knee, he lowered his mouth to hers once more. Her lips were molten fire, her tongue a dervish of desire. Her hands strayed to his buttocks and kneaded them as she'd knead dough for making bread.

For a virgin Camilla was remarkably uninhibited. Fargo's doubts mounted. So did his hunger as his manhood bulged against his pants. He stopped thinking about the Killamak, stopped thinking about their predicament, and devoted himself to the carnal delights at hand. Their kiss lingered on and on, their bodies growing hotter by the minute. At long last Camilla drew back to catch her breath, panting heavily, and fanned her face with a hand.

"My goodness! What you do to me."

Fargo began to undo the fasteners on the back of her dress. Many were missing, ripped off when her garment was torn, so it only took a few moments to loosen it enough to slide it off. He reached up, and for the first time Camilla had reservations. She grasped his wrist and peered deep into his eyes.

"You will be gentle, won't you? Like you promised?"

"I would never hurt you." Fargo started to inch the dress off, but she didn't let go of his arm.

"It's just that I don't have a lot of experience in this regard," Camilla told him.

Fargo smiled to encourage her and she dropped her hand so he could continue.

"The only other man I've ever been with treated me much too roughly," Camilla said softly.

"Other man?" Fargo said.

"He liked to squeeze me so hard it hurt." Camilla paused. "I would never have expected it of Professor Petticord."

Petticord? Fargo drew back in surprise. "Your teacher from college? The one who was with you when you were caught by the Killamak?"

"Artemis was more than a teacher. He was my mentor. My friend. As sweet a person as you'd ever want to meet." Camilla gazed at the top of the compartment. "It was on a dig. One night we were in his tent, sitting around sipping brandy, and before I knew it, he began fondling me. I was so scared I didn't know what to do so I didn't do anything. And, to be honest, I sort of liked it. But it was over much too soon. Afterward, I cried. Artemis apologized. He said he didn't know what had gotten into him, and he begged my forgiveness."

Fargo remembered a comment by someone at the Kemp mansion. "Wasn't he old enough to be your father?"

"So? Artemis was a good-hearted, kind human being. I didn't care how old he was, or that he had a wife. I only knew I adored him. The second time we did it was better than the first, and so were all the times after that. But he was always rough. I never could understand why."

Fargo wondered how many other female students the randy professor had dallied with over the years. And what Lucius Kemp would say if he learned the niece he had put on a pedestal was no more virtuous than his other nieces and nephews? A thought jarred him. Camilla knew she was the heir-apparent. She also must know why; Ronnie and Beda and the others did. Yet she hadn't owned up to her indiscretions. She had let Lucius go on believing she was a virgin when she wasn't. She was after her uncle's money just like all the rest. Leaning on an elbow, he chuckled to himself.

Camilla misunderstood. "What's so funny? The idea of the professor and I being secret lovers? I'll have you know he was more than willing to leave his wife for me. That's how serious we were. But he couldn't, not with her health problems. He was afraid the shock would kill her."

"Her health?" Fargo said.

"You wouldn't know it to look at her, but his wife suffers from a lung condition. Artemis confided that they kept it a secret because they didn't want everyone to feel sorry for her."

Fargo smothered a laugh. Camilla was supposed to be smart. She had graduated from a prestigious university with some of the highest grades in her class. She was strong-willed and independent. Yet she had fallen for one of the oldest ruses around.

"Anyway, now you know why I want you to be gentle. I never did like it as rough as Artemis did."

"Really?" Fargo covered her right breast and squeezed. Not lightly, either.

Camilla came partway up off the platform. "Ohhhhhhhhh! Yessssssss!"

Fargo squeezed her other mound. The gleam that lit her eyes belied her claim. She dug her fingers into his flesh as if seeking to rip his arm off, and her mouth fused on his, hotter than ever. Replacing his left hand with his mouth, he inhaled her rigid nipple and pulled with his lips, stretching her breast taut.

"Harder! Do it harder!"

Fargo removed her clothes and tossed them to one side. A musky scent filled his nostrils as she threw her legs wide and reached for him.

"I need this, need this so much," Camilla breathed. "I can't ever get enough. I want to feel what it's like one more time before I die."

Fargo slid between her legs. Balancing on his knees, he licked her silken legs. He slowly licked steadily higher until his mouth brushed her moist slit. At the contact she cried out, placed both of her hands behind his head, and pushed him hard against her.

"More! I want more! Use your tongue! Like that! Ahhhhhhhhh!"

Accommodating her, Fargo looped his arms around her thighs to hold her bucking hips still. The Killamak were bound to hear, but that fitted his plan perfectly. They wouldn't be expecting trouble and would let down their guard.

"Oh God!" Camilla exclaimed. "You have no idea what you're doing to me!" To demonstrate her point, she pumped up off the furs, nearly dislodging him, and ground her womanhood against his mouth. "Oh! Oh! Deeper! Please! Deeper!"

Fargo's lip brushed her swollen knob, triggering a whirlwind of wildly shaking limbs and raking nails. She spurted, and he tasted her sweet nectar. Her thighs constricted like twin pythons onto his temples and ears. He held on as best he could, licking and flicking all the way home. By then she had subsided and lay moaning and trembling, her arms and legs limp.

Fargo was in no rush. The longer they took, the less likely the Killamak were to suspect a trick. He ran his hands up over her flat stomach to her melons. Camilla sighed and smiled. Sliding upward, he lay on top of her, his pole gouging a thigh. She shifted and sought to impale herself on him but he wasn't quite ready.

"Make me forget," Camilla pleaded. "Make me forget the horror of it all."

Fargo compromised. He kissed her breasts, her shoulders, her throat. He sucked on her tongue. He stroked her sides, rubbed her back, slid his palms up and down her legs. He did everything except touch Camilla where she yearned to be touched the most, and her hunger rose accordingly. She tossed her head and groaned, her nails digging furrows in his back. Her hips were in constant motion, rocking up and down, enticing him to take that next consummate step.

Fargo's manhood was pulsing. He held out as long as he could, until his need could no longer be denied. Holding himself steady, he aligned the tip of his member with her wet core and teased her one last time.

"Ahhhh! Yes! Put it in!"

By gradual degrees Fargo fed himself into her. She became impatient and elevated her bottom, but he drew back to entice her to the heights of anticipation.

Camilla was practically beside herself. "Please!" she begged. "I can't take much more of this! Do it, damn you!"

Grinning, Fargo molded his hands to her bottom, tensed his legs, and rammed up into her. Camilla's mouth gaped wide but no sounds came out. For a few moments she was completely still, transfixed by the raw pleasure coursing through her veins. Then she uttered an inarticulate cry and clasped him to her as if she were drowning and he was her only hope of staying afloat.

Fargo didn't move, other than to nibble at her hair line and to delicately nip at her right ear. Suddenly Camilla exploded into motion, her red-hot body the fulcrum to his lever. She heaved upward, bearing him with her, her legs pumping rhythmically, seeking to attain the pinnacle that much sooner. But Fargo refused to gush too soon. Pacing himself, he repeatedly sheathed his iron sword in her mink-lined scabbard.

"I never knew! I never knew!" Camilla declared, without saying exactly what it was she hadn't known. She kissed him, she stroked him, her hands and mouth moving faster and faster to match the frantic pumping of her finely sculpted legs.

The platform under them rattled to the pounding of their bodies. The curtains fluttered as if in a strong breeze. Fargo couldn't have been happier. The more noise they made, the less likely the Killamak were to anticipate trouble.

"Harder!" Camilla prodded. "Harder and faster!"

Fargo speared himself in to the hilt, lifting her off the furs, and she screeched like an alley cat. Any modesty she possessed had evaporated in the red-hot heat of passion. She was absorbed in their lovemaking to the exclusion of all else. At that instant Fargo couldn't help thinking that she wasn't any different than Beda or Pandora. Or Ronnie, for that matter. She was a normal woman with normal urges, not the saint her uncle made her out to be.

"I'm almost there!"

So was Fargo, but he held the surging tide back as long as he could. Camilla's legs rose higher and her heels locked behind his back. She bit his shoulder. She cupped him low down, and it was the catalyst both of them needed.

The compartment blurred. His mouth grew dry. his body prickled madly. All a prelude to his climax. They both moaned and groaned as the moment came. The furs, the platform, the longhouse receded into nothingness. There was just the two of them, lost in a world of their own, their senses reeling from the assault of undiluted bliss.

Fargo rocked until he was drained. As he slowed, Camilla sagged, perspiration sprinkling her forehead, her hair damp. She tried to kiss him but lacked the energy to raise her head. A twisted smile creased her face.

"Thank you. Thank you so much."

Easing off her, Fargo rolled onto his side. He was tired and sweaty and craved sleep, but instead he hitched at his pants, buckled his gunbelt back on, and sat up. The Killamak would expect them to rest a while but that was exactly what they shouldn't do. Flattening, he crawled to the front curtain.

Camilla shifted to see what he was doing. "Where are you going?" she demanded. "We have all night together, remember?"

"We're getting out of here," Fargo whispered, and cracked the curtain enough to scan the central aisle. He didn't see any warriors. All that stood between their compartment and the throne was a single cooking fire tended by a middle-aged woman holding a large wooden dipper. Near her squatted a girl of twelve or so who was playing with a small doll.

"Are you crazy?" Camilla said, sitting up. "We'll be killed that much sooner."

"Get dressed," Fargo commanded. All they had to do was reach the bench with the guns. Once he had the Colt in his hand, he would blast their way out. If he died, he would die as he had always imagined he would, not hog-tied and helpless, but with guns ablazin'.

"I wish you would reconsider," Camilla said, tugging into her underthings. "Tenecicomesh will be furious. He's liable to sacrifice us tonight instead of tomorrow night."

Fargo motioned for her to hurry up. He glanced both ways to confirm the guards were gone, then rose into a crouch. It was another minute before Camilla sidled next to him. Touching a finger to his lips, he eased the curtain open far enough for him to slide a leg over the edge of the platform.

A startled grunt to his left was his first inkling he had blundered.

As it turned out, Tenecicomesh *had* left guards, a pair of beefy warriors who had sat down with their backs to the next compartment. Uttering beastlike growls, they shoved to their feet and brandished heavy war clubs.

17

The die was cast. Skye Fargo had to make his bid for freedom right then and there. If he climbed back into the compartment he might never get a better chance. So as the two burly warriors rose to confront him, he sprang. He smashed his right fist full into the face of the foremost Killamak, knocking him back against the other. Both staggered, but neither went down. They were short but they were immensely powerful, and what they lacked in height they more than made up for in corded sinews.

Grabbing the first man's war club, Fargo tore it free. He had to dispose of them quickly, before they yelled to warn the rest. Pivoting, he swashed the club against the first man's temple and the warrior toppled, taking his companion down with him.

A scream pierced the longhouse, courtesy of the woman at the cookfire.

Fargo turned. Camilla Kemp had slid from the compartment and was riveted in consternation. Seizing her by the elbow, he flew toward the bench beside the throne.

The little girl leaped out of his path, but not her mother. Snarling like a she-bear, the big-boned Killamak threw herself at him with the wooden dipper raised to strike.

Fargo hit her. He drove the knobby end of the hardwood club into her gut and she collapsed onto her hands and knees. But she wasn't to be denied. As he bounded past, she shrieked and flung her arms around his right leg, bringing him to an abrupt halt.

"Behind you!" Camilla bleated.

The second warrior was rising. Fargo shook his leg to dislodge the woman but she clung to him with the stubborn persistence of a riled wolverine, all the while screeching for help. All along the central aisle curtains were being jerked open and hairy heads were poking out.

Camilla was the same shade as a bed sheet. "Do something!" she beseeched him.

Left with no recourse, Fargo slammed the war club against the Killamak woman's head. She slumped, and he kicked her aside and broke into a run, pulling Camilla along after him. She was petrified and moved woodenly, slowing him down. "Run, damn it!" he bellowed, and let go so he could go faster. Every second was crucial. Shouts of alarm were spreading from one end of the longhouse to the other and warriors were rushing from both directions.

Fear lent wings to Camilla's feet. She stayed on his heels, and nearly collided with him when he stopped and bent over the bench. "Whatever you're going to do, you had better do quickly!"

Fargo thought he remembered exactly where his revolver had been but he didn't spot it amid the pile. He was about to snatch up a Smith and Wesson when he spied the Colt. Its smooth grips fit his calloused palm as if they were a natural extension of his hand. He spun the cylinder to verify the cartridges hadn't been removed, and whirled.

The second guard was almost on top of them, war club hiked high.

Fargo shot him through the chest. Pivoting, he fanned two swift shots at a pair of warriors and both sprawled to the dirt.

Pandemonium ensued. Women and children screamed and dived for cover. The rest of the onrushing warriors slowed, brandishing their weapons and whooping in a feral frenzy. A bow string twanged and a long shaft sliced through the curtain on Fargo's right. Spinning, he sent a slug into the forehead of the Killamak responsible.

Among the two dozen guns on the bench was a Spencer. Hoping to high heaven it was loaded, Fargo shoved the Colt into his holster and jammed the rifle's stock to his shoulder. He fired as rapidly as he could work the lever, dropping two warriors on the right and another on the left, the shots booming like a cannonade.

Somewhere someone roared commands in the Killamak tongue. It sounded like Tenecicomesh. The warriors melted into adjacent compartments and drew the curtains after them.

Fargo had to hand it to the wily chieftain. Tenecicomesh knew clubs and bows were no match for guns in the closed confines of the longhouse. Within moments the central aisle was empty save for a bawling infant strapped to a cradleboard, neglected by its mother.

"You did it!" Camilla marveled.

Fargo knew better. They weren't out of danger yet. Far from it. "Can you use one of these?" he asked, picking up the Smith and Wesson. He tossed it to her and she awkwardly caught it.

"I've never shot a gun before, but I can try."

"Watch behind us," Fargo instructed. "If anyone rushes us, shoot." Snagging a Remington pistol, he wedged it under his belt Then, swinging the Spencer from side to side, he glided toward the compartment where they had left the Delaware. He was surprised the young warrior hadn't already emerged. "Nayokona!" he called, but there was no reply.

With most of the curtains drawn, Fargo couldn't tell which compartments were occupied and which weren't. A noise to his left caused him to spin, but it was only a little boy curious about the uproar. A curtain to his right moved but no one appeared.

"There's one trying to sneak up on us!" Camilla bawled, and the Smith and Wesson cracked.

Fargo started to glance back, but the barbed tip of an arrow protruded from behind a curtain in front of them. He fired into the hide at chest height and was rewarded with a strangled outcry and a loud thud. "Nayokona!" he yelled again. "Can you hear me?"

"Skye!" Camilla shrieked.

A sinewy Killamak had burst from a compartment on the other side and was hefting a lance to throw it. Twisting, Fargo snapped off a slug that drilled the man's sternum. For a few seconds afterward all was still, but it wouldn't be for long. The Killamak weren't about to let them leave.

Further down, the curtain to the compartment Nayokona was in opened and out shuffled the young Delaware. He had a hand pressed to his side and was wincing in pain. In his other hand was a war club. "When I heard the first shot I jumped my guard," he said, nodding at the curtain. A crescent-shaped moccasin poked from underneath it. "He was a skilled fighter."

"Use this." Fargo slipped Nayokona the Remington. "And don't waste a shot." They hastened toward the entrance and saw that the heavy barrier was braced against the opening, blocking them in.

Another loud command from across the way was relayed from compartment to compartment, on down the length of the longhouse.

"That was Tenecicomesh," Camilla translated. "He told the others to wait, that once we're in the forest we'll be easy to bring down."

"That's what he thinks," Fargo said, moving faster.

Camilla clutched at her throat. "The chief is right. There are too many of them. In the woods, in the dark, we won't stand a chance."

"We won't stand a chance in here if they changed

their minds and decide to rush us all at once," Fargo pointed out. A nearby curtain started to billow outward and he swung the Spencer, but it was only an old Killamak woman who took one look and jerked back as if she had been scalded with hot water.

Fargo passed the last compartment. He kicked at the log bracing the wooden barrier but it wouldn't budge.

"Permit me." Nayokona squatted, curled his free arm around the log, and lifted. Weakened by the beating he had endured and his scrape with the guard, he was unable to move it far enough. Without being asked, Camilla stepped up and added her strength to his. Between them, they pushed the log to one side and it rolled to the ground with a resounding crash.

The solid slab of wood was still wedged against the opening. Nayokona took one side, Camilla the other. Planting their feet, they strained mightily. Their faces became red, their necks corded, but all they accomplished was to slide the barrier a few inches to the right.

"We can't do it by ourselves," Camilla said.

Fargo was loathe to relinquish the Spencer, but there was no other way out of the longhouse except for the other opening at the far end, which had also been barricaded. Shoving the rifle at her, he barked, "Watch the Killamak." Then he bent his shoulder to the foot-thick slab, nodded at the Delaware, and threw every ounce of strength he possessed into moving it. The thing had to weigh upwards of three hundred pounds. If fire ever broke out, the Killamak would be hard pressed to make it out of their dwelling alive.

A fire. In his excitement Fargo nearly lost his hold. Muscles rippling, he redoubled his effort and the slab slid another two feet. "That's far enough." He reclaimed the Spencer and covered the central aisle. "Ladies first," he said. "Keep your eyes skinned for sentries."

Camilla stooped, shifted sideways, and wriggled through. Nayokona went next. A few heads popped out of curtains and Fargo fired a shot into the roof to discourage them from mounting an attack. The heads were promptly withdrawn, except for that of a girl of eight or so who gaped at him in mesmerized fascination.

The nearest cookfire was ten feet from the entrance. Fargo ran to it and picked up a burning brand by the unlit end. He cocked his arm, then hesitated, glancing at the girl. The longhouse would go up like a tinder box; Killamak were bound to perish. Hopefully, none would be children. "I'm sorry," he said, and tossed the flaming brand as far as he could, onto the overhead shelf on the left. Grabbing another, he threw it to the right and it fell next to a curtain. Almost instantly the hide caught and flames licked upward.

Moving swiftly, Fargo threw several more. By then smoke was pouring from the shelf and several compartments were on fire. Screams rose in strident terror, and heads poked into the open.

Fargo didn't waste any more ammunition. He backpedaled to the entrance, tucked at the knees, and slid outside.

The night was cool, the sky a quiltwork of stars. Nayokona and Camilla had only gone a few yards, where they stood quietly waiting for him. "Run like hell," Fargo yelled, and sprinted toward the gate. Movement atop the palisade pinpointed a sentry, an archer who was notching a shaft to the string of his bow. Fargo thumbed back the Spencer's hammer, slowed for the barest instant, and fired. The warrior staggered and sank to a knee but didn't collapse. Fumbling at a bone-handled knife at his waist, he moved toward a rickety ladder. Fargo worked the Spencer's lever and stroked the trigger a second time, but the result was a metallic click. The magazine was empty. Tossing the rifle aside, he drew his Colt. The warrior had reached the ladder and was descending. Fargo took deliberate aim, and when the warrior twisted to look in their direction, he shot the Killamak through the head.

By now an uproar of thunderous proportions engulfed the longhouse. Women and children keened in mortal terror. Warriors were shouting and roaring at the top of their lungs. The fire was spreading rapidly, fueled by the dry elm bark. Reddish-orange flames licked the roof and the sides, and thick columns of grayish smoke billowed into the sky.

"You set it on *fire*?" Camilla asked in astonishment.

"We needed to slow them down," Fargo said as he seized hold of the gate. Nayokona lent a hand.

Camilla pointed at the rapidly spreading conflagration. "But there are women and children in there! They'll be roasted alive!"

"If their men know honor, they'll leave us be so they can save their own," Fargo said. Another second, and the gate was wide open. He gave the palisade a once-over, saw no warriors, and grabbed her hand. "Let's light a shuck."

"It's not right," Camilla said, digging in her heels. "We should help them."

Fargo yanked so hard she almost fell, hauling her toward the murky wall of vegetation. "Are you loco? Would you rather they take us hostage again?" He nodded toward the platform. "Would you rather they tie us on their altar and smash our brains out?"

"No, but—"

"Then *run*!" Fargo said, and propelled her toward the trees. She complied, but she was none too happy. Nayokona was already well ahead of them, dashing determinedly for cover. Fargo brought up the rear, running sideways so he could keep an eye on the longhouse.

Smoke was pouring from the entrance. So were Killamak. Coughing and sputtering, over a dozen had made it out, and more were joining them. Several collapsed on the grass, overcome. Others turned to help those who were still inside. A bawling girl was next, the same girl Fargo had seen inside, and he was glad she was safe. After her came a heavyset woman, then several warriors in a row.

Tenecicomesh wasn't one of them. Fargo didn't see him anywhere. He hoped the vicious chieftain ended up burnt alive. Without Tenecicomesh to lead them, confusion would run riot, and it was less likely the Killamak would give chase. Then, at the very moment the foliage closed about him, Fargo saw the leader stagger from the longhouse.

Doubledamn! Fargo thought, and devoted himself to covering as much ground as the three of them could, as rapidly as they could. Nayokona was moving to the southeast at a steady dog-trot, a pace he could probably sustain indefinitely. Camilla ran lithely, her tattered dress swirling about her milky legs, affording a flash of creamy thigh now and again.

Fargo was preoccupied with listening for sounds of pursuit. Sooner or later it would come. It was inevitable. Tenecicomesh would thirst for revenge on those who had destroyed the tribe's home.

The seconds dragged into minutes and the minutes piled on as they ventured deeper into the woods. Camilla flagged but gamely persevered. Fargo only had to help her once, when she tripped over an exposed root and almost fell.

They had covered at least five miles when Camilla finally slowed. Exhausted, she called out, "I need to rest! I can't go on like this!" Breathing heavily, she ambled over to a log and sat down.

Fargo stopped, turned, and tilted his head. Other than the spectral sigh of the wind and the rustling of leaves, the night was uncommonly quiet. "You get five minutes," he said. "That's all." They couldn't afford more.

Nayokona had halted and was leaning against a tree. "The Shadow People will want our blood for what we have done," he commented. "They will not bother to capture us alive this time."

Camilla placed a hand to her bosom and greedily sucked in air. "Maybe not," she said. "Maybe they'll take our escape as a bad omen and let us go."

"There is a saying among my tribe," the young Delaware said. "To kill one of the Shadow People is to invite death into your lodge." He stared to the northwest. "They never forgive, never forget. Harm one, and the tribe will not rest until the killer is food for the worms."

The way Fargo saw it, they had one hope, and one hope alone. Owen Hamilton and a dozen seasoned backwoodsmen were supposed to be waiting for him less than twenty-five miles from where they stood. If they could link up with Hamilton, they might make it out alive. He mentioned it to the others.

"Twenty-five miles is a lot of ground to cover," Camilla groused.

"Better to cover it than be buried in it," Nayokona said. "If we push on through the night and into the new day, we can reach them by tomorrow evening."

Fargo perched on the log beside Camilla. "How are you holding up?"

"Physically? Well enough, I guess," she wearily answered. "But I doubt I'll ever fully recover emotionally. Seeing my friends murdered. Seeing my mentor sacrificed. It will haunt my dreams for the rest of my life."

"Not if you don't let them," Fargo said.

Camilla looked at him, her brow puckered. "You've witnessed atrocities almost as bad, I take it?"

"Worse."

Snorting in disbelief, Camilla said, "How can anything be worse than watching someone you care for have their brains bashed out?"

"You've never seen Apaches at work. Or what Comanches do to settlers." Fargo saw she was still skeptical, so he elaborated. "In the Green River a few years back, a Blackfoot foot party was caught in Crow territory. Hundreds of Crows surrounded them and they had nowhere to go. The Blackfeet held out for hours but eventually were overrun. The wounded were laid out in rows, and the Crows went from man to man, gouging out their eyes, cutting out their tongues, chopping off their noses and their ears, slicing open their stomachs and ripping out their intestines. I saw it all, every gory detail."

"My word," Camilla said, appalled. "How do you manage to sleep at night, then? Doesn't it get to you?"

"I've learned to shut it from my mind," Fargo said. "If you refuse to think about it, the nightmares will go away."

"I'll try," Camilla said, but she didn't sound confident.

Nayokona interrupted by saying, "We should move on. The Shadow People must be on our trail by now."

"We'll push on until dawn," Fargo proposed. By then they would be far enough from the village to justify resting for a couple of hours.

The night passed at a tortoise pace, a nerve-racking eternity of exertion and dread. They never knew when unearthly shrieks would herald the arrival of the Killamak. All three of them were tired and sore, Camilla most noticeably, when a pink band infused the eastern horizon with the promise of impending dawn.

"If we don't stop to rest, I'll keel over from exhaustion," she announced.

"A little ways yet," Fargo said. He wanted to press on until they came to more open country but they had miles of dense woodland to navigate yet. "A couple of hours rest is all we can spare. I'll keep watch while the two you get some sleep."

"That would not be fair," Nayokona said. "You

stand guard the first hour. I will stand guard the second."

Not a minute later they came to a small clearing. Camilla slowed to a walk, ambled to the center, slumped down in the knee-high grass. "I can't take another step. Go on without me if you want, but I'm worn out."

Fargo decided not to argue. Stepping to a flat boulder, he sat facing west so he could watch their back trail. "You must be looking forward to seeing your father and your uncle again," he said, as much to bolster her spirits as to give her cause not to oversleep.

"And my brother," Camilla said, curling onto her side and closing her eyes. "Don't forget him."

From out of the undergrowth bordering the south edge of the clearing came a mocking chuckle. "He hasn't forgotten you, missy."

Fargo leaped up and pivoted, but he was too slow. Three men had risen from hiding, their rifles leveled. Their rustic clothes and unkempt hair and beards pegged them as backwoodsmen, but something told him they weren't with Owen Hamilton's bunch.

Nayokona went to brandish the Remington.

"I wouldn't do that, if I were you, Injun," warned the scruffiest of the trio. "We've got orders to take the little miss and anyone with her alive, but if you don't send that six-shooter, I'll splatter your red guts from here to sundown."

For a second Fargo thought the young warrior would defy them but Nayokona did as he was instructed.

"Now you, mister," the scruffy spokesman said. "Toss your lead-pusher this way. And no fancy stuff, savvy?"

Camilla was on her feet, confusion and anger contorting her features. "What's the meaning of this? Who are you? What do you want?"

"The name is Skinner, ma'am," the man said.

"These are my pards. We were hired to track down the Trailsman, here, and step in when he found you."

"Hired by whom?" Camilla asked.

"Whom?" Skinner snickered. "Don't you talk elegant!" He nodded at one of his companions, who drew a revolver and fired three evenly spaced shots into the air. To the southeast, a few seconds later, banged three answering shots.

"You have no idea what you've just done," Fargo said. The Killamak would now know right where to find them.

"Sure I do," Skinner said. "We just signaled our employers. They're not far behind and should be here lickety-split." He jerked his Sharps a shade higher as Camilla started to raise the Smith and Wesson. "Behave yourself, missy. Do as the others did and chuck your artillery over to me."

The third man was glaring at Fargo. "We found Willy, you bastard. We know it was you who put two holes in him the size of walnuts. That's where we picked up your trail."

Willy? Fargo recalled the bushwhacker he had shot. "You've been following me ever since?"

Skinner was the one who answered. "We lost the sign a while back, shortly after we found where you had tangled with some Injuns wearin' the strangest moccasins I ever did see. We've been lookin' for more ever since." He grinned. "This mornin' we were up early and hadn't gone a quarter of a mile when, lo and behold, we spotted you comin' through the trees yonder."

"Right into our laps," crowed the third backwoodsman.

Hooves drummed in the distance. Fargo counted fourteen riders galloping toward them, the last leading a string of pack horses and a few saddled mounts. This, then, was the group of whites Nayokona had spotted the other day, the group that went out of its way to avoid Owen Hamilton's bunch. In the lead were faces he recognized. Young faces. *"The young ones,"* Willy had called them.

Camilla was bewildered. "It can't be!" she exclaimed as the riders drew rein and smirked at her in malicious glee. "Beda? Ronnie? Pandora? What on earth is going on?"

The siblings looked at one another and cackled.

Pandora interested Fargo the most. Her hair was now the same sandy color as Beda's, but there was no doubt it was the same woman who had posed as Bethany Wingate at the Imperial Inn and tried to murder him. She caught him studying her, and winked. "Did you miss me, handsome?"

Ronnie pushed a jaunty cap back on his head and regarded Camilla as he might a slug. "Well, well, well. So the reports of your demise were premature, my dear cousin. We'll have to remedy that, won't we?"

"What do you mean?" Camilla said, her confusion almost pitiable.

"Haven't you figured it out yet, sweet sister?" asked a fourth rider, who kneed a bay up alongside Ronnie.

"Laurel!" Camilla grinned and eagerly took a step toward him, but his harsh expression stopped her in her tracks. "Why are you looking at me like that?"

"Can't you guess?" her brother rejoined, and sighed. "I regret your life has to end, but that's what you get for being a paragon of virtue."

"I don't understand," Camilla said, her lower jaw quivering. She was close to tears. "Aren't you here to rescue me?"

"Hardly," Beda Kemp said. Like her sister, she wore a smart riding outfit and a peaked hat pinned to her hair to hold it in place. She glanced at Fargo. "I know you understand. Why don't you enlighten her, Trailsman?"

"I wish *someone* would!" Camilla mewed.

Under the wary gaze of Skinner and his friends,

Fargo moved toward her. "It's the inheritance," he explained. "With you out of the way, they think your uncle will select one of them to be his new heir."

Beda leaned on her saddle horn, her red lips crooked in delight. "Your disappearance, dear cousin, was a godsend. When we got together at Uncle Lucius's, we realized how much we all hate you. And how much each of us wants the fortune for our own. So we entered into a secret pact to ensure you never returned."

Camilla extended a limp hand toward her brother. "You too, Laurel?" she asked in bleak despair.

Laurel shrugged. "Anything to increase the odds."

It wouldn't stop there, Fargo reflected. Once Camilla was eliminated, the four of them would turn on one another.

"Have you any last words before we put you out of your misery?" Pandora inquired. "A last request, perhaps?"

Before Camilla could respond, from the shadowy bowels of the deep woods wavered an inhuman shriek.

18

Dawn had not quite broken, but the cloud-shrouded sky had brightened enough to sprinkle the darkling woods with splashes of pale, eerie light. More bestial shrieks filled the gloom, cries Skye Fargo knew all too well.

"What on earth?" Ronnie Kemp blurted, stiffening. He glanced at Skinner. "What the hell are they?"

"I've never heard the like," the scruffy cutthroat admitted.

"Could they be wolves?" Pandora Kemp asked. Her mount was prancing in nervous fear that spread to some of the other horses.

Skinner was scratching his head. "That doesn't sound like any wolves I ever heard. Coyotes, neither."

"Maybe they're dogs," Beda suggested.

Nayokona turned to the west and squared his shoulders. "Death comes," he somberly informed them. "Death for all of you. And you have only yourselves to blame. Your evil has brought the Shadow People down on your heads."

"Stupid Injun," Skinner said. "Talk sense."

"He is," Camilla declared. She was quaking like a reed, her complexion as white as paper. "It's the Killamak. They've caught up to us."

Laurel was the only one of the four conspirators who seemed to appreciate the significance of her revelation. "The lost tribe? Those savages you were trying to find?" he said in rising alarm. "Don't tell me they actually exist?"

As if to offer their own proof, fierce shrieks lifted in collective chorus. Out of the shadows materialized loping figures; squat, powerful, painted figures, as green as the vegetation they traversed with animal speed and agility. Like a great pack of two-legged beasts, they swooped toward the clearing and those who had presumed to invade their domain.

Pandora Kemp screamed. Beda was frozen by shock. Ronnie started to rein his horse around to get out of there. Only Laurel kept his wits about him and shouted to their hired underlings, "What are you waiting for? Open fire, damn you! Drop those heathens before they get any closer!"

Fargo saw Skinner and the others fan out along the edge of the clearing into a skirmish line. They took aim, some kneeling, some standing. At a yell from Skinner ten rifles cracked in a withering volley, and forty feet out two of the onrushing warriors pitched forward in a spray of scarlet. But only two. The remaining Killamak vanished in the blink of an eye. One instant they were there, the next they weren't.

"Where in tarnation did they go?" Skinner hollered, puzzled. He and the rest of the riflemen raised their heads to scour the undergrowth. "They can't just vanish into thin air."

Unnoticed by anyone else, Fargo nudged Camilla. "Stay close to me," he whispered. "Any moment now all hell is going to break loose."

"I'm scared," Camilla said.

Fargo needed to get his hands on a gun, any gun. His Colt, the Remington, and the Smith and Wesson were only five or six feet away, lying where they had been tossed. He sidled toward them.

"What do you think you're doing, handsome?" Pandora Kemp trained a derringer on him. "The next step you take will be your last."

"You're going to need my help," Fargo said. "You have no idea what you're up against. Your men can't stop them."

"Care to place a wager on that?" Pandora responded with a sneer.

A heartbeat later the woodland resounded to a single earsplitting shriek, and at the signal the Killamak rose and charged. They were closer now, a lot closer, so close that Skinner and his men were only able to squeeze off a few shots before the green horde was in among them. War clubs rained in a torrent. Lances were flung with deadly accuracy. Bow strings twanged in uneven rhythm.

Bedlam reigned. It was every man for himself as the hired killers and the Killamak battled in a wild melee of ferocious proportions. Rifles boomed. Pistols cracked. Knives gleamed and glittered.

Pandora Kemp's sorrel shied and reared, nearly throwing her. Beda's animal snorted and plunged, and Ronnie tried to grab the reins. Laurel kept control of his and reined around to flee.

Fargo sprang to his Colt. A stocky Killamak was hurtling toward him, brandishing a bloody war club. He snapped off a shot that dropped the warrior in midstep, then scooped up the Remington and tossed it to Nayokona. The Smith and Wesson he held onto. Camilla was in no condition to use it. She was backing toward the east end of the clearing, a hand over her mouth, overcome by panic.

Fargo backpedaled to overtake her and the young Delaware fell into step at his side. Bodies sprinkled the grass, whites and Killamak alike, convulsing and thrashing and pumping their life's blood.

Howling and roaring, warriors broke through the defenders and flew toward the Kemps. Pandora extended her derringer and fired. She hit the man she aimed at, but she hit him in the shoulder, not in a vital organ, and before she could fire again he leaped high into the air and tackled her about the waist. She screamed as she plummeted.

Beda was tugging on her reins and slapping her legs against her dun. She wheeled him halfway around but got no farther. Another Killamak leaped, his steely arms clamping fast, and like her sister she was borne to the earth in a swirl of limbs and lace.

Ronnie whipped out a pearl-handled Beaumont-Adams revolver and squeezed off a shot at the warrior who had grabbed Beda. Unfortunately, he never saw the Killamak who killed him. A long lance transfixed him from rib cage to spine and the revolver slipped from his nerveless fingers. Dead in the saddle, he slumped over the saddle horn.

That left Laurel. He was almost to the trees. He, too, had drawn a pistol, but he was more intent on escape. The coat he wore, a brown hunting frock with gold trim, made an excellent target, and an arrow sheared through it smack between his shoulder blades. Another ripped into the nape of his neck. Unguided, his horse raced under a low limb and he was sent toppling.

Fargo had seen it all as he darted in among the pines. He had caught up to Camilla, and when she wailed "Laurel!" and tried to run to her brother, he gripped her wrist and pulled her after him. "Forget it! He's beyond help!"

"No! Let me go!" Camilla struggled to wrest loose. "I have to try and help! He might still be alive!"

Fargo ignored her plea. A riderless horse galloped past, and another, a gelding, was fast approaching. "Here!" he shouted, shoving Camilla at Nayokona. "Hold onto her!" Wedging the Smith and Wesson under his belt, he moved to intercept the gelding. But the frightened animal wanted no part of him and swerved wide, out of reach. Cursing, he looked for others, but they were trotting off in other directions. Swivelling, he quickly rejoined the Delaware and the heiress. "Keep running and don't look back."

Camilla was sobbing and whining. She plodded listlessly along, her heart crushed. Nayokona had to spur her to greater speed with repeated tugs. He wasn't rough, but he was far from gentle.

Fargo tried to recall if he had seen Tenecicomesh during the battle, and couldn't. The leader was the one they had to worry about, the one who wouldn't give up until they were recaptured or dead. Every ten or twelve strides he checked behind them, but no one was on their trail. Yet.

"The Killamak—" Camilla said, but couldn't finish. Sniffling, she sobbed long and loud, tears dripping from her chin.

"What about them?" Fargo said, not paying much attention. He had more important things to worry about.

"Didn't you see? They took Beda and Pandora alive." Camilla blubbered like an infant. "My cousins will be sacrificed. Their brains will be eaten."

"It couldn't happen to two nicer people." The way Fargo saw it, they deserved their fate.

"We should do something," Camilla said. "We should go back and try to save them."

"And get ourselves killed?" Fargo argued. "You're not thinking straight. Your cousins were about to have you gunned down in cold blood. You don't owe them a damn thing."

Harrowing minutes wasted away. They pushed themselves to their limit, until they were breathing raggedly and their legs were wooden. On a rise under a giant oak, they finally stopped. Camilla groaned and sat straight down, exhausted. Nayokona leaned against the trunk, his face slick with sweat. Fargo surveyed the rough terrain they had crossed but saw no sign of the

Killamak. "I can't believe they'll let us get away," he muttered.

Camilla heard him. "After a battle they always tend to their dead before they do anything else. It will delay them a while."

"How long?" Fargo estimated they needed most of the day to reach the stream where Hamilton was waiting.

"I can't rightly say. Sorry."

Fargo glanced at the Delaware. In broad daylight the vicious beating Nayokona had suffered was more apparent. Bruises and welts covered his chest, arms, and face. The worst was a ten-inch patch of solid black-and-blue low on his left side. "How are you holding up?"

"I refuse to die before Tenecicomesh," Nayokona said grimly. "He was the one who slew my father. I will not rest until I have done the same to him."

Camilla started to sniffle again. "I wish I'd never lived to see this day," she said sadly. "My own brother wanted me dead! Pandora, I could understand. Beda, too. But Laurel and I were always close as could be. How could he betray my trust? My love?"

"Money," Fargo said. "Lots and lots of money." Greed was the oldest vice known to man. Or almost. He gazed at her thighs, and was reminded of an older one.

"The irony is that I never asked to be Uncle Lucius's heir," Camilla said. "One day, out of the blue, he called the entire family together and announced he had chosen me. I was as stunned as everyone else." She dabbed at an eye. "From that day on things were never the same. My cousin would hardly speak to me. I was an outcast in my own family."

"Why didn't you go to your uncle and ask him to divide up the inheritance equally?" Fargo asked.

"Uncle Lucius might have misunderstood," Camilla

said. "He might have thought I wasn't grateful enough, and picked someone else."

Fargo stared at her.

"Why are you looking at me like that? You wouldn't have done any different. Being the wealthiest person in America is an important responsibility."

"Sure it is."

Camilla's tears dried up like dew under a blistering sun. Pushing to her feet, she fumed, "What are you insinuating? That I'm no better than Beda or Pandora? That I'm as money-hungry as they were?"

"Your words, not mine," Fargo said, and turned his back to her. He was sick and tired of the whole business, and he regretted ever agreeing to help out. He should have stayed west of the Mississippi River where he belonged.

"You can go to hell," Camilla said.

Movement in the trees below gave Fargo something else to think about. Green shapes were flitting through the forest, dead on their trail. "They're coming," he said. "We run or we die."

They ran. Through tangles and thickets and brush that clawed at their clothes and their skin. Over logs and deadfalls and gullies. Up one slope and down another. The luxury of choosing the easiest route was denied them. They were racing for their lives, the Reaper at their backs. Or, to be more exact, a pack of reapers. Green-skinned, beetling-browed, cannibalistic abominations from another day and age, creatures who should have died off long ago.

Camilla began to lag. She was wheezing through her nose, and from time to time she tottered as if drunk.

Fargo slowed to pace her. Moments later so did Nayokona. They swapped glances. Both of them realized that they were merely delaying the inevitable. They couldn't outrun the Killamak any more than they could outrun bloodhounds. "We have to make a stand," Fargo said, and when a small meadow yawned before them, he jogged out into the open and halted. "This will have to do."

"Here?" Camilla could barely get the word out. Bending over, her hands on her knees, she gulped for breath. "But they'll see us."

"And we'll be able to see them," Fargo said. In the open they stood a fighting chance. Not much of one, but better than amid the trees. He drew the Colt and the Smith and Wesson and gave the latter to Camilla. "You'll need this."

"We're going to die, aren't we?"

"Maybe not right away. Maybe they plan to take us alive so they can repay us for the lives we took and the damage we caused," Fargo speculated.

Nayokona cocked the Remington. "They are not taking me alive. I will honor the memory of my father and my father's father by dying as a Lenape should."

Fargo slipped the Arkansas toothpick from its ankle sheath. "Stand back to back," he directed, and the three of them shifted so their shoulders were touching. "Protect whoever falls as best you can."

"I am glad to have met you," Nayokona said. "You have the heart of a Lenape."

Off in the dank depths of the vegetation a green figure bounded into sight. Then another, and another. Eight, nine, ten wolfish silhouettes, with more in their wake. Too many for the three of them to overcome. Girding himself for the end, Fargo said, "Make every shot count."

Camilla looked ready to bolt. "I don't want to die," she said plaintively.

"Who does?" The Killamak were close enough for Fargo to recognize the warrior at the head of the pack. "Tenecicomesh," he said. The leader had shed the eagle-feather headdress and the bearskin robe and wore a breechclout like the rest. He carried a huge club and had a knife in a sheath on his right hip. Only one of the warriors had a bow and none had a lance.

"Remember," Nayokona said. "Tenecicomesh is mine." He raised the Remington in both hands.

The Killamak were still out of effective pistol range and the wily Tenecicomesh knew it. He slowed and barked commands, and the other warriors diverted to the right and left, forming a crescent shape much like that of their moccasins. The warrior with the bow made no attempt to use it.

"I think you're right," Camilla said. "I think they intend to take us alive."

"Or pound us to a pulp," Nayokona remarked.

Warriors were wagging their war clubs or pounding their chests or both. They snarled and hissed, building themselves into a frenzy. Loudest of all was Tenecicomesh.

"Any second now," Fargo said.

"May our ancestors welcome us with open arms," Nayokona intoned.

A howl from Tenecicomesh launched the attack. Stepping in stride so they maintained the crescent formation, the Killamak advanced, slowly at first, then faster and faster. At another howl from their chief they launched themselves forward, roaring and shrieking, their eyes agleam with bloodlust.

Fargo fired at a warrior next to Tenecicomesh. The slug bored the Killamak between the eyes and he keeled forward. The rest never broke stride.

Nayokona and Camilla fired but only one warrior tottered and crashed to the earth.

On came the savage green tide. The Killamak were astoundingly fast. They were almost to the center of the meadow when Fargo squeezed off his second shot. Another deformed gargoyle fell, but there were plenty more left to take his place.

Fargo fired, dodged a club, fired again, ducked, fired a fourth time. The Smith and Wesson and the Remington were also booming. Several of the Killamak dropped, but nowhere near enough. Fargo used his fifth shot on a warrior who nearly dashed his skull in. His sixth bullet catapulted a screeching warrior head over heels. All he had now was the toothpick, a slender knife against war clubs and blades twice as long. He shifted to avoid a blow, sank the toothpick into green ribs, sidestepped, and cut a hairy forearm open from wrist to elbow.

Camilla screamed. She was on the ground, a pair of warriors attempting to strip her of her revolver.

Fargo turned to help her, but a brawny arm caught him around the waist. Another locked onto his leg. The earth rushed up to meet him and air whooshed from his lungs. Knobby fingers closed on his right wrist. Someone tried to pin his left arm. Slashing wildly, he rolled free, pushed up onto a knee, and hacked like a madman, forcing the Killamak back and ripping the abdomen of one who wasn't swift enough.

Out of the corner of an eye Fargo glimpsed Nayokona and Tenecicomesh locked in fierce combat, rolling back and forth in the grass. A glimpse was all he had, because the next moment three Killamak were on top of him and knives streaked to counter his own. He cut, parried, swung to the right and sank the toothpick deep into a muscular leg.

A muscular arm forked Fargo's neck from behind and he was jerked erect. He twisted to dislodge the warrior, but the Killamak was too strong. Whipping an elbow back, he connected with unyielding ribs. The man stumbled a half step but didn't go down.

Others were converging. One swung a war club at Fargo's face. By arching up onto his toes, Fargo contrived to have the club strike the arm that was holding him. Bone crunched, and the Killamak behind him let go. Spinning, Fargo slashed him across the throat, spun again, and drove the toothpick into the stomach of the warrior holding the club. For a moment he was in the clear, but only for a moment. A two-hundred-pound wall of sinew slammed into him, shoulder first, and he was bowled over. Before he could rise several others piled on, an avalanche of heavy bodies too much for anyone to resist. He was mashed flat against the dirt and the Arkansas toothpick was torn from his fingers.

Camilla screamed louder than ever.

Fargo struggled to rise but it was impossible. Nails ripped at his right hand, prying at the Colt. The Shadow People had won. Another minute and it would be all over. They would tote him to their village and eat his brain. The West would never know what became of him. He would die unmourned and be soon forgotten.

Then a gun blasted. Fargo thought it was Nayokona's Smith and Wesson until it boomed again. It was a rifle and it wasn't alone. Other rifles cracked, sparking yowls of outrage from the Killamak. Fargo heard the rush of feet, heard the thud of war clubs and the whiz of an arrow. The pressure on his back lifted and he rolled over.

Owen Hamilton and a line of stalwart backwoodsmen were working their weapons with the precision and discipline of a veteran militia. A wave of Killamak frothed toward them, and like inbound surf were dashed apart on the breakers of heavy caliber slugs. A few warriors reached the line, and hand-to-hand contests were waged on life-or-death terms.

It was all over so fast, Fargo could hardly credit his senses. Two-thirds of the Killamak were down, dead or dying, and those still alive turned tail rather than be exterminated.

"After them, boys!" Owen Hamilton hollered. "Give the devils their due!"

The buckskin brigade raced to do his bidding, firing on the run. More Killamak died before they could gain cover. Pursued and pursuers sped into the woods and were soon lost from sight, the crackling cadence of rifles dwindling with distance.

Fargo had twisted to watch. He jumped when a huge hand fell on his shoulder, and glanced up into the friendly features of Owen Hamilton.

"You're alive! Thank goodness. Too bad about the others."

The others. Fargo slowly rose, his ears ringing, the blood hammering in his veins. A few feet away lay Nayokona and Tenecicomesh locked in a crimson embrace. The young Delaware's left temple was caved in from the blow of a war club, but somehow he had throttled Tenecicomesh with his bare hands. They were both dead.

Fargo pivoted. Camilla Kemp was spread-eagle on her back, her eyes glazing, her throat gashed from ear to ear, the handle of a knife jutting from her chest.

"Is that who I think it is?" the big backwoodsman asked.

Bleakly nodding, Fargo closed his eyes and put a hand to his forehead. He had tried, honestly tried.

"We were following the Kemp outfit when we heard shots and came as quick as we could," Hamilton said. "I'm sorry it wasn't quick enough."

"How did you know about the Kemps?" Straightening, Fargo lowered his weary arms. Beyond Hamilton, at the tree line, stood a knot of horses, and among them, incredibly, was the Ovaro.

"One of my men was out hunting yesterday and spotted their camp. When they moved out, so did we." Hamilton bobbed his head at the pinto. "We found your animal in a ravine with its reins tangled in some brush."

"I owe you," Fargo said. More than he could ever possibly repay.

"Shucks. I only did what you would have done." Hamilton gazed sorrowfully down at Camilla. "What a shame. How do you reckon her uncle will take the news?"

"Not very well," Fargo predicted.

*   *   *

Webster walked Fargo to the burnished bronze gate to bid him good-bye. "I'm terribly sorry about how things turned out, sir," the butler said sincerely. "When the messenger from Mr. Hamilton arrived with the news, Mr. Kemp was devastated. His heart couldn't take the strain. I was with him when it happened, and he died just like that." Webster snapped his fingers to demonstrate.

"I should have come myself," Fargo said. But he'd needed a day to rest up before returning to New York City, so Hamilton had sent a rider on ahead.

"It wouldn't have made a difference, sir," Webster assured him. "Camilla was Lucius's pride and joy. He doted over her. In his eyes she was the only one who was worth a damn, to use his own words."

"If he only knew," Fargo said, and hiked his right boot to the corresponding stirrup. Pulling himself up, he settled into the saddle and looked back one last time at the vast estate with its gardens and trimmed lawns and stately mansion. All Kemp's riches, all his power, and in the end it hadn't mattered one bit.

"How's that, sir?" Webster asked.

"Nothing." Fargo saw no reason to reveal the truth.

"I'm also sorry I can't authorize payment of the money you're due," the butler said. "Lucius wasn't dead five minutes when Dalbert and Berton rushed off to see their lawyers. Now they're both claiming to be the legal heir, and they've persuaded a judge to issue an injunction freezing all their brother's funds until the court decides. It could take years."

"I'm not sticking around that long." Fargo had seen enough of the East to last him a good long while.

"This isn't right," Webster said. "You put your life in peril. You nearly died. And for what? So two pompous old fools can spend the rest of their days squabbling over riches they'll probably never receive."

Fargo lifted the reins. "Texans have a saying. Be

thankful for fools. Without them, none of us would amount to a damn."

Webster laughed. "If you don't mind my nosiness, sir, where will you head from here? Back to St. Louis?"

"No. My cards have gone cold. I think I'll follow the sun until I reach the Rockies." Fargo clucked to the pinto and rode out the gate. He planned to make one important stop along the way, at a certain sleepy hamlet in Pennsylvania. A few nights under the sheets with Cheryl Taylor and he might be able to forget the ordeal he had been through.

Buffalo could fly, too.